"Captures the messy, awkward, all-consuming
emotions of a teen's first love."
—*Entertainment Weekly*

"You could probably learn a thing or two from [Henry]
and Grace's emotional odyssey."
—*Teen Vogue*

"The author pulls no punches . . . emotionally engaging."
—*Kirkus Reviews*

"Eloquently conveying the complexity of love and grief,
debut novelist Sutherland creates a story filled with
intriguing and memorable characters."
—*Publishers Weekly*

"Emotionally complex, funny, filled with well-realized
and diverse characters and realistic motivations,
Sutherland's debut will stick with readers."
—*Booklist*

"This book delves far deeper than the typical high school ro-
mance, and its savvy wordplay and Henry's self-deprecating
charm will win over fans of Stephen Chbosky's *The Perks of Being
a Wallflower* and John Green's *The Fault in Our Stars*."
—*School Library Journal*

"The love story of Henry and Grace is going to
kick you in the emotional gut."
—*Bustle*

also by
krystal sutherland

A Semi-Definitive List of Worst Nightmares
House of Hollow

chemical hearts

krystal sutherland

PENGUIN BOOKS

PENGUIN BOOKS
An imprint of Penguin Random House LLC, New York

First published in the United States of America by G. P. Putnam's Sons,
an imprint of Penguin Random House LLC, as *Our Chemical Hearts*, 2016
Published by Penguin Books, an imprint of Penguin Random House LLC,
as *Our Chemical Hearts*, 2017
Published by Penguin Books, an imprint of Penguin Random House LLC,
as *Chemical Hearts*, 2020

Visit us online at penguinrandomhouse.com

LIBRARY OF CONGRESS CATALOGING-IN-PUBLICATION DATA IS AVAILABLE.

Printed in the United States of America

ISBN 9780593109670

10 9 8 7 6 5 4 3 2

Design by Annie Ericsson

For my family, for everything, forever.

CHAPTER 1

I ALWAYS THOUGHT the moment you met the great love of your life would be more like the movies. Not exactly like the movies, obviously, with the slow-mo and the hair blowing in the breeze and the swelling instrumental soundtrack. But I at least thought there would be something, you know? A skipped beat of the heart. A tug at your soul where *something* inside you goes, "Holy shit. There she is. Finally, after all this time, there she is."

There was none of that when Grace Town walked into Mrs. Beady's afternoon drama class ten minutes late on the second Tuesday of senior year. Grace was the type of person who made an impression on any room she walked into, but not for the kind of reasons that generate instant and undying affection. She was of average height and average build and average attractiveness, all things that should've made it easy for her to assimilate into a new high school without any of the dramatic tropes that usually inhabit such storylines.

But three things about Grace immediately stood out, before her ordinariness could save her:

1. Grace was dressed head to toe in guys' clothing. Not the tomboy, skater-girl kind of look, either, but legitimate dudes' clothing that was way too big for her. Jeans that were meant to be skinny were held on her hips by a belt. Despite it being only mid-September, she wore a sweater and a checkered shirt and a knit cap, and a long leather necklace with an anchor on the end.

2. Grace looked unclean and unhealthy. I mean, I'd seen junkies that looked in better shape than she did that morning. (I hadn't really seen that many junkies, but I'd seen *The Wire* and *Breaking Bad*, which totally counts.) Her blond hair wasn't brushed and was badly cut, her skin was sallow, and I'm almost certain if I'd smelled her at any point during that day, she would've reeked.

3. If all this wasn't enough to really screw over her chances of fitting in at a new high school, Grace Town walked with a cane.

And that's how it happened. That's how I first saw her. There was no slow-mo, no breeze, no soundtrack, and definitely no skipped heartbeats. Grace hobbled in ten minutes late, silently, like she owned the place, like she'd been in our class for years, and maybe because she was new or because she was weird or because the teacher could see simply by looking at her that a small part of her soul was cracked, Mrs. Beady said nothing. Grace sat on a chair at the back of the black-walled drama room, her cane resting across her thighs, and said nothing to anybody for the entire class.

I looked at her twice more, but by the end of class I'd forgotten she was there, and she slipped out without anyone noticing.

So this is certainly not a story of love at first sight.

But it *is* a love story.

Well.

Kind of.

CHAPTER 2

THE FIRST WEEK of senior year, before Grace Town's sudden apparition, had passed by as uneventfully as high school possibly can. There'd been only three minor scandals thus far: a junior had been suspended for smoking in the girls' bathroom (if you're going to get suspended for something, at least make it something not cliché), an anonymous suspect had uploaded footage of an after-school fight in the parking lot to YouTube (the administration was freaking out over that one), and there were rumors going around that Chance Osenberg and Billy Costa had given each other an STD after having unprotected sex with the same girl (I wish I was making this up, dear readers).

My life had remained, as always, entirely scandal-free. I was seventeen years old, a weird, lanky kid, the type you might cast to play a young Keanu Reeves if you'd already spent the majority of your budget on bad CGI and craft service. I'd never so much as secondhand-smoked a cigarette, and no one, thank

God, had approached me about doing the no-pants dance sans a prophylactic. My dark hair skirted my shoulders, and I'd grown particularly fond of wearing my dad's sports coat from the eighties. You could say I looked something like a male Summer Glau crossed with Severus Snape. Subtract the hook nose, add in some dimples, and hey presto: the perfect recipe for one Henry Isaac Page.

I was, at the time, also uninterested in girls (or guys, in case you were wondering). My friends had been in and out of dramatic teenage relationships for close to five years now, but I had yet to even have a real crush. Sure, there'd been Abigail Turner in kindergarten (I'd kissed her on the cheek when she wasn't expecting it; our relationship rapidly declined after that), and I'd been obsessed with the idea of marrying Sophi Zhou for at least three years of elementary school, but after I hit puberty, it was like a switch inside me flipped, and instead of becoming a testosterone-driven sex monster like most of the guys at my school, I failed to find anyone I wanted in my life in that way.

I was happy to focus on school and getting the grades I needed to get into a semi-decent college, which is probably why I didn't think about Grace Town again for at least a couple of days. Maybe I never would've if it wasn't for the intervention of one Mr. Alistair Hink, English teacher.

What I know about Mr. Hink is still very much confined to what most high schoolers know about their teachers. He had bad dandruff, which wouldn't have been half as noticeable if he didn't insist on wearing black turtlenecks every day, the color of which clearly displayed the fine white dust on his shoulders like snow falling on asphalt. From what I could gather from his naked left hand, he was unmarried, which probably had a lot to do with the dandruff and the fact that he looked remarkably like Napoleon Dynamite's brother, Kip.

Hink was also fiercely passionate about the English language, so much so that on one occasion when my math class was let out five minutes late and thus ate into our English lesson, Hink called up the math teacher, Mr. Babcock, and gave him a lecture about how the arts were no less valuable than mathematics. A lot of students laughed at him under their breaths—they were mostly destined for careers in engineering or science or customer service, I suppose—but looking back, I can pinpoint that afternoon in our sweltering English classroom as the moment I fell in love with the idea of becoming a writer.

I'd always been decent at writing, at putting words together. Some people are born with an ear for music, some people are born with a talent for drawing, some people—people like me, I guess—have a built-in radar that tells them where a comma needs to go in a sentence. As far as superpowers go, grammatical intuition is fairly low on the awesomeness scale, but it did get me in with Mr. Hink, who also happened to be in charge of running and organizing the student newspaper I'd volunteered at since sophomore year in hopes of one day becoming editor.

It was about midway through Mrs. Beady's Thursday drama class in the second week of school when the phone rang and Beady answered it. "Henry, Grace. Mr. Hink would like to see you in his office after school," she said after chatting for a few minutes. (Beady and Hink had always been friendly. Two souls born in the wrong century, when the world liked to make fun of people who still thought art was the most extraordinary thing humanity ever had or ever would produce.)

I nodded and purposefully didn't look at Grace, even though I could see in my peripheral vision that she was staring at me from the back of the room.

When most teenagers get called to their teacher's office after school, they assume the worst, but like I said, I was tragically free of scandal. I knew (or hoped I knew) why Hink wanted to see me. Grace had been an inmate at Westland High for only two days, hardly long enough to have given another student trichomoniasis and/or handed out any after-school beatdowns (although she *did* carry a cane and look angry a lot).

Why Mr. Hink wanted to see Grace was—like much else about her—a mystery.

CHAPTER 3

GRACE WAS ALREADY waiting outside Hink's office when I got there. She was dressed in guys' clothing again today, different stuff this time, but she looked a lot cleaner and healthier. Her blond hair had been washed and brushed. It made a remarkable difference to her appearance, even if having clean hair made it fall in uneven chunks around her shoulders, like she'd cut it herself with a pair of rusted hedge trimmers.

I sat down next to her on the bench, entirely too aware of my body, so much so that I forgot how to sit casually and had to purposefully arrange my limbs. I couldn't get my posture right, so I kind of slumped forward into an awkward pose that made my neck ache, but I didn't want to move again because I could see her looking at me out of the corner of her eye.

Grace was sitting with her knees pressed up against her chest, her cane wedged between them. She was reading a book with tattered pages the color of coffee-stained teeth. I couldn't see the title, but I could see that it was full of poems. When she caught me looking over her shoulder, I expected her to close the book or angle it away from me, but instead she turned it ever so slightly toward me so that I could read too.

The poem Grace was reading, I assumed over and over again because the page was dog-eared and food-stained and in generally bad shape, was by a guy called Pablo Neruda, whom I'd never heard of before. It was called "I do not love you," which intrigued me, so I started to read, even though Hink had not yet succeeded in making me like poetry.

Two lines in particular had been highlighted.

I love you as certain dark things are to be loved,
in secret, between the shadow and the soul.

Hink stepped out of the office then, and Grace snapped the book shut before I could finish.

"Oh, good, I see you've met," said Hink when he saw us together. I stood up quickly, keen to unravel myself from the weird position I'd folded my body into. Grace shuffled to the edge of the bench and rose slowly, carefully distributing her weight between her cane and her good leg. I wondered for the first time how bad her injury was. How long had she been like this? Was she born with a bad leg or did some tragic accident befall her in childhood? "Well, come inside."

Hink's office was at the end of a hall that might've been considered modern and attractive sometime in the early eighties. Pale pink walls, fluorescent lighting, painfully obvious fake plants, that weird linoleum that's supposed to look like granite but is actually made up of hundreds of little bits of plastic filled in with clear laminate. I followed Hink, my steps slower than they normally would be, because I wanted Grace to walk next to me. Not because I wanted her to, like, *walk next to me*, you know, but I thought she might like it, that it might be a nice thing to do, for her to be able to keep up with someone. But even when my pace felt maddeningly slow, she still hung back, hobbling two steps behind me, until it felt like we were in a race to see who could go the slowest. Hink was ten steps in front of us by then, so I sped up and left her behind and must've looked like a total weirdo.

When we reached Hink's office (small, bland, green-tinged; so depressing it made me think he was probably part of a fight club on the weekends), he ushered us inside and motioned for us to sit in the two chairs in front of his desk. I frowned as we sat down, wondering why Grace was here with me.

"You're both here, of course, because of your exceptional writing abilities. When it came time to pick our senior editors for the newspaper, I could think of no two better—"

"No," said Grace Town, cutting him off, and her voice was such a shock to me that I only just realized it was the first time I'd heard her speak. She had this strong, clear, deep voice, so different from the broken and timid image she portrayed.

"I beg your pardon?" said Hink, clearly taken aback.

"No," Grace said again, as if this were explanation enough.

"I . . . I don't understand," said Hink, his gaze flicking to me with this pleading look in his eyes. I could practically hear his silent scream for help, but all I could do was shrug.

"I don't want to be an editor. Thank you, really, for thinking of me. But no." Grace collected her bag from the floor and stood.

"Miss Town. Grace. Martin came to me specifically before the start of the school year and asked me to look at your work from East River. You were going to take over as editor of their newspaper this year, I believe, if you hadn't transferred. Isn't that right?"

"I don't write anymore."

"That's a shame. Your work is beautiful. You have a natural gift for words."

"And you have a natural gift for clichés."

Hink was so shocked that his mouth popped open.

Grace softened a little. "Sorry. But they're just words. They don't mean anything."

Grace looked at me with this kind of disapproving expression I wasn't expecting and didn't understand, then slung her backpack over her shoulders and limped out. Hink and I sat there in silence, trying to process what'd just happened. It took me a good ten seconds to realize that I was angry, but once I had, I, too, collected my bag and stood quickly and made my way toward the door.

"Can we talk about this tomorrow?" I said to Hink, who must've guessed that I was going after her.

"Yes, yes, of course. Come and see me before class." Hink shooed me out and I jogged down the corridor, surprised to find that Grace wasn't there. When I opened the far door and stepped out of the building, she was already at the edge of the school grounds. She could move goddamn fast when she tried. I sprinted after her, and when I was within earshot, I shouted, "Hey!" She turned briefly, looked me up and down, glared, and then kept on walking.

"Hey," I said breathlessly when I finally caught up with her and fell in step beside her.

"What?" she said, still speed walking, the end of her cane clicking against the road with every step. A car behind us beeped. Grace pointed violently at her cane and then waved them around. I'd never seen a vehicle move in a way I'd describe as *sheepish* before.

"Well . . . ," I said, but I couldn't find the words to say what I wanted to say. I was a decent enough writer, but talking? With sounds? From my mouth? That was a bitch.

"Well what?"

"Well, I hadn't really planned this far into the conversation."

"You seem pissed."

"I am pissed."

"Why?"

"Because people work their asses off for years to get editor, and you waltz in at the beginning of senior year and have it offered to you on a platter and you turn it down?"

"Did you work your ass off?"

"Hell yeah. I've been buttering Hink up, pretending I'm a tortured teen writer who really relates to Holden Caulfield since I was, like, fifteen."

"Well, congratulations. I don't understand why you're angry. There's normally only one editor anyway, right? The fact that I said no doesn't impact you at all."

"But . . . I mean . . . Why would you say no?"

"Because I don't want to do it."

"But . . ."

"And without me there, you'll get to make all the creative decisions and have the newspaper exactly how you've probably been envisioning it for the last two years."

"Well . . . I guess . . . But . . ."

"So you see, this is really a win-win for you. You're welcome, by the way."

We walked on in silence for a couple of minutes longer, until my anger had entirely faded and I could no longer remember exactly why I'd chased after her in the first place.

"*Why* are you still following me, Henry Page?" she said, coming to a stop in the middle of the road, like she didn't give a shit that a car could come hurtling toward us at any second. And I realized that, although we'd never been introduced and never spoken before today, she knew my full name.

"You know who I am?" I said.

"Yes. And you know who I am, so let's not pretend we don't. Why are you still following me?"

"Because, *Grace Town*, I've walked too far from school now

and my bus has probably already left and I was looking for a smooth way to exit the conversation but I didn't find one, so I resigned myself to my fate."

"Which is?"

"To walk in this general direction until my parents report me missing and the police find me on the outskirts of town and drive me home."

Grace sighed. "Where do you live?"

"Right near the Highgate Cemetery."

"Fine. Come to my place. I'll drop you."

"Oh. Awesome. Thanks."

"As long as you promise not to push the whole editor thing."

"Fine. No pushing. You want to turn down an awesome opportunity, that's your decision."

"Good."

It was a humid afternoon in suburgatory, the clouds overhead as solid as cake frosting, the lawns and trees still that bright, golden green of late summer. We walked side by side on the hot asphalt. There were five more minutes of awkward silence where I searched and searched for a question to ask her. "Can I read the rest of that poem?" I said finally, because it seemed like the least worst of all my options. (Option one: So . . . are you, like, a cross-dresser or something? Not that there's anything wrong with that; I'm just curious. Option two: What's up with your leg, bro? Option three: You're definitely some kind of junkie, right? I mean, you're fresh out of rehab, yeah? Option four: Can I read the rest of that poem?)

"What poem?" she said.

"The Pablo whoever one. 'I do not love you.' Or whatever it was."

"Oh. Yeah." Grace stopped and handed me her cane and swung her backpack onto her front and fished out the threadbare book and pushed it into my hands. It fell open to Pablo Neruda, so I knew then for sure that it was something she read over and over again. It was the line about loving dark things that I kept coming back to.

> *I love you as certain dark things are to be loved,*
> *in secret, between the shadow and the soul.*

"It's beautiful," I said to Grace as I closed the book and handed it back to her, because it was.

"Do you think?" She looked at me with this look of genuine questioning on her face, her eyes narrowed slightly.

"You don't?"

"I think that's what people say when they read poems they don't understand. It's sad, I think. Not beautiful." I couldn't see how a perfectly nice love poem was sad, but then again, my significant other was my laptop, so I didn't say anything. "Here," Grace said as she opened the book again and tore out the page with the poem on it. I flinched as though I were in actual pain. "You should have it, if you like it. Pretty poetry is wasted on me."

I took the paper from her and folded it and slipped it into my pocket, half of me horrified that she'd injured a book, the other half of me elated that she'd so willingly given me something that clearly meant a lot to her. I liked people like that. People who could part with material possessions with little or no hesitation. Like Tyler Durden. "The things you own end up owning you" and all that.

Grace's house was exactly the type of place I expected her to live. The garden was overgrown, gone to seed, the lawn left to grow wild for some time. The curtains on the windows were drawn and the house itself, which was two stories tall and made of gray brick, seemed to be sagging as if depressed by the weight of the world. In the driveway there was a solitary car, a small white Hyundai with a Strokes decal on the back windshield.

"Stay here," she said. "I've got to get my car keys."

I nodded and stood by myself on the front lawn while I waited for her. The car, like everything else about her, was strange. Why did she walk (or hobble, rather) fifteen minutes to school every day if she had a license and a readily available vehicle? Every other senior I knew was desperate for the privilege of driving to the mall or McDonald's during lunch, escaping the confines of the school grounds. And then, in the afternoons, bypassing the bus line and rolling right on home to food and PlayStations and sweet, sweet comfortable sweatpants.

"Do you have your license?" Grace said from behind me. I jumped a little, because I hadn't even heard her come out of the house, but there she was, car keys dangling off her pinkie finger. These, too, had Strokes paraphernalia attached to them. I'd never really listened to their stuff before, but I made a mental note to look them up on Spotify when I got home.

"Uh, yeah, actually. I got it a couple of months ago, but I don't have a car yet."

"Good." She threw me the keys and walked to the passenger side of the car and pulled out her phone. After twenty seconds or so, she looked up from her screen, her eyebrows raised. "Well? Are you going to unlock the car or not?"

"You want *me* to drive?"

"No, I thought it would be hilarious to hand you the keys and stand here until someone invents teleportation. Yes, Henry Page, I want you to drive."

"Uh, okay, I guess. I'm a bit rusty, but yeah. Okay." I unlocked the car and opened the door and sat in the driver's seat. The inside of the car smelled like her, the musky, masculine scent of a teenage boy. Which was very confusing for me, to say the least. I started the engine—so far, so good—and took a deep breath.

"I'll try my best not to kill us both," I said. Grace Town did not reply, so I laughed at my own joke—a single, awkward "ha"—and then I put the car in reverse.

My grandmother would've looked cooler driving than I did on the journey home. I hunched over the steering wheel, sweating, hyperaware that I a) was driving someone else's car, b) hadn't driven any car at all for months, and c) had only scraped through my driving test because my instructor was my violently hungover second cousin twice removed, and I'd had to stop three times to let him vomit on the side of the road.

"Are you *sure* you passed your driving test?" Grace said, leaning over to check the speedometer, which revealed I was sitting five miles under the speed limit.

"Hey, I only had to bribe *two* officials. I *earned* my license." I swear I might've almost seen her smile. "So you came from East River, huh?"

"Yeah."

"Why'd you change schools in senior year?"

"I'm all about adventure," she said dryly.

"Well, we are a particularly thrilling institution. I can definitely see the appeal."

"Hink seems like a riot. I bet he gets into all sorts of shenanigans."

"Life of the party, that one."

And then, thank God, it was over. I pulled up in front of my house and relaxed my fingers from the steering wheel, aware for the first time of how tightly I'd been clenching my muscles.

"I don't think I've seen anyone drive that tensely since . . . Do you need a minute to compose yourself?" she said.

"What can I say? I'm a rebel without a cause."

I expected Grace to slide over to the driver's side, but she told me to turn the car off. We both got out and I handed her the keys and she locked the door like she meant to come inside. I hesitated. Was I supposed to invite her in? But then she turned to me and said, "Okay. Good-bye. I'll see you tomorrow. Or maybe not. Who knows where I'll be," and she started hobbling down the street in the complete opposite direction from which we'd come.

"There's not much down there but a storm-water drain and a cemetery a block away." (The graveyard was close enough that its proximity had resulted in several counseling sessions in elementary school due to a brief yet intense period when I was convinced my great-grandfather Johannes van de Vliert's ghost was trying to kill me.) Grace didn't say anything, didn't look back, just lifted the hand that wasn't holding her cane as if to say *I know* and kept on walking.

I watched her, entirely puzzled, until she disappeared around the next street corner.

"Hola, broseph," said my sister, Sadie, the moment I closed the front door behind me.

"Jesus, Suds, you scared the crap outta me," I said, clutching at my chest. Sadie was twelve years older than me, a celebrated neuroscientist, and was generally considered both the golden child and black sheep of the family simultaneously. We looked a lot alike: black hair, slightly buggy eyes, dimples when we smiled. Except Suds was *slightly* more cutting edge than me with her septum piercing, tattoo sleeve, and intricate dreadlocks, all souvenirs from her rocky teenage years.

"Haven't seen or heard from you in, like, two days, kid. I was starting to think Mom and Dad had murdered you and buried you in a shallow grave." This was, of course, a strategic lie. Suds was going through a fairly shitty divorce from her fairly shitty doctor husband, which meant she spent about 90 percent of the time she didn't spend at the hospital at our house.

"Sadie, don't be ridiculous," Dad said from the kitchen, dressed in his usual getup of a Hawaiian shirt, male short shorts, and black spectacles. (His fashion sense had rapidly declined after he'd moved his carpentry workshop into the backyard three years ago. Honestly it was a miracle to find him in something other than pajamas.) Sadie and I got our hair from him. Or at least, I assumed we did. The ever-present stubble on his chin was dark, but he'd been bald for the majority of my life. "We'd make his grave at least four or five feet deep. We don't half-ass murder in this house."

"Toby and Gloria can attest to that," Sadie said, referring to an event six years prior to my birth that involved a pair of goldfish, insect spray, and the accidental yet untimely death of her aquatic pets.

"Twenty-three years, Suds. It's been twenty-three years since your goldfish died. Are you ever going to let it go?"

"Not until I have my vengeance!" Sadie yelled dramatically. A toddler started crying from the back of the house. Sadie sighed. "You'd think after three years I'd start getting used to this whole motherhood thing, but I keep forgetting about the damn kid."

"I'll get him," I said, dumping my schoolbag and heading down the hallway to where Ryan usually slept in Sadie's old room. The kid had been, much the same as me, an accident and a surprise. Mom and Dad had only ever planned to have one child: twelve years after they had Sadie, they got stuck with me.

"Ryan, man, what's up?" I said when I pushed open the door to find my two-and-a-half-year-old nephew, whom Dad babysat on weekdays.

"Henwee," he rasped, rubbing his eyes. "Where's Mama?"

"Come on, I'll take you to her."

"Who's the girl, by the way?" Sadie asked as I walked back down the hallway holding Ryan's hand.

"The girl?"

"The one who drove you home." As she scooped Ryan up, Sadie had this thin, lopsided grin on her face. I'd seen that look many times before, when she was a teenager. It always meant trouble.

"Oh. Grace is her name. She's new. I missed my bus, so she offered me a ride."

"She's cute. In a weird, Janis Joplin, will probably die at twenty-seven kind of way."

I shrugged and pretended I hadn't noticed.

CHAPTER 4

ONCE RYAN WAS settled, I went down to the basement, which Sadie had turned into her teenage den of iniquity more than a decade ago (and I'd inherited upon her departure for college). It wasn't fancy. It kind of looked like a postapocalyptic fallout shelter. None of the furniture matched, the concrete floor was covered with a patchwork of faux-Persian carpets, the refrigerator was older than my parents, and there was a poorly taxidermied elk head on the wall. Everyone claimed not to know where it came from, but I had a sneaking suspicion Sadie had stolen it as a teenager and my parents were either too embarrassed or too impressed to return it to its rightful owner. Maybe both.

My two best friends were, as always, already down there, playing *GTA V* on my PS4. They were, in order of appearance (i.e., seating order on the couch):

- Murray Finch, 17, Australian. Tall and tan and muscular with curly blond hair to his shoulders and a seedy teenage mustache. His parents had immigrated to the States like six years ago, but Muz still (purposefully) sounded like Steve Irwin and said things like "g'day" and "drongo" and "struth" on a regular basis. He was of the strong opinion that *Crocodile Dundee* was the best thing to ever happen to Australians. Girls loved him.

- Lola Leung, 17. Dark-skinned, dark-eyed, dark-haired (cropped short). My next-door neighbor for my entire life, and a self-described "diversity triple threat": half Chinese on her dad's side, half Haitian on her mom's, and one hundred percent gay. For as long as I could remember, La had been "randomly selected" to appear front and center in all of our school's promotional material, including but not limited to front cover of the yearbook, on the billboard outside school, on the website, and even on bookmarks that were handed out at the library. She'd also been my first kiss three years ago. Two weeks later she'd come out as a lesbian and entered into a long-term, long-distance relationship with a girl named Georgia from the next town over. People still thought my kissing skills were the reason she decided to start batting for the other team. I was still trying not to be offended. (Girls also loved her.)

At the foot of the stairs, I leaned on the banister and watched them. "I love that even though I failed to make it onto the bus and was possibly dead and/or dying, you two still saw fit to come to my house, eat my food, and play my games without me. Did my father even notice I wasn't with you?"

"Let's be honest," Lola said, twisting around on the couch to grin at me. "Justin does love us more than he loves you."

"Who's the sheila, mate?" said Murray without looking away from the screen, where he was plowing a tank over a line of police cars. "Saw you going off after her like a raw prawn."

"Roll back the slang, Kangaroo Jack," I said, crossing the room to boot up Sadie's old iMac computer, which was, after almost two decades of service, still wheezing along with life. "There are no unsuspecting American girls in the room for you to charm." Murray was, for the most part, capable of speaking like a normal human being, but he'd discovered somewhere along the way that sounding like a bushman from the outback endeared him to the womenfolk. Sometimes he forgot to turn it off.

There was only one folder on the iMac's desktop, entitled "Missing/Funeral/Manhunt Headshots," that contained attractive pictures of everyone in the room (plus Sadie), to be used in the event that any of us disappeared/died/became wanted felons. Our parents had strict instructions to access the photos and provide them to the media before journalists went snooping on Facebook and picked random, unfortunate-looking pictures we'd been tagged in against our will.

"Muz raises a very good point, though," La said. "Who was the strange girl you were sprinting after? Did you think to yourself, 'Here's finally one that can't get away,' but then she proved you wrong?"

"Ha-ha. I can't believe you both saw that." I grabbed a can of Coke from the refrigerator and went back to the computer, where Facebook was loading pixel by painful pixel. "Her name is Grace Town. She's new. Hink offered her editor but she turned it down, so I got pissed and went after her."

"Her name is Grace Town? Like *Gracetown*?" said Murray as he, too, cracked a can of Coke and took a swig. "Christ. Poor chick."

Lola was already on her feet. "Hink offered her editor over you? That *bastard*. No way am I designing that glorified newsletter if you're not in charge!"

"No. Calm down. He gave it to us *both* but she turned it down because she—and I quote—'doesn't write anymore.' The way she said it was so ominous."

"Oh," Lola said. Murray yanked her back down to the couch. "Maybe bad things happen when she writes. Oh! Maybe the things she writes come true? Or maybe she has a voodoo curse on her so that every word she writes breaks a bone in her leg and that's why she walks with a cane?"

"Let's take a shufti at old FB, shall we?" Murray said. "Nothing like a little cyberstalking to clear these things up."

"Way ahead of you." When I typed Grace's name in the search field and hit return, a list of all the people I knew with Grace in their name showed up. Sadie Grace Elizabeth Smith was the first, followed by Samantha Grace Lawrence (we went to elementary school together), Grace Park (some kind of distant relative) and Grace Payne (I had no idea). Underneath them was a list of exact matches—five or so genuine Grace Towns—none of whom I had mutual friends with, and only one of whom lived in my geographical area.

I slouched forward. "None of them are her."

"Wait, what about that one?" Lola said, pointing.

I clicked the profile picture of the closest geographical Grace Town, a girl in a red dress with red lipstick and loose curls in her honey-blond hair. She was smiling brilliantly, her eyes closed, her head tilted back in laughter so that the sharp lines of her collarbones were visible beneath her skin. It was a good handful of seconds before any of us recognized her. Because it *was* her. It was the same Grace Town who had driven me home. The lips were the same, the shape of her face.

"Holy *shit*," Murray said. "Blokes would be on her like seagulls at a tip."

"Translation: She's an attractive female who likely gets a lot of attention from males," Lola said. "And lesbians," she tacked on after a moment, leaning closer to the screen. "Damn. She's got that Edie Sedgwick thing going on. That girl is stupid hot."

And she was. On Facebook, Grace Town was tall and lean and tan, with the kind of limbs that makes you think of words like *gracile* and *swanlike* and *damn, son*. *It must be an old picture*, I thought, but no. According to the date it was uploaded, it'd only been a little over three months since Grace had changed it. I scrolled through the five other public profile pictures, but each of them told the same story. None were more than a few months old, but the person in them was very different from the one I'd met. Her hair was much longer, down to her waist, and fell in soft, clean curls. There were pictures of her at the beach, pictures of her in makeup, pictures of her smiling this incredibly wide smile, the kind that models smile in ads when they're super jacked up about eating salad. There was no cane at her side, no black circles under her eyes, no layers upon layers of guys' clothing.

What had happened to her in the last three months that'd left her so changed and broken?

Sadie called us upstairs then, to help Dad finish dinner before Mom got home from the art gallery she curated in the city. ("Thank Christ. I could chew the crutch out of a low-flying vulture," Murray said.) All of us quickly forgot about the mystery of Grace Town for a few hours as we ate and did the dishes and watched Netflix together, as was our Thursday-night routine. It was only after I'd said good-bye to my friends and gone back down into the basement and noticed the screen of the poor iMac still wheezing with life that I thought of her again, but once I did, I was hooked.

I didn't brush my teeth that night. I didn't shower or change out of my clothes from school or go to say good-bye to Sadie and Ryan when they finally left around midnight. Instead, I stayed in the basement and spent the rest of my night listening to every song the Strokes had on Spotify.

You say you wanna stay by my side, crooned Julian Casablancas. *Darlin', your head's not right.*

If I'd been older or wiser or if I'd paid more attention to the dramatic teenage feelings my peers had described to me the first time they'd had crushes, I might not have misdiagnosed the burning, constricting sensation in my chest as indigestion from the four overfried chicken chimichangas I'd had for dinner instead of what it actually was: an affliction far more serious and far more painful.

That was the first night I dreamed of Grace Town.

CHAPTER 5

WHEN I KNOCKED on Hink's open door the following morning before school, he smiled and waved me into his office.

"Good job with convincing Town to take the job, Henry," he said. "That was a very nice thing of you to do. She's had a rough time, the poor kid."

"Wait, she's doing it?" I said.

"She came to see me half an hour ago to tell me you'd changed her mind. I don't know what you said to her, but it had an impact."

I raised my eyebrows. "She said *I* changed her mind?"

"The two of you should start planning your first issue ASAP. December seems a long way off, but it'll catch up to you. I put the fear of God into some of my juniors in English yesterday, so you should get a handful of volunteer writers to help you out. Mainly the ones who need extracurricular activities to scrape their way into college, so I can't guarantee they'll submit anything legible, but it's a start."

"What do you mean by 'She's had a rough time'?"

"Oh, you know. Changing schools in senior year. Always tough. Anyway, go get set up in your office. Your log-in details are on a Post-it note in front of your computer. Town's already in there. And Leung as well. You already know each other, I believe?" Hink gave me the look that people always gave me when they knew I'd been the last male to put my lips on Lola Leung's lips before she'd gone AWOL from the masculine species.

"Yeah." I cleared my throat instead of doing what I wanted to do, which was to say, *She was always a lesbian! Don't you know how human biology works?* "Lola's my next-door neighbor."

"Neighbor. Yes, of course. No need for introductions, then. Go settle into your office and we'll have a meeting early next week to get started on the first issue." Hink went back to whatever was on his computer screen then (fight club scheduling? haikus?) like he hadn't just dropped a Grace-sized bombshell.

I turned and walked numbly to the small office that the student newspaper staff worked out of. It was a fishbowl. The wall parallel to the corridor was all glass and the door (also glass) didn't lock, presumably to prevent any rabid teenage coitus from taking place on the furniture, a strategy that had failed spectacularly with last year's editor, who used to have sex with his girlfriend on the couch on a regular basis. There was, thank God, a blanket now covering the suspicious stains that had accumulated on the upholstery by the start of summer vacation.

Lola was sitting at the Mac reserved for the designer, her chunky-booted feet up on the desk as she browsed ASOS and sucked a lollipop. Grace was sitting at a small desk pressed up against the glass wall, away from the editor's desk. I guessed it'd been shoved in the room sometime in the last half hour, in an effort to accommodate Grace Town's sudden change of mind.

"Hey," I said as I walked into the room, feeling a strange, unfamiliar pang of excitement at the sight of her. There was something deeply confusing about looking at Grace, like that feeling you get when you see a colorized photograph of the Civil War or the Great Depression and realize for the first time that the people in them were real. Except it was reversed, because I'd seen the colorized Grace on Facebook, and here was the sepia version—the hard-to-grasp version—ghostlike and ashen in front of me.

Grace nodded without speaking.

"Hola, hombre!" Lola said, waving her lollipopped hand in my direction without looking away from her screen.

I sat at the editor's desk. Turned on the editor's computer. Logged in to the editor's account. Savored, for a moment, the feeling I had worked for two years to achieve.

It was quickly interrupted when Grace turned around on her computer chair to face me. "I'm not going to write anything. That's the deal. No editorials. No opinion pieces. You want something said, you say it yourself. Everything else I'll help you with, but I don't write any words."

I glanced sidelong at La, who was concentrating very intently on looking like she was ignoring our conversation. The voodoo-curse theory was starting to look more and more plausible. "I can deal with that. I'm hoping not to do much writing myself, actually. Hink said we should be able to get some juniors to volunteer."

"I already talked to Hink. I'm going to be assistant editor. You worked for this for years; it should be your baby."

"Okay."

"Good."

"Well, uh, I guess you should read our policies and procedures, our editorial guidelines and our charter. They're all saved in the shared drive." Lola and I had both read them when we'd volunteered at the paper the previous year. "You get a log-in yet?"

"Hink gave me one before you walked in."

"You're good to go, then."

"Straight to the point. I like it." Grace swung back around on her chair, opened the shared drive, found the documents I'd been talking about, and started to read them.

Lola did one slow, deliberate three-hundred-sixty-degree swing around on her office chair, her eyes wide and brows raised, but I shook my head at her and she sighed and went back to ASOS.

There wasn't much to do that first morning except for planning, so I put my Spotify playlist on shuffle. The first song to play was "Hey" by the Pixies. *Been trying to meet you,* crooned Black Francis. I turned up the volume a little and hummed along to the tune as I logged into my email (thinking about how I should really rewatch *The Devil Wears Prada* now that I was editor, get some tips) until I caught a tiny movement in the corner of my eye. I looked up to find Grace Town mouthing the words. *If you go, I will surely die,* she mimed absentmindedly, scrolling through the newspaper's thirty-page policy and procedures document about topics we weren't allowed to cover (no sex, no drugs, no rock 'n' roll, nothing relevant to real-life teens in general, etc.).

"You know the Pixies?" I asked her after the first chorus. Grace looked up and over her shoulder at me but didn't speak right away.

"'You met me at a very strange time in my life,'" she said eventually. When I said nothing, she cocked her head slightly and said, "*Fight Club*? 'Where Is My Mind?'?"

"I know. I got it. *Fight Club* is, like, one of my favorite movies."

"Me too."

"Really?"

"Yeah. Why are you so surprised?"

"Most girls—" I began. Lola snapped up her hand.

"Be *very* careful what you say next, Henry Page," she said. "Very few good things come out of sentences that begin with 'Most girls.'"

"This is true," Grace agreed.

"Uh. Well. I was *going* to say that a lot—not most, but a lot—of the girls I know don't like *Fight Club*."

"I like *Fight Club*, you bigot," Lola said.

"Most girls don't like intelligent films?" Grace said. "Or girls that *do* like *Fight Club* are special snowflakes and therefore better than the rest of the womenfolk?"

"Oh God, no, that's not what I meant. The girls here—they probably haven't even seen *Fight Club*, you know? They've never even watched it."

"I am a female and I have seen *Fight Club*," Lola said.

"There you go. Of the two women in the room, one hundred percent of them have seen *Fight Club*. Your 'most girls' statistics might need some reevaluating."

"I'm going to stop talking now," I said, "lest more of the patriarchy vomits out of my mouth."

Grace grinned. "We're teasing you, Henry."

There was a beat of silence—these would become a constant fixture in our conversations—in which I tried desperately to keep the conversation going beyond its natural point of death.

"Why'd you change your mind?" I said quickly.

Grace stared at me, the remnants of her smile fading. "I don't know," she said finally. Right at that moment, the bell for first period rang, and—even though we technically didn't have to go to it because it was designated newspaper time—Grace Town stood up and packed her things and left the room.

"Did you hear that?" I said to La after Grace was gone. "She likes the Pixies *and Fight Club*."

"Pretty sure I like the Pixies and *Fight Club*, you giant bag of dickweed."

"Yeah, but you're a devious lesbian who steals boys' first kisses and then forever emasculates them by coming out of the closet two weeks later."

"Speaking of, I forgot to tell you something. Madison Carlson legit asked me the other day how bad a kisser you must be to turn a girl off mankind forever."

"I hope you politely explained that sexual orientation is predetermined and that you were already a lesbian when you kissed me."

"Oh no, I told her you have a crooked penis and that after I saw it I could never contemplate seeing another."

"Thanks, bro."

"Anytime," Lola said as she, too, stood and packed up her things. At the doorway she stopped and glanced back at me, her head cocked in the direction Grace Town had left in. "I like her, Henry. There's, I don't know . . . something about her."

I nodded, and said nothing, but because Lola was my best friend, and because we'd known each other all our lives, she smiled. Because, even without speaking, even without words, she knew exactly what that nod meant: *I like her too.*

CHAPTER 6

THAT AFTERNOON AFTER my last class, when the bell rang, I walked out of the classroom and—shoving my books into my bag—almost ran headfirst into Grace Town. I didn't realize until later that she must've asked Lola where my locker was. I'd certainly never told her, and the only other human I'd seen her speak to was Mr. Hink, who didn't know either.

"Henry," she said.

"Hello," I said slowly.

"Do you want a lift home?"

"Okay."

"You still have to drive yourself, though."

"Uh. Sure?"

Grace turned without another word and made off down the hallway without checking to see if I was following (I was, of course). When we made it to the football field, she sped up, which made her limp much more pronounced, her movements slightly wild. It was a stride I could only accurately describe as Mad-Eye Moody–esque. I jogged every fifth step to keep up with her. At the edge of the school grounds I looked back to where Lola and Murray were waiting (as always) in the bus line to catch a ride to my house. I waved. They both raised their right arms and saluted me in unison. Grace Town did not see, thank God.

Out on the street, the silence was broken only by the occasional passing car and the steady click of Grace's cane against the road, until she eventually spoke. "So what's your story, Henry Page?" she said. There was, once again, an undercurrent of anger that I didn't understand, like Grace was disappointed in me for some reason. "Give me all the gory details."

"I, um. Well." I got stage fright. "I like piña coladas and getting caught in the rain?" I said weakly.

"Don't you find it strange that whenever anyone asks you to describe yourself, you draw a blank? It should be the easiest thing in the world to talk about—I mean, you *are* you—but it isn't."

"Yeah. I guess. Although it's kind of like asking someone, 'How was Europe?' after they've spent three months there, you know? There's a lot to cover."

"This is true. Shall we narrow it down? Let me ask you a question."

"Okay."

"It's going to be intensely personal, so feel free not to answer if you don't want to."

"Uh . . . Okay," I said, steeling myself for questions about my sexual orientation or my unnatural predilection for wearing my father's black coat even in the heat, which seemed to be, when meeting strangers, the two most popular courses of inquiry.

"What's your favorite color?"

Not what I was expecting. "Um . . ." I'd never really had a favorite color. Or maybe I had too many to list. All colors were created equal as far as I was concerned. "I don't give colors preferential treatment? What about you?"

"Alice in Wonderland's dress blue."

"So, like, sky blue?"

"No, not at *all*. I hate sky blue and baby blue and periwinkle, but Alice in Wonderland's dress blue is perfect."

"Is that the technical name for the shade, then? Is that what they put on the color wheel?"

"Well, I guess you could also say it's vintage fifties car blue, but Alice is easier. I can handle cornflower blue in a pinch."

"You've thought about this a lot."

"I like to have answers ready when people ask me about myself. I mean, if I don't know who I am, how is anyone else ever supposed to?"

I racked my brain, trying to pull something out of the black void it seemed to become when Grace Town was within a ten-foot radius. "Green. Green is my favorite color."

"That's utterly boring."

"Fine. The kind of faded, acid green color of my sister's

eyes when she's in sunlight. My nephew has exactly the same shade. That would have to be my favorite."

"Better."

A beat. "Are you going to ask me anything else?"

"No. I don't think I will."

"That was the strangest game of twenty questions I've ever played."

"It wasn't a game of twenty questions. I only wanted to ask you one thing."

When we got to Grace's house, we performed the same routine as yesterday. I waited outside on the lawn while she slipped inside and collected her keys. I drove her car to my house, said good-bye, then watched her walk away in the wrong direction, down a road that would lead her to nowhere. As soon as I walked in the door, I hated myself for not inviting her inside. As soon as I walked down the steps into the basement, I remembered why that would be a bad idea.

"Well, dig a ditch and bury me in it," Murray said, clapping me on the back at the foot of the stairs. "If you haven't gone and got yourself a frother."

"She just drove me home," I said.

"Oh my actual God," Lola said as I dropped my backpack and slumped onto the couch. "There's definitely something brewing there, Page."

Murray bounded into my lap, his obscene muscle mass crushing my legs as he threaded his arms around my neck and pressed his forehead to mine. "Are you sure there's nothing going on? Because we may have spied on you from the grimy basement window and seen you staring deeply into each other's eyes."

"Guys, you both need to chill out," I said as I tried to detach Murray, without much success. "She's a total weirdo. I think she's lonely and she hasn't made any friends yet, so she's latched on to me because I was nice to her."

"You weren't nice to her, though," La said, frowning. "You chased her across a field while screaming obscenities at her."

"That's quite an embellishment."

"It's his fiery passion that she's fallen for," Muz said, his hair bouncing as he pressed his fists to my heart. "His vehement hunger for life."

"She hasn't *fallen* for me. I don't think she even really likes me. She glares at me a lot. It's really confusing."

"Ask her to come hang out Monday afternoon after school," Lola said, stroking her chin. "Bring her to the lions' den. Let *us* be the judges of that."

"As long as Murray promises not to pull this shit." Muz was now rubbing his hair all over my face and chest and arms. "Can you . . . Ugh, Murray. C'mon, get off!"

"I'm scenting my territory!" he insisted. "I can't lose you!"

I looked at Lola. "This is why I'm single."

La shook her head. "I promise you, it's not."

So I went limp and let Murray anoint me with his greasy

mane, certain that if Grace ever witnessed the weirdness that
went on in this room, she'd run the other way.

Which seemed like a good enough excuse to never, ever,
ever invite her over.

Later that night, when the rabble had left, I pulled up Grace
Town's Facebook profile on the iMac and let the mouse pointer
hover over the "Add Friend" button for about ten minutes before I finally shut my eyes and clicked. My heart beat wildly
at the sight of the "Friend Request Sent" notification, but I
only had to wait a handful of seconds before I got a response.
*Grace Town has accepted your friend request. Write on Grace's
timeline.*

Naturally I stalked her page, but everything, barring those
few publicly available profile pictures, had been bleached from
her timeline. No status updates. No check-ins. No life events.
No tagged photos. Apart from her 2879 friends (how does anyone even know that many people?!), Grace Town was a virtual
ghost.

After Grace had left the office that morning, I'd started
emailing PR companies around town, seeing if any of them
would let any of the shitty junior writers from the *Westland
Post*, as the paper had been dubbed when it started back in the
eighties, interview some of the shitty bands they represented.
It seemed like a good enough reason to start a conversation
with her.

HENRY PAGE:

Just thought I'd let you know I've locked in the Plastic Stapler's Revenge for an interview next week.

GRACE TOWN:

How exciting. I've always been anxious to hear the pressing thoughts of avenging stationery. When?

Not sure yet. Some of our junior volunteers should start crawling out of the woodwork soon. I predict that exactly two illiterate people and the feral cat that lives in the ceiling above Principal Valentine's office will actually offer to help out. I'll see if any of them are up to the task.

Excellent. Gather some minions. Order them to do our bidding. (My money is on the cat.)

I love that we get minions.

Do you think this is what Kim Jong-un feels like?

It's all part of the brainwashing process.

We're building an army.

First Westland High . . . then the world.

Drink the Kool-Aid, my minions! It's delicious!

Yes.

How you doing anyway? You settling in?

Are people being nice?

Were you sad to leave East River or was it kind of mixed emotions?

Most of my friends had already graduated. That made it easier to leave, but still, I miss it.

The East River kids do have a reputation for enjoying a good time. Weren't some of the seniors arrested last year for constructing and then riding a motorized picnic table around campus?

I don't like to say it but . . . #YOLO

I'll let that one slide, but only once.

Never again. I swear it.

Very good. I'm glad we have an agreement.

scraps idea for regular YOLO article

Hey, if you're happy to put your name on it, go right ahead.

No, no. I'm good.

The conversation ended there. Grace was still online for another hour, but I couldn't think of anything else to say, so I left it at that.

There were, of course, methods of finding things out about people from other schools if you were so inclined. Madison Carlson, in particular, seemed to run an interschool goods and information trading service so large and complex that she could've given the Silk Road a run for their money. Madison's boyfriend went to East River, which apparently gave her unparalleled access to the lives of the East River elite (I made a mental note to ask her to write a *Gossip Girl*–style column for the newspaper). But what Madison Carlson giveth, Madison Carlson taketh away. If I so much as breathed a casual inquiry about Grace Town's past life, the rumor that I kind of, maybe, sort of liked her would be known school-wide within a day.

Grace Town, for now, would have to remain a mystery.

CHAPTER 7

ON MONDAY AFTERNOON, after the final bell rang, Grace was already waiting outside my locker. How she managed to escape her last-period class early on such a frequent basis I don't suppose I'll ever know, but after that day she was always there when I walked out.

"Lift?" she said, her expression and tone betraying that she was (confusingly?) unhappy to see me, like she'd been hoping I wouldn't there today.

"Sure," I said warily.

And so began the routine that would pattern our relationship. We walked to her house together, Grace abusing any cars that beeped at us to get out of the way. She made me wait on the overgrown front lawn while she got the keys from inside. Once she'd found them, she threw them to me and made me drive myself home. In the car, she'd either stare straight ahead, stony-faced and unspeaking, or ask me questions like:

"What's your favorite song?"

And I'd say things like: "Why are these questions so hard to answer?"

And she'd say things like: "Because right now you're trying to think of a song that's both cool and socially acceptable to say it's your favorite. Usually a minimum of twenty years old, because anything newer than that is generally considered pop trash."

"Well, now that I know you're judging me, I'm not going to be able to pick anything."

"That's what getting to know someone is about. Judging them."

"So you really *are* judging me right now?"

"Always. Look, tell me a song that makes you feel something."

"Fine. 'Someday' by the Strokes," I said, remembering the night I'd fallen asleep with Grace's favorite band playing in the background.

"Risky choice. Definitely not twenty years old yet, but indie enough that you might get away with it."

"What's yours? 'Stairway to Heaven'? 'Smells Like Teen Spirit'? Something equally awesome and classic, I suppose?"

"'She Will Be Loved' by Maroon 5."

"That . . . is not what I was expecting."

"What can I say? Whenever I hear it, it reminds me of being happy."

Yikes. If that was her idea of a happy song, what did she listen to when she was sad? Funeral marches? "Where do you hear it? Do they even *play* that on the radio anymore? Does anyone even *listen* to the radio anymore?"

"Ha-ha."

"Not a Strokes song, then?"

"What do you mean?"

"The Strokes? You seem to be a big fan too." Grace was still frowning like she didn't understand. "You have decals on your car. On your key ring. It's your phone background."

"Oh yeah. The Strokes. Yeah. I had a friend who was a big fan. He used to listen to their stuff all the time."

"Your friend liked the Strokes so much that you put decals on your car?"

"It's his old car, actually."

"What about your phone?"

"It's his old phone too."

"Right."

After we got out of the car, I said, on an impulse, "Do you want to come in?"

Grace said, "Why?"

And I said, "Um. We could, like, hang out and stuff? I don't know, like, if you wanted?"

"I go somewhere in the afternoons."

"Sure. Yeah. I noticed that. Well, I'll see you tomorrow, then."

Grace sighed. "Meet me back here once the sun has set."

"Why?"

"Don't you want to hang out?"

"Uh, yeah, I guess."

"So let's hang out. Tonight. Once the sun has set, meet me back here. Okay?"

"Are we, like, doing something illegal or . . . ? Just the whole after-sunset thing seems very diabolical."

Grace smiled her tired smile. "I'll see you tonight, Henry Page." Then she turned and limped off down the street and disappeared around the corner.

For some reason, I didn't tell my basement-dwelling friends that Grace was meeting me that night. Whatever was happening between us felt very thin, very fragile, not the type of thing to be discussed and dissected by a group of people. Because, deep down, I think I honestly believed it would go nowhere and I didn't want to have to deal with the inevitable embarrassment that would come if I told my friends I very nearly almost liked a girl and it turned out she didn't like me back. So I faked feeling sick, and they begrudgingly went home to their own families to eat their own dinners instead of being freeloading succubuses (*succubi*?) like they normally were.

After they were gone, all that was left to do was tell my parents.

Now, I know most teenagers are supposed to hate their parents or at the very least think they're uncool or whatever, but I was always too in awe of my mom and dad for any of that. My parents had one of those creepy, pre-*Frozen*-Disney-movie-type love-at-first-sight stories. They met at a KFC (okay, so maybe not *quite* Disney) after school when they were barely tweens. Dad, being the cocky little kid I assume he was, asked for Mom's hand in marriage on the spot (offering her a piece of fried chicken instead of an engagement ring—definitely, definitely *not* Disney).

You've probably read stories like that before, about old-timey folk proposing marriage on the first date and all. But this is legit. And it worked. They didn't get married for another eleven years, but they never dated anyone but each other from that day onward. They eloped in India on a Christmas Day when they'd barely finished college, each dressed in swimwear and painted in henna. I had a Polaroid photo of them feeding mangoes to elephants. So theirs was an incredible love. Speaks volumes of Colonel Sanders' secret recipe.

But it wasn't their Nicholas Sparks–esque, so-perfect-it-kind-of-makes-you-sick relationship that I loved most about them. It was the way they were. I'd seen hormonally ravaged teenagers who weren't as giddily in love as my parents, and—instead of making me dry retch, like it was apparently supposed to—I loved their love.

They'd been hippies when Suds was a kid, an artist and a carpenter living in an abandoned warehouse. Maybe the hellish experience of raising Sadie to adulthood had stripped any resistance from their systems, but they'd always been nothing but incredibly cool and open toward me.

So when I said to my mom, Daphne, when she got home from the gallery: "Mother, I'm going out tonight and I'm not sure what time I'll be home or where I'm going exactly. I'm not a hundred percent certain, but I may possibly be engaging in illegal activities. Is that okay?"

She just said: "An adventure, huh? Excellent. I was starting to worry about you. Sadie had been arrested three times by your age, and look how she turned out."

"Thanks, Mom. I knew you'd support me."

"In anything except murder and the use of prohibited substances that require injection."

"Oh, good, 'cause I've been meaning to see if you wanted to invest in this mobile meth lab business I've been working on for the past few months."

"Of course, darling. Do me up a compelling spreadsheet and I'll take a gander at the figures. Will you require emergency getaway transportation from your possibly illegal activities this evening?"

"I'm not sure yet. Can I keep you posted? I shouldn't be out too late. I don't want to keep you and Dad up."

"If I don't answer my phone, just get the police to drop you home. We'll pretend to ground you for a month."

"Thanks, Mom."

She kissed my forehead. "For real, though. Don't break any laws. And call me if you need me, okay?"

"Will do."

The afternoon passed far too slowly after that and then, in the minutes leading up to sunset, far too quickly. All of a sudden it was dark and I was walking toward the front door, shouting good-bye to my parents, searching my thoughts for conversation starters, questions I could ask Grace to keep the small talk going. I always got stage fright in front of her, my brain turning into a cavernously empty pothole that couldn't scrounge up useful thoughts to save itself.

Outside, Grace's car had disappeared, as it had the two afternoons she'd driven me home last week. I waited by the mailbox, shuddering against the surprisingly chilly evening breeze. Five minutes passed before I caught a flicker of movement in the corner of my eye. A small, dark figure stood at the end of my street, beckoning me into the blackness. From that distance I couldn't see their face, only the outline of their strangely wide shoulders. It wasn't the silhouette of something I wanted to follow into the dark. When I didn't move, Grace exaggerated her summoning motion so that she was using her whole arm and her cane to call me to her. I jogged over, zipping up my jacket against the cool. As I drew closer, I could see she was still dressed in her typical boyish attire, topped with a football jacket that was so large on her, she could've worn it as a dress. Had she driven home to get it and then walked all the way back here?

"Do you have a bus pass?" she called when I was within earshot. Not hello. Never hello.

"Not on me, no, sorry."

"That's okay. I'll be your sugar mama and pay your fare."

"Where are we going?"

"You'll see."

"As long as we're not, like, leaving the state or anything."

"You'll see."

And then instead of setting off back down my street, Grace turned and started making her way into the long grass where the street ended.

"Are you serious?" I said. "There's a gully down there. It's a storm-water drain."

"Shortcut" is all Grace said, plunging farther into the darkness.

"I mean, are you okay with your leg and everything?" I shouted after her, not knowing if it was politically correct or not to even *mention* that I'd *noticed* she walked with a limp. "The ground is really uneven!"

"Shortcut!"

Grace started swatting the grass away with her cane then, like she was an explorer hacking her way through a jungle. I followed the trail she cut through the greenery, keeping close enough to her so that if she stumbled I'd be able to catch her, but—even though her limp was more pronounced—she never did.

We followed the drain for ten minutes, making small talk about the newspaper, until the gully spat us out on the main road near a bus stop. We sat and waited for a bus in fluorescent light, me kind of expecting it to be a Greyhound that would take us halfway across the country, but the one Grace hailed was the one that went into the city. She paid my fare like she said she would, and then we sat in the disabled seating section, which Grace said was (and I quote) "the one perk of being a cripple."

The city at nighttime was spectacular. I'm all for mountains and forests and glass-clear rivers, but there is something about the million burning lights of a city in the dark that just gets to me. Maybe because it reminds me of the galaxy.

When we got off the bus, Grace led me straight to the closest convenience store.

"We require snacks," she said. "My treat."

"You are too kind to me. Keep taking care of me like this and I'll become a kept man." I chose some M&M's and Coke. Grace picked a bag of salt-and-vinegar chips (which—I know it sounds weird—just totally *suited* her), a Vitaminwater, and a loaf of cheap white bread. Then we walked. We walked for so long, I started to think that this *was* the hanging out and that we didn't actually have an actual destination, but Grace wouldn't let me eat my snack yet, despite my protests.

Eventually she came to a stop at a tall iron fence with a thick hedge growing on the other side and said, "Ta-da."

"It's a . . . fence. I mean, it's a very nice fence. And I admire the workmanship. But it's a fence."

"What's behind the fence is what we came for."

"Which is?"

"I am so pleased you asked. Behind this fence is one of this city's best-kept secrets. Did you know that before the subway was built, a steam train line used to run right through the business district?"

"I did not, but now that you mention it, I suppose it makes sense."

"Behind the fence is the last steam train station in the city. It's been permanently closed to the public for decades."

"Then why are we here?"

Grace kept an entirely straight face as she put her loaf of bread down at her feet, held her cane in her right hand like a javelin, and launched it over the hedge.

"Oops. I'd better go get that," she said. Then she stepped up onto the fence with her good leg and hauled herself up.

"What are you *doing*?" I said.

"Trespassing, obviously. C'mon."

"What if someone calls the police?"

"I'll tell them I lured you here and seduced you into breaking the law."

"Yeah. Like that's gonna work."

"C'mon, Henry. You have shiny hair and dimples and I dress like Aileen Wuornos." She paused to take a breath as she climbed. "The cops *will* believe you. Have you never broken a law before?"

"I've jaywalked once or twice in my time."

"So badass."

"And I've been involved in at least three incidences of underage drinking."

With a final grunt and wince of pain as she put weight on her bad leg, Grace straddled the top of the fence. She'd done this before. "Henry."

"I really want to go to college."

"Climb the fence."

"You know I've made it through seventeen years of my life without being peer pressured? My parents warned me about it in elementary school, but I never experienced it. I was starting to believe it was a myth."

"Henry Page. Climb. The. Fence."

"And, like, it's a really accurate description of what it is. I'm feeling very pressured by my peer right now."

"Henry, haul me that goddamn loaf of bread and then get your ass up here right now!"

"Fine!" I threw the bread over, then wrapped my hands around the iron bars and pulled myself up, which was difficult, because I could no longer feel my legs due to what I assumed was an impending panic attack. "Oh my God, oh my God, oh my God," I said over and over again as I climbed. Grace disappeared on the other side of the hedge. "I'm going to be arrested. I'm never going to college. I'm going to be a felon. My parents are going to kill me."

Once I reached the top of the iron bars, it became clear that there was no easy way to climb down the other side, so I kind of straddled the hedge and then rolled. It did not go well. I hit the ground, hard, lost my balance, and ended up on my knees. Grace's cold laugh could only accurately be described as a cackle, this kind of raucous clucking more befitting of a crow than a human being.

"You sound like a Disney villain," I said as I stood and

brushed the dirt from my clothes, which only made Grace cackle more.

"I warn you, child. If I lose my temper, you lose your head! Understand?!" Grace said. "Congratulations, Henry. You're officially trespassing."

I looked around. Apart from a few trees stripped naked from the cold—or possibly long dead—there appeared to be little more on this side than an empty field.

"Where is this mysterious train station you speak of?"

Grace pointed with her cane and set off in front of me. "Just down the hill."

And it was. Not ten seconds after we'd started walking, a small, sodium-lit building came into view, nestled away in the blackness.

"It looks like a crypt," I said.

"Well, it is a crypt. In the philosophical sense. All old buildings become crypts the moment they're finished. A shrine to a time that's already dead."

"You are very weird, Grace Town."

"I know."

"I don't mind it."

"I know."

When we reached the building, we came to a tall gate made in the same elaborate design as the fence.

"Come," said Grace. "We're only trespassing at the moment. Now it's time for the breaking and entering."

"Grace, no, come on, that's really—" I said, but the gates

swung open at her touch and she walked through them and looked back at me and winked.

"They haven't been locked for years."

We walked through a short, dim tunnel out onto a single open platform that was, shockingly, lit from above by burnt sodium lights. The station was in a much better state than I expected it to be. It was mostly clean of graffiti and not overgrown by any kind of vegetation.

"Uh, as far as abandoned buildings go, this one seems to be in pretty un-abandoned condition," I said. The ceiling was a series of high arches made of frosted glass, the ground checked marble in black and white, the walls of the building eggshell and emerald green tiles. "Are you sure this isn't a leftover set from *The Great Gatsby* or something?" I said as I took it all in, because it really was that beautiful.

"It's a historical landmark, so even though people aren't allowed here anymore, they still try and look after it. C'mon, you still haven't seen the best part." Grace knelt at the station door then, an ornate piece of wood painted red, and started picking the lock with a hairpin.

"Okay, now, that *is* breaking and entering."

"The best thing about historical landmarks is"—there was a *ping* as the lock clicked open—"all original fixtures. Hundred-year-old locks are child's play."

"Are you aware that you're slightly terrifying right now?"

Grace ignored me, turned on the flashlight on her phone, and stepped into the dark. I followed her through a series of empty, pitch-black rooms, deeper and deeper into the bowels of the old building, until we came to a cast-iron spiral staircase that corkscrewed into the ground.

"Look up," Grace said as we started descending the stairs. Above us was another domed glass roof, but one of the panels was shattered to reveal a spray of white stars. A rare sight in the city.

We couldn't go all the way down the stairs because the basement was flooded. Grace sat on the second-to-last step, took off her shoes, and put her feet in the water. Then she tore off a little piece from the loaf of bread and flicked it into the water. It floated on the surface for a few seconds before I heard a *bloop* and it was sucked under.

"What the hell was that?" I said, backing up the stairs.

"Calm down, it's only fish. Come down here. Sit really still and they'll come up to you."

It felt a lot like the trash compactor scene from *Star Wars*, but I'd already come this far, so I did what she said. I went down the stairs. I took off my shoes. I sat next to her, close enough that our clothing brushed when either of us moved. I put my feet in the cold water. I sat still. I didn't speak. I watched as Grace tore off more bread and let it float above our toes. A few minutes passed, and then the fish came, these small, silver streaks about the size of my palm. They darted in and out of our legs, their slick bodies brushing our ankles. Grace put out more bread and more fish came, until all the water around us was alive with silver.

"This is awesome," I said, but Grace hushed me so I wouldn't scare the fish away. I fell quiet and just watched them, and watched her, and tried not to think about how soft her lips would feel if I kissed her.

When the bread was gone, Grace leaned back against the stairs with her arms behind her head, so I did the same.

"Have you ever had a girlfriend, Henry?" she said.

The question kicked my heart into overdrive. "Uh, no, not really."

"Why not?"

"I . . . Um . . . Shit, I'm really not good at this sharing business."

"I noticed. Why is that? I thought you were a writer."

"Exactly. I'm a writer. I could go home and write you an essay on why I've never had a girlfriend, and it would be awesome. But I . . . kinda suck at telling stories when they're not on paper."

"So you draft everything? Filter everything?"

"Well, it sounds depressing when you say it like that, but yeah. I guess."

"That sucks. You lose the rawness, the truth of who you are if you pass everything through a screen first."

"I guess you're right. If rawness is what you want, at least. I struggle to get the exact message I want across unless I write it down."

"Why don't you try?"

"How?"

"Give me the unedited draft of why you've never had a girlfriend. Blurt it out."

"Because . . . So many reasons. Because I'm seventeen. Because I don't mind being alone. I like it actually. I've been surrounded by teenagers who are always in and out of these dramatic, toxic relationships and that's never held any appeal for me. I want what my parents have. Extraordinary love."

"You understand that you're missing out on a lot of awesome stuff by choosing to be that way, though, right? Sometimes you don't know things are going to be extraordinary until they are."

"Well, yeah. I mean . . . I guess."

"As long as you're aware. That was a decent first draft, by the way. You can revise your answer and give it to me again in text form if you feel the need."

"I'll keep you posted. I might send you an essay sometime in the next few days."

"Okay, Henry Page, I have asked you three questions now. The magic number. It's your turn to ask me something."

"What should I ask you?"

"Asking what to ask me kind of defeats the purpose of the game. Ask me something you want to know."

"What happened to your leg?"

Grace turned her head to face me. We were only inches apart. I could feel the warmth of her breath on my lips. "*That* is a boring question."

"Why?"

"Because the answer has no relevance to me as a human being. Here I am asking you very deep stuff about your favorite color and song and singledom, and you go straight for the obvious physical stuff."

"I can ask something else if you'd like."

Grace looked toward the stars. "I was in a car accident like three months ago. It was bad. The car flipped hood to trunk seven times. I spent about a month in the hospital afterward, getting pins and skin grafts and stuff in my leg. For a week I was mostly unconscious, for a week I wanted to die to end the pain. And then I started to get better. I learned to walk again. I have a series of gnarly scars. No, you cannot see them. Did I cover everything for you?"

"That sucks."

"It really does. But everything happens for a reason and all that jazz, yada, yada, yada." She rolled her eyes.

"You don't believe everything happens for a reason?"

Grace snorted. "Look up at that, Henry. Look up at that, honestly, and tell me you believe that our lives are anything more than a ridiculous cascade of random chances. A cloud of dust and gas forms our planet, a chemical reaction creates life, and then all of our cavemen ancestors live just long enough to bone each other before they die awful deaths. The universe is not the magical place people like to paint it as. It's excruciatingly beautiful, but there's no magic there, just science."

I stared at the stars for a little while longer, mainly thinking about caveman sex. "How'd you find this place anyway?"

Grace sat up a little, opened her chips, and started eating them. "A friend brought me here years ago, when we were kids. We were both troublemakers and breaking in here made us feel like rebels. We used to come here all the time and talk for hours. Now I come here whenever I want to be reminded of how insignificant I am in the grand scale of the universe."

"Sounds like lots of fun."

"Space is the best cure for sadness that I know."

"Feeling insignificant isn't exactly a great cure for un-happiness."

"Hell yeah it is. When I look up into the night sky, I re-member that I'm nothing but the ashes of long-dead stars. A human being is a collection of atoms that comes together into an ordered pattern for a brief period of time and then falls apart again. I find comfort in my smallness."

"I don't think you're on the same page as the rest of hu-manity, Town. You're supposed to be terrified of oblivion, same as the rest of us."

"The best thing the universe ever gave us is that we'll all be forgotten."

"Oh, come on. Nobody *wants* to be forgotten."

Grace leaned back again and looked up at the sky. The quote "I have loved the stars too fondly to be fearful of the night" came to mind. My spine shuddered slightly as I watched her. "I kinda like the idea," she said. "That when we die, despite any pain or fear or embarrassment we experienced during our lives, despite any heartbreak or grief, we get to be dispersed back into nothingness. It makes me feel brave, knowing I'll get a blank slate at the end. You get a brief glimmer of consciousness to do with what you will and then it's given back to the universe again. I'm not religious, but even I can appreciate that that's redemption, on the grandest scale. Oblivion isn't scary; it's the closest thing to genuine absolution of sin that I can imagine."

"Jesus. No wonder Hink wanted you on the newspaper."

"See? Good things come out of first drafts sometimes."

"I bet your writing is incredible. Why'd you stop?"

"Oh, you know. The usual cliché. Post-traumatic stress disorder, I suppose. Very boring, plot wise."

I wanted to say *You're kind of extraordinary—I mean, seriously weird, but also extraordinary,* but instead I said, "What sins does a seventeen-year-old girl need absolved?"

"You'd be surprised." Grace sat up, a small, mischievous smile on her face. "Do you want to know a dark secret from my past?"

"Oh God, I knew it. You buried a body down here, didn't you?" I said as she stood and held out her hand and pulled me to my feet. "Who was it? A random homeless person? A teacher from your old school? Is that why you transferred?"

We walked together, slowly, her still holding my hand, halfway back up the spiral staircase, where she crouched to show me something scratched into the metal.

"I was, once upon a time, a vandal." Grace moved her hands aside to reveal a set of crudely engraved letters. It read *G + D 4evr*. "Voilà."

"You did this?"

"Yep. When I was, like, ten."

"Grace Town. I don't know how I feel about you anymore. What's the *D* stand for?"

"A boy."

"Was he your boyfriend?"

"More of a crush, at the time."

"Forever, huh? You guys still together, then?"

"As it turns out, forever is not as long as I thought it would be."

Grace traced her fingers over the letters, trancelike, as though she'd forgotten entirely that I was there. "I should probably head home," she said quietly. "Thanks for hanging out. I used to come here all the time, but it's not the same when you're alone."

"Sure. Anytime. We can come here whenever you want."

"I'll see you tomorrow."

"You all right?"

"Yeah. Just . . . old memories, you know? My mom lives in the city. I might crash with her tonight. You all right to get the bus on your own?"

"Oh my stars, Grace Town, however will I make it home unaccompanied?"

"I'll take that as a yes."

Grace started to climb, but after taking three steps, she paused and looked back at me. "I'm glad I met you, Henry."

"I'm glad I met you, Grace."

Then I stood there and watched her leave, the light from her phone growing dimmer and dimmer as she was swallowed by the drowning dark, until there was nothing left of her at all, not even a sound, and I was alone in the blackness.

My feelings were like a knot inside my gut. Normally I knew exactly what my emotions were. Happy, sad, angry, embarrassed: they were all easy enough to catalog and label. But this was something new. A kind of web of thoughts that had offshoots in all directions, none of which made particular sense. A huge feeling, a feeling as big as a galaxy, a feeling so large and twisted that my poor little mind couldn't comprehend it. Like when you hear that the Milky Way is made up of 400 billion stars, and you think *Oh, shit, that's pretty big* but your puny human brain will never really be able to comprehend how gigantic it is because we were built too small. That's what it felt like.

I knew when girls liked me. Or, at the very least, I knew when girls were flirting with me. Grace Town wasn't flirting. Grace Town didn't like me. Or, if she *was* and she *did*, she wasn't expressing it in any way I was used to.

I also knew when I liked girls. Abigail Turner (from kindergarten) and Sophi Zhou (from elementary school) had been obsessions. Infatuations. Grace didn't feel like that. I wasn't even particularly sure I was attracted to her. There was no burning desire there. I didn't want to tear off her clothes and kiss her. I just felt . . . drawn to her. Like gravity. I wanted to orbit her, be around her, the way the Earth orbits the sun.

"Do not be an idiot, Henry," I said as I turned on my phone's flashlight and climbed the rusty spiral staircase toward the night sky, thinking of Icarus and his hubris and how appropriate the metaphor was (I was kind of proud of it, actually). "Do not fall for this girl."

When I got home (Mom picked me up, bless her), I opened up the Notes app on my phone and wrote:

> Draft Two
> Because I have never met anyone that
> I wanted in my life that way before.
> But you.
> I could make an exception for you.

CHAPTER 8

"MPDG," SAID LOLA Tuesday afternoon after school. She was lying upside down on my couch, boots on the headrest, head dangling off the edge, halfheartedly playing *FIFA*. "That's some serious MPDG behavior right there."

"What's MPDG?" Murray said.

"Manic Pixie Dream Girl. I mean, she takes Henry on an adventure to an abandoned railway station filled with fish and then talks about the universe? Real people don't do that."

"Well, she did," I said, "and it was kind of awesome."

"No, this is *bad*. MPDGs are dangerous territory."

"Wait, so how do the fish live underground?" Murray said. He'd been stroking his peach fuzz with a befuddled look on his face ever since I'd mentioned them. He must have washed his hair the night before (a rare occurrence), because it had reverted to its natural state: a lion's mane with the consistency of cotton candy. It enveloped much of his shoulders and face, to the point that he'd had to borrow several hair clips from La to keep it out of his eyes. "Is it like an enclosed ecosystem or something? How'd they even get there?"

"Probably connected to some kind of water source nearby," Lola said. "Birds land in the water with fish eggs stuck to their legs, something like that."

"Do you think they're edible? Maybe we should go fishing. What kind of fish were they, Henry? Trout? Bream?"

"Guys, can we focus here? I'm freaking out."

"Why?" Murray said.

"I think I like her." It wasn't easy for me to say. It wasn't something I'd normally admit to. Maybe, because it was senior year, I wanted some scandal. Not "contracting an STD from my shared love interest and earning the nickname the Trichomoniasis Trio" levels of scandal, but something. I was always on the outskirts of the teenage drama, always listening to Lola's and Murray's stories of love found and love lost, but I was never a participant.

For the first time, I wanted in. For the first time, someone might be worth it.

"Oh boy," Lola said.

Muz wiped a fake tear from his eye. "I've waited so long for this auspicious moment. Our little ankle biter finally becomes a man."

"What do I do?" I said.

"Does she like you? I mean, could you see something happening?" Lola said.

"Well, she did take me to her secret fishpond and talk to me about death. Maybe, in her brain, that means she's super into me?"

"Not necessarily. If she *is* an MPDG, she probably takes everyone there."

"Grace isn't a Manic Pixie Dream Girl, okay? If she were, she would wear sundresses and have bangs and ride a Dutch bike with baguettes in the basket and smile a lot. She's not quirky; she's straight-up weird. Actually, I think she might be depressed."

"Okay, lover boy, I wasn't trying to insult you."

I didn't tell La what I was really thinking: that Grace had turned up at school that morning in the same clothes she'd worn last night, her hair a nest piled at the top of her skull, her eyes rimmed red and puffy from a sleepless night. Girls who lied about having family in the city and occasionally slept in the streets hardly seemed capable of fitting the Manic Pixie Dream Girl archetype.

Murray swung his arm over my shoulder. "Look, mate. The most important thing is to not be too hasty. You get one opportunity with this. You balls it up and you'll be in some strife. Give it time. You only met her a week ago. Just assess the situation. Take note of her body language. Get to know her before you crack onto her, right?"

"That is strangely the wisest thing you've ever said," said Lola.

"As we'd say Down Under, there's no point pushing shit uphill with a rubber fork on a hot day."

"Are these real Australian sayings or do you come up with this stuff yourself?" I said.

"It's genetic," Muz said, grinning. "We're born with it already in our blood."

"And what's this crap about 'I go somewhere in the afternoons'?" Lola said. "What does that even mean?"

I shrugged. "No idea. She gets out of the car, wanders down the street, and disappears. Two or three hours later, the car vanishes too. I don't know if she comes back for it or if someone else drives it away or what."

"That's some enigmatic fuckery right there," Murray said.

"Grace Town is a riddle wrapped in a mystery inside an enigma," I said.

"We *could* solve it. I mean, I know we ain't no Madison Carlson, but we *could* give it a red-hot go."

"We could," La said slowly. "Follow her. See where she goes. Suss out the sitch."

"That's a bit Christian Grey–ish, don't you think?" I said.

"Dude, you aren't gonna sniff her hair while she sleeps. We're just gonna trail her for five minutes to see where she goes. She might be visiting her *boyfriend* or something." I could tell by the way Murray enunciated the word *boyfriend* that he knew the mere mention of a possible lover would be enough for me to agree. He was right.

"Seventeen goddamn years without peer pressure and suddenly I get smacked down with it twice in two days. Fine. Let's get our creep on."

Muz clapped his hands. "It's settled, then. Tomorrow afternoon, after school, we shall be parked and ready in a car outside your house to begin our stealth operation."

"I'm the only one with a license, though," I pointed out, "and I very much intend to be hiding on the floor of the backseat. So which one of you cretins, exactly, is going to drive?"

"Don't worry," Lola said, unlocking her phone. "I have a brilliant idea."

"I. Cannot. Fucking. Believe I let you talk me into this," Sadie said from the driver's seat as I scrabbled into the foot well of the backseat of her SUV. Lola and Murray were already strapped in and ready to go. "I'm a twenty-nine-year-old neuroscientist and I'm aiding and abetting my teenage hoodlum brother to stalk his disabled crush. What went so drastically wrong in my life?"

"Dude, what shoes are you wearing, pointed rodeo boots with spurs?" I said to Murray as he pulled the door closed and I tried to get comfortable on his feet, which was difficult, because his shoes were trying to eviscerate my kidneys.

"They're kicks, bro, calm your tits. Stop being dramatic and sit next to me."

"Never! I must protect my identity. La, I really wish you'd climb in the back so Grace can't see you."

"And miss seeing this train wreck unfold firsthand? Not likely," Lola said.

I twisted around, unable to find a spot that didn't feel like I was being filleted. "Ugh, Sadie, just drive!"

"Patience, John Hinckley Jr. 2.0, we're following a girl who walks with a cane," said Sadie as she started the car and slowly pulled away from the curb.

I conceded to being uncomfortable for the entire trip and rested my cheek in the dirty foot well. "I swear I'm not going to shoot the president anytime soon."

"Say what you will, but if you book flights to Washington and start watching a lot of Jodie Foster movies, we *will* report you to the NSA," Lola said.

"What's happening?" I said as the car rolled to a slow stop. "Can you see her?"

"Yeah, she's right up ahead. Just picked a few flowers from someone's front garden. Freakin' MPDGs." I could practically hear Lola shaking her head. "Don't worry, I don't think she's gonna shake us."

"I'm more worried about her *seeing* us than shaking us."

"If we get busted, we'll tell the cops that Sadie is obsessed with Grace and made us come along for the ride so she could slaughter us all in some kind of violent Satanic ritual."

"Oh, ha-ha," Suds said. "I hate you all, bunch of little weirdos."

"Sounds like something a Satanist would say. Do you

frequently have congress with the beast or is it on more of a casual basis?"

Sadie mussed Lola's hair. La laughed and swatted her away.

"Damn, she's taking a shortcut," Murray said. "Where does that alley lead?"

"Only thing on the other side of the alley is the cemetery," Sadie said.

Murray jabbed me in the ribs. "I flippin' knew it! She goes to a boneyard every afternoon? We're dealing with some kind of genre fiction here for sure. Anybody wanna stack bets? What do we think? Is she a vampire? A ghost? One of those new age zombies that can love?"

"I'll wager ten dollars on fallen angel," Sadie said. "They're so hot right now."

"I'm gonna go out on a limb here. What's mermaid paying, Muz?" Lola said.

"Mermaids don't live in graveyards, you bloody drongo."

"Fine. Demon mermaid from hell who haunts the cemetery swamp that floods whenever it rains. What are the odds?"

"One hundred thousand to one."

"Excellent. Put me down for ten. Can almost taste dem dolla dolla bills."

"What about you, lover boy?" Murray said, leaning down. "What do you think your girl is? Witch? Alien? Werewolf? . . . Weredropbear?"

"Weredrop what?" Lola said.

"Real problem back home. Sydney's bloody infested with 'em. Everyone walks 'round with Vegemite rubbed behind their ears to keep from getting mauled. It's a flippin' tragedy, the amount of good blokes and sheilas we've lost to weardropbearism."

I lifted my head from the foot well. "Would you all please shut up and remember that we're on a very serious intelligence gathering slash stalking mission? Suds, go around to the end of Beauchamp Road—we can catch her on the other side."

"Way ahead of you, pipsqueak," Sadie said as I felt the car cut a wide U-turn onto the appropriately yet unimaginatively named Cemetery Drive.

"There it is," Lola said. "The dead center of town."

"I hear people are dying to get in," Murray said.

"I don't know about that," I said. "I hear everyone inside is pretty stiff."

"There she is," Lola said, smacking my shoulder. "Henry, get up, she's far enough away that she won't see us."

Murray yanked me up from the foot well by my coat and—with much effort and grunting—I eventually sat up beside him. Grace was a little ways away, walking along a row of headstones, the cluster of motley garden flowers grasped in her left hand. She'd taken her knit cap off and let her hair out so that the breeze caught it and it reflected the afternoon light and took on the color of sour buttercream. She stopped and tucked a wayward strand behind her ear and knelt at a grave that was already garlanded with dozens of blooms in various stages of decomposition. And then she sunk down into the grass on her stomach, her head resting on one arm, her fingers twirling blades of grass, her feet kicked up behind her. Even at this distance I could see her lips moving—Grace was talking, singing maybe, to an invisible someone beneath the earth.

All of us sat transfixed for a minute, sedated by the stillness that comes with seeing an intensely private moment that doesn't belong to you. Then Sadie shook her head and put the car into drive. "We weren't meant to see this, Henry. This wasn't for us."

I nodded. "Take us home, Suds."

I sat on the front windowsill all afternoon, reading a book and watching a storm roll in, waiting for the mystery of the disappearing car to be solved. Just after sunset, when the sky was bruised with a lightning storm, a car slowed in front of our house. I watched through the glass as a short bald man got out of the passenger side and ran through the rain to Grace's Hyundai. As he opened the door, he looked up, saw me looking at him, and raised his hand. I mirrored his gesture. The man nodded and got into the car and turned it around and drove off into the bucketing downpour, his brake lights like a demon's eyes in the darkness.

CHAPTER 9

THERE WAS NO WAY for me to broach the subject of the cemetery with Grace without admitting that we'd followed her there, so, like a sane, logical, and emotionally healthy person, I decided to try and forget what I'd seen. Instead I followed Murray's advice about getting to know her, which turned out to be harder than it sounded, because Grace Town was possibly the strangest human being alive.

Over the next couple of weeks, we ate lunch together almost every day, sometimes with my friends, sometimes—when I got the feeling that she didn't want to be around other humans—alone. This new ritual began much the same way that her driving me home had: the day after the graveyard incident, out of nowhere, Grace materialized at our table in the cafeteria and asked if she could sit with us.

Vampire, mouthed Murray as Grace sat down next to Lola. I kicked him under the table.

With Murray's pep talk about body language in my head,

I tried to take note of how Grace held herself around me. I found myself pulled toward her—I leaned across tables, angled my legs in her direction. Grace never mirrored my movements. She always sat straight or bent back, her legs crossed away from me. Every time I fell into her gravity, betrayed by my own body language, I drew back, careful not to give too much of myself away.

The editorial process worked like this: each year, four newspapers were released, one at the start of each term. The one in circulation now was the final one that last year's editor, Kyle (the aforementioned couch defiler), had put together. The last issue Grace and I would preside over would be released the summer after both of us had graduated. It would be our legacy, the wisdom we would impart to the fresh batch of seniors.

As well as recapping important events from throughout the term, each issue had a theme, usually some variant of one of four übervanilla high school flavors: "Friendship!" "Journeys!" "Acceptance!" "Harmony!"

Kyle, who wore a cape to school and hung a Guy Fawkes mask in the newspaper office, pushed the boundaries with abstract themes like "circles," "red" (Taylor Swift made many appearances), "uncanny," and "faded." This was frowned upon by the teachers, who preferred the newspaper to be nothing but hardcore "your teenage years are the best of your life" propaganda, but beloved by the students, who got to read about something other than "forging lifelong bonds" and "marching triumphantly into the future" for a change. And when I say *beloved*, I mean that at least 45 percent of them bothered to pick up a copy, which, if you know anything about teenagers and their penchant for not giving a shit about anything school related, kind of means Kyle's papers were runaway best sellers.

In pursuit of a Perfect Theme that would blow Kyle's legacy out of the water, the newspaper required a lot of work in closed spaces. Hink let us have free rein over the content ("You're both good kids; I trust you'll keep to the charter," he said in our first and only planning meeting, perhaps rather foolishly), which required Grace and me to have regular after-school brainstorming sessions. I'd roll my office chair over to her small desk and we'd sit side by side, me drinking Red Bull or coffee (we had special access to the teachers' lounge, *aw yiss*), her drinking peppermint tea, each of us filling in the newspaper's pagination with our increasingly shitty ideas. "New beginnings"? "Fresh starts"? "Becoming the person you're meant to be"? "Forever young"?

I wondered, during the long, hazy afternoons of those first couple of weeks, if she was as hyperaware of her body as I was of mine. Every accidental brush of skin as we reached over each other, every bout of raucous laughter that would leave one of us burying their forehead into the other's shoulder. Some days, Grace instigated the accidental contact. Other days she held herself like a marionette, every movement deliberate and measured to ensure our skin never touched, that we weren't sitting too close to each other.

Normally I was pretty good at reading people, but Grace

Town was an anomaly, a black spot on my radar. I hate to go all *Twilight*, but I could suddenly empathize with how Edward found such a dullard interesting (not that Grace was dull—she was sharp and witty, with a humor so dark it could've played Batman). But I finally understood Old Sparkly's attraction to Bella. The less I could read Grace—the less I understood about her—the more enraptured I became. I needed, desperately, to understand what was going on in the dark, twisted, hilarious halls of her mind.

Some days we felt like old friends. Some days she put in her earbuds and didn't speak to Lola or me except to say good-bye. Some days she didn't show up at all. I took the good with the bad, all the while getting sucked deeper into the tornado that was Grace Town.

On the Good Grace Days, the days when she was willing to engage, I was able to ascertain that:

- Grace Town used to run track (like, for *fun*). Or at least she had before the accident.
- Grace Town did not drink coffee.
- Grace Town spent her free time reading Wikipedia pages about serial killers and plane crashes.
- Grace Town's birthday was the weekend after Thanksgiving.
- Grace Town liked *Breaking Bad* and *Star Wars* and *Game of Thrones*, but not *Star Trek* or *Doctor Who* (which was almost a deal breaker, but not quite).

We only had one class together (drama), which I was fairly sure she was going to fail because she never left her seat at the back of the room and Beady never made her participate. Despite it being senior year and everyone freaking out about college acceptances, GPAs, and SAT scores, my first few weeks of classes went okay. I knew I'd get A's from the teachers who'd taught me before (Beady, Hink, my Spanish teacher Señor Sanchez), but the rest were all new to me and required a fair amount of buttering up to ensure I got anything close to good grades, because most were still—more than a decade later—holding a grudge against the Page family name.

The start of every school year was the same. The teachers who'd been at Westland long enough to have taught my sister always had the same reaction when taking attendance for the first time. They'd call my name. Recognize the last name *Page*. Look up in horror. See me, see how much I looked like Sadie, know for certain that we were siblings. Mom hadn't been exaggerating when she'd said Suds had been arrested three times by the time she was my age, but she got into even more trouble at school than she did with the law. Expelled (informally) and reenrolled five times for (among other things): selling cigarettes, stealing a video camera, setting a home economics kitchen on fire (Sadie maintained that this was a legitimate accident), successfully distilling moonshine (for eight months) in a science classroom cupboard, and finally, successfully growing marijuana (for three years) in the science department's greenhouse. (Perhaps it's no surprise she ended up a scientist—she did spend a lot of time working on "science projects" as a teenager, albeit illegal ones.)

The reason she was allowed to return time and time again? Because Sadie Page was, for all intents and purposes, a genius. I guess Westland wasn't ready to dump their one shot at having a Nobel Prize–winning graduate, no matter how much trouble she was. Principal Valentine had a soft spot for her less destructive shenanigans (legend has it she took Sadie's moonshine home after it'd been confiscated and still has a shot of it at the end of every school year), and Sadie's grades weren't just exceptional, they were astounding. Her report cards, along with the words *deviant* and *nuisance*, also said things like *mathematically precocious* and *disturbingly brilliant*. So, yeah. Being a Page came with a reputation for being an evil genius, neither of which I was, so I had to work my ass off to be seen as a) not a juvenile delinquent and b) slightly above average in the intelligence department.

I'd always hated this fact before. Now it gave me an excuse to spend as much time as possible studying, which of course required company, which of course included Grace. The last week in September, we walked to McDonald's together most lunchtimes to "study," which generally consisted of silly literature deconstructions ("What I like most about *Animal Farm* is that there is no frou-frou symbolism. It's just a good, simple tale about animals who hate humans," I said, echoing Ron Swanson from *Parks and Rec*, which earned a laugh and a forehead buried into my shoulder) and even sillier math problems

("What did you get for question six?" I said. Grace checked her book. "Purple, because aliens don't wear hats.")

Those first few weeks of working on the newspaper were the best. Something about the three of us being holed up in that little fishbowl of a room together was magic. Not a lot of work got done, but that didn't matter, because our print deadline was months away. The leaves had only just started to change color and the sun was still warm in the middle of the day, which meant we had all the time in the world. All the time in the world to wait for the Perfect Theme to fall into our brains. We knew it would be awesome when it came to us, and we'd be so consumed by its brilliance that we'd get the newspaper done in no time. So we advised our junior writers (four had eventually volunteered—a new record) to concentrate on the content that didn't have to fit the theme: interviews, event recaps, photo pages. Mostly we didn't work at all, because—on the Good Grace Days anyway—just being around each other was way more fun.

We made each other watch a slew of YouTube videos. The girls had never seen Liam Neeson going to Ricky Gervais for advice on "improvisational comedy" but we all watched it together, three times over, in fact, because it was so funny. We traded memes. We sent each other Snapchats ten times a day. In-jokes fell into place as easily as breathing. I was amazed at how quickly a person could become an essential part of your life. By early October, only four short weeks after meeting her, Grace and I practically had our own language. We could speak entirely in movie quotes or GIFs if required. We snuck Nerf guns into the office and had mini wars before and after school. We swapped our favorite books (mine: *The Road* by Cormac McCarthy, hers: *84, Charing Cross Road* by Helene Hanff), both horrified that the other had not yet read such a staggering work of literary perfection.

One afternoon in the first week of October when Lola was feeling particularly generous toward my cause, she announced that she needed Grace and me to model as guides for cartoons she was drawing for art class. The three of us went out into the empty football field at dusk, Lola with her camera around her neck, and proceeded to take a set of progressively more ridiculous photographs. They weren't as animated as La wanted them—Grace couldn't do the *Dirty Dancing*-style pose with her injury—but we all ended up collapsed in a laughing fit on the grass by the end of it.

"You owe me big-time," Lola said the next morning before class, pressing a photograph to my chest as she stalked past my locker. It was a candid moment captured in black and white. Me with my eyes closed, my head tilted downward, a small smile playing on my lips. Grace had her arm slung around my neck and was looking directly into the camera, in the middle of a laugh that crinkled her nose. I'd never seen her smile so wide. I hadn't known she was capable.

I quickly hid the picture in my biology textbook, sure that if Grace ever caught me with it, she'd file a restraining order. But when I got to the newspaper office in the afternoon, something had changed. It took me a few minutes to figure out what. There was a small rectangle taped to the glass in front of Grace's desk. A photograph. I had to get out of my chair and go over to it to see what it was. A blond girl and a dark-haired boy captured in gray scale, the girl kissing the boy's cheek while he grinned, his chin grasped loosely in her hand. They didn't look like us. Not a lanky, awkward kid and an unwashed tomboy who walked with a cane. Lola had captured something I'd never seen in either of us before.

We were characters out of a movie.

We were thoroughly alive.

And we were absolutely beautiful.

"I think I need a pseudonym," I said that Thursday, talking to Grace across our office. "I don't know, it feels like now that I'm so busy and important as editor, I shouldn't really be writing under my own name." We still had not, in fact, managed to be particularly productive. The Plastic Stapler's Revenge had finally been interviewed by an overenthusiastic junior, Galaxy Nguyen (he'd been allowed to choose his own name when he came over from Vietnam as a kid—badass), and we had a handful of articles submitted by our three other volunteer writers (usually covering topics they were unsettlingly passionate about, like Magic: The Gathering or cats).

Still, there was no need to panic yet.

"I accept the challenge of finding you an incredible nom de plume," Grace said with a small, seated bow. And that is how, some fifteen minutes later, I started composing my first article under the name of Randy Knupps (I'd bargained Grace down from Randy Nips, which Hink, although naïve, probably would've picked up on). But it was the moment she said, "I wanna get in on this pseudonym business. Maybe we can make it a family affair? I'll be Dusty Knupps, your Knupply wife, and Lola can be Candy Knupps, our Knupply daughter," that got my heart pulling two beats a second.

"The Knupps family newspaper. I like it."

"Actually, you know what? I think I'm ready to take our relationship to the next level."

"Oh?" I said, my heart beating so fast I couldn't discern one beat from the next.

"I think it's time we gave Lola a little brother or sister. Let's adopt a fish."

So we spent the rest of the day preparing for the arrival of our adopted aquatic baby. Lola made it a grand fishy palace out of clay in art class, Grace and I went to the pet store and bought it a tank and a water plant, and we even drew up a custody agreement, stating that our as of yet unnamed fish child would live at the office during the week and then at Grace's and my houses on alternating weekends.

In the evening, the three of us broke into the abandoned train station, and Grace used her skills as a fish whisperer (i.e., she fed them lots of bread) to gather a school of quicksilver bodies at the foot of the stairs.

"I am Grace of House Town, mother of gill-bearing aquatic

animals," she said as she slipped the net we'd bought at the pet store into the water and scooped up a small, shimmering fish.

"What should we call it?" I said as Grace transferred it into a plastic bag already filled with basement water.

"It looks like a he," Lola said, taking the bag from Grace and examining the fish swimming lazily inside. "An exotic, fabulous male. Let's call him Ricky Martin."

"Ricky Martin *Knupps*," I corrected. "Don't exclude your brother like that, La."

Ricky Martin Knupps, tragically, didn't live out the night. It turned out that the clay Lola had used to make his grand palace wasn't exactly fish-safe, and we found him floating belly-up in the morning, already long gone from this world.

"It's me," I whispered when Grace showed me his tiny corpse. "It's my fault. There's a fish-killing curse upon my family."

"He's with Toby and Gloria now," La said, resting a hand on my shoulder.

Grace carried RMK in a Tupperware container in her backpack until lunchtime, and we held a small yet solemn funeral for him under the bleachers, all of us humming "Livin' la Vida Loca" as we filled in his tiny grave, which is marked to this day with a fishing hook (poor taste, I know).

After scrubbing out the tank and ditching the murder castle in favor of several more plants and some aquarium-safe Ewok figurines, we finally brought home our forever baby,

Ricky Martin Knupps II, also captured from the train station fishpond.

"He has your eyes," Grace said as we all sat in the office and watched him swim around his new nontoxic home.

"He has your fins and gills," I said, and the playfulness of the situation sent a surge of adrenaline through me and I reached out and held her hand, like new parents might, like it was the most natural thing in the world.

"You guys are really fucking weird," Lola said.

"You're going to be a great dad to Ricky Martin Knupps II," Grace said, her fingers still knotted with mine. I wondered, in that moment, if it was possible for human beings to go supernova—my atoms felt like they were emitting a shock wave of heat and light as they came unstuck from each other. "Let's never tell him about the first Ricky Martin Knupps, though."

After that, I decided unconscious body language was bull-shit, probably dreamed up by some crackpot psychologist that'd been dead for half a century (I'm looking at you, Freud). Grace never really gave me any solid hints that she *like* liked me, and she never asked me to hang out alone again like we had the first night we went to the abandoned train station. But she drove me home every day after school. And on the week-ends we texted constantly, even though we didn't see each other.

So body language must be crap. It didn't matter that she didn't unconsciously cross her legs toward me; she *consciously* held my hand as we watched the fish swim around his bowl, for much longer than she needed to, the pad of her thumb moving back and forth across my skin.

Fake family noms de plume and adopted pets were what really counted, and in the world of Randy Knupps, Grace was already my wife and the mother of our fabulous aquatic child, Ricky Martin Knupps II.

CHAPTER 10

THE DECISION TO engage the services of Madison Carlson, supersleuth/interschool rumrunner, came about on a Tuesday in the second week of October, after Murray had failed to hear from his ex-girlfriend for nine consecutive days, and playing "Wonderwall" (very poorly) on his guitar outside her house had resulted not in reconciliation but several phone calls to the police and a low-speed foot chase through suburbia.

Sugar Gandhi, the love of Murray's life (who'd broken up with him at the end of junior year), was a girl actually named Seeta Ganguly, whose name he'd either misheard entirely or flat-out refused to pronounce. Either way, he'd taken to calling her Sugar Gandhi (I was 99 percent sure it was super racist, but Sugar Gandhi had insisted we call her that after she'd heard it for the first time, so I *guess* it was okay?) and so had we. Their relationship had been brief—five months of Murray learning to cook biryani and samosas, and "You're a top sheila, honest" posted to her Facebook wall on a fairly regular basis.

Alas, as teenage relationships are wont to do, their grand love story didn't last. Seeta told Murray her parents wanted her to date a "nice Indian boy" (this was, I suspect, an elaborate lie inspired by *Bend It Like Beckham*, constructed in order to spare Murray his feelings).

Muz had been trying to win her back ever since, but to do that, he needed insider information. Enter Madison Carlson.

Of all the girls in our high school, Madison was the most terrifying, the most blond, the most curvy, the girl who made you feel the shittiest about yourself just by existing because girls like her and guys like you were creatures from different tiers of the animal kingdom. Her Instagram account had an absurd amount of followers, and designers sent her free stuff all the time, and she flew to New York every month to do fashion shoots and have meetings with Very Important People. Rumor had it she already made more money than her parents and was going to pay for her college degree outright.

"Uh," I said when I approached her at her locker on Tuesday morning.

"Hey," said Madison, giving me a weird look, which I suppose was warranted considering my smooth greeting.

"Christ, Henry, you're never gonna cop a root at this rate," Murray said, elbowing me out of the way before taking Madison's hand and curtsying deeply. "Miss Carlson. Like a boomerang, I keep coming back to you."

"What do you want?" Madison said.

"Intel. From East River. Price is no object, and by that I

mean we have eight dollars and seventy-five cents between us and will happily treat you to a supersized meal at a fast-food chain of your choosing."

"You want *gossip*? We aren't in middle school, Murray. I don't do that anymore."

"Mads. Mate. You still date that clodhopper of a bloke that goes there—which is a travesty, by the way—so that means you know a thing or two. Seeta Ganguly. Senior at East River. Suss out the sitch with her love life. Your payment"—Murray slipped something into Madison's jeans pocket—"will be lucrative."

Madison took out the folded paper and inspected it. "This is an expired coupon for Pizza Hut."

"There's plenty more where that came from." Murray leaned in and whispered close to Madison's ear. "Rendezvous tomorrow afternoon at your locker. You know where it is. Oh, and if anyone asks—we were never here." Murray walked backward into the crowd then, and tried to do one of those Jason Bourne disappearing-into-thin-air tricks, but we both saw him dive into the girls' bathroom.

"He's not funny," Madison said. "Can you please tell him that he's not funny?"

"Sorry you had to witness that."

"I'll ask about Seeta. And tell Murray I actually broke up with Sean, like, two months ago."

"Sure. Uh, and . . . could you also maybe . . . Grace Town. Murray wants to know why she left East River."

"Murray wants to know, does he?"

"He's a passionately curious man."

Madison closed her locker. "I'll see what I can do."

Approximately twenty-four hours later (Madison Carlson really didn't screw around when it came to gossip), we were back in front of her locker.

"Did you speak to Seeta?" Murray said. "Has she taken a lover? Who must I kill?"

"When I talked to her, she mentioned a psychotic Australian ex-boyfriend who her dad called the cops on, but apart from that, no, Seeta is single," said Madison.

"Everything's coming up Milhouse."

"You're going to go to jail, Murray. Your obsession isn't romantic, it's disturbing."

"Hey, it was her old man who called the cops, not her. She messaged me and said she wanted to talk, but then her folks confiscated her phone."

"Whatever."

"And Grace?" I said.

"Leave her alone, Henry. Trust me. You don't want to get mixed up in that."

"Now come on, Mads," Murray said. "Don't be cliché. You know your reluctance to divulge information is only going to make us more inquisitive. Help the plot move a little faster and spill the bloody beans already."

"All I know is that her family's screwed up, and there was something about a car accident a few months ago. That's everything, okay?"

"For your time," Murray said as he handed Madison another Pizza Hut coupon.

"Wow, this one is actually still valid."

"Don't say I never get you anything nice."

Madison sighed and looked from the coupon to me and then back again. "Definitely don't go to the East River track around nine p.m. on Tuesday nights. You definitely won't see anything there."

"East River track. Nine p.m. on Tuesday. Thanks," I said. "Hey, while we're here . . . would you wanna write for the newspaper? We need something along the lines of a *Gossip Girl*–style column."

"I'd rather write film reviews or something."

"Oh yeah? What would you want to review?"

"Modern classics, maybe? *Fight Club*, *Inception*, *The Matrix*, *Pulp Fiction*. All the good ones."

I narrowed my eyes. "Did Lola put you up to this?"

"Up to what?"

"Uh. Never mind. That'd be awesome. No rush, we don't go to print until early December. Thanks."

"Yeah, thanks, cobber," Murray said. He clapped her on the back.

"I hate you both," said Madison, but her gaze lingered on Murray for a heartbeat too long, and I got the distinct impression that Madison Carlson did not hate him—not even close, not even a little bit, not even at all.

• • •

It came that Wednesday evening. The first ever personal message from Grace, unprompted and not about the newspaper, popped up on my phone as I caught a bus home from Murray's place close to midnight.

GRACE TOWN:

> How was Simba? Did he face his demons and save the day?

I'd been to see *The Lion King* musical with Sadie and Ryan the night before. I'd only mentioned it to Grace once, in passing, maybe a week ago. It'd been a fun night. After the show we'd posed with a statue of Rafiki and gone to a place that made ice cream with liquid nitrogen near the theater in the city.

"Look, Henwee, look!" Ryan had said when the lady handed him a paper bowl of mint ice cream bigger than his head. "Life is grand," he'd said very seriously as he inspected his dessert. Sadie and I had almost fallen over laughing.

HENRY PAGE:

> It was good! But they added songs and stuff and I was like, "Next." Then Scar was trying to bang Nala and it kinda ruined my childhood.

> Oh wow. I could've lived without hearing that.

Exactly. And little things changed. Like Timon and Pumbaa dressed in drag and did the Charleston instead of the hula. Like, why change it? And Zazu doesn't sing "I've Got a Lovely Bunch of Coconuts."

That is an outrage. Please tell me Rafiki was still a BAMF, though?

Rafiki was still on fleek.

Did you just.

Do I have to remind you about #YOLO?

You win this round, Page.

So Lola just messaged me and told me she was very pleased with our modeling skills. Definitely one for the resume.

Naturally.

I believe I was even cut from one picture in favor of "Grace, copied three times."

Lola has excellent taste.

Sometimes I wonder if there's more to life than being really, really, really ridiculously good-looking.

We'll have to test out your Blue Steel next time.

Exactly.

looks at pagination

What is this . . . a newspaper for ants?

HA.

People on the bus now think I'm a crazy person because I laughed out loud.

I'm okay with it.

PS. Principal Valentine dropped by the office this afternoon. Woman is scary as balls. I had to pretend like we've actually settled on a theme. I told her we want to keep it a secret because it's going to blow her mind. Need to decide ASAP.

How long were you at the office for?
Sorry I wasn't at school today.

I'm on my way home. Present tense. I spent most of the afternoon at Murray's, editing one of Galaxy's pieces about the disappointing texture of chicken served at the cafeteria. A truly riveting article.

Yikes.

I suddenly feel deep sympathy for Miranda Priestly. (Might have watched The Devil Wears Prada last weekend.)

How did one person edit the newspaper all by themselves in the past?

Amphetamines?

Makes sense.

We should organize some speedballs for print day.

From what I hear about him, I wouldn't be surprised if Kyle kept a stash somewhere in the office.

I'm sure those business cards Hink gave us have some decent residue on them. Maybe give 'em a lick?

Look at that subtle off-white coloring. The tasteful thickness of it. Oh my God, it even has a watermark!

Business class. It's the only way to fly.

Maybe instead of getting into hard drugs, we could become tortured alcoholics? More appropriate for writers. I think we should start drinking in the office every afternoon. Let's get a mini fridge and fill it with beer.

We can hide it under Lola's desk. She's small. She probably won't even notice.

"You can't sit there, sorry, beer sits there."

"We have no designer this year because we replaced them with beer."

#BeerBeforePeople

Sounds like a government campaign.

Hillary Clinton, 2016: Beer before people.

Only Hillary could pull that off.

Damn straight.

I'd vote for that.

As would I. Anyway, have a nice night. Lift tomorrow afternoon?

Yeah, for sure. Catch you on the flip side, kid.

And then, on Thursday, like a miracle descending from the heavens, there came news of The Party. (Much like World War I, it only became known as The Party later on in the year. Before it had actually occurred, The Party [i.e., WWI] was known as Heslin's Party [i.e., the Great War].) Heslin's Party/The Party began as a rumor that escalated to a lunchtime conversation topic that escalated to a full-fledged event when James Heslin made it Facebook official less than twenty-four hours after the initial speculation had begun. The whole year was invited, along with half the juniors (the hot, female half, naturally). Us seniors, despite the occasional personality clash, generally all got along pretty well. Maybe we were an anomalous bunch, or maybe high school movies have been lying to us all along, but all I know is that the "jocks" sometimes hung out with the "nerds" and that most people were nice to most other people most of the time.

Anyway, The Party, to be held on Friday night, was all anyone was talking about for the rest of the day. Lola and Murray were going, naturally. La's girlfriend, Georgia, was even driving over from the next town to attend. I wasn't much for parties normally, but this one. This one.

I wanted desperately for Grace Town to go and I wanted to sit with her all night while music thumped through my chest, away from the quiet, fishbowl room that was our office and the quiet, boyish room that was Grace's car.

I opened the Notes app on my phone, and under the second draft I wrote:

Draft Three

Because I never realized that you could fall in love with humans the same way you fall in love with songs. How the tune of them could mean nothing to you at first, an unfamiliar melody, but quickly turn into a symphony carved across your skin; a hymn in the web of your veins; a harmony stitched into the lining of your soul.

CHAPTER 11

"I AM GOING to The Party," I announced to her on Friday morning before class. (In retrospect, I probably said "Heslin's Party" at the time, but I digress.) Grace looked up from her computer screen, where she was scrolling through Tumblr, as per usual.

"You're definitely going?" she said.

"I'm definitely going," I answered. I put my things down and turned on my computer and watched her as she turned back to her screen. Now was the moment of revelation. Either she really liked me or she didn't. Either she felt for me how I felt for her, or she didn't. A minute ticked by, and then a minute more, and right when I thought I'd be stuck going to some shitty party by myself—I had to go now, you can't just announce that you're going to a party and then not go—Grace said, without looking at me, "I think I'll go too."

I knew then. Grace Town, beautiful, mysterious, damaged, and thoroughly, thoroughly *weird*, liked me. The shaky body language and the lack of flirting meant nothing, because she was coming to the party and parties meant alcohol and dimly lit rooms and maybe after a drink she would lighten up a little and then we could talk about the cemetery and the car crash and everything.

Grace wasn't looking at me, so I watched her without blinking and said, "Cool," in the most casual voice I could muster.

"Are you going to drink?" she said.

I wasn't much of a drinker. I'd been truly drunk only once before, when I was sixteen. Murray had coerced me into drinking tequila with him, to test the legitimacy of the "one tequila, two tequila, three tequila, floor" theorem. Over the course of the evening I discovered that "one tequila, two tequila, three tequila, floor" is wildly inaccurate. It's more like one tequila, two tequila, three tequila, vomit all over your clothes, cry while your father puts you in the shower, vomit some more, cry and ask your mother to cook you "salmon eggs," whatever that is, be put to bed by your mother, decide you're going to escape your parents' totalitarian regime, vomit in the garden while escaping, be put back to bed by your father, floor.

Not quite so neat and tidy as the saying would have you believe.

But I said, "I might have a drink or two," because I had a feeling Grace would be drinking and I wanted to do that with her, to watch her as she sipped her alcohol and observe the way it changed her. I wanted to know what kind of drunk she was. Angry? Probably. Flirty? Probably not. Sad? Almost definitely.

"I can get us drinks," Grace said, and I said, "Cool," again and then the bell rang and she packed up her stuff and left without another word.

One thing was clear: only five short weeks after I'd met her, Grace Town was already stuck on repeat in my head.

Fall had kicked into high gear by the time Friday afternoon rolled around. The sunshine had a hazy quality to it, tinted by the gold and orange leaves that sifted down from the trees whenever the breeze blew. Everything for the party had been organized: the booze, the location (Heslin's parents were out of town for the weekend—so cliché, but whatever).

All there was to do was tell my parents my plans for the evening, which went something like this:

Me: "Father, I intend to engage in illegal underage drinking again tonight."

Dad: "Good lord, Henry. It's about time. Do you need a ride?"

Someone had decided it was a good idea, and our rite of passage as seniors, to drink on the school football field before migrating to Heslin's for the party. By the time I arrived, around sunset, half a tub of punch had already been consumed by the stumbling attendees. And when I say *tub*, I mean a legitimate bathtub that someone had bought or stolen from somewhere and filled with a concoction of cheap vodka, even cheaper wine, and "fruit drink" (high schoolers don't have the cash for *actual* juice).

Grace was there when I arrived, sitting cross-legged by herself against a tree at the edge of the field, her cane resting across her lap. There were two plastic bottles in front of her, one empty, the other half-full of some strange pastel yellow liquid.

"Henrik," she said when she saw me. I don't remember at what point we'd assigned each other Germanic/Russian nicknames, or why, but we had, and I loved it.

"Evening, Grakov," I said.

"I procured you an instrument of intoxication." She handed me the empty plastic bottle and nodded toward the tub of punch, from which Murray was drinking with his bare hands while he gave a demonstration to a small crowd of onlookers on the correct safety technique of drinking from crocodile-infested billabongs. When attending public gatherings, he tried to wear as much "safari clothing" as possible, in an effort to evoke Steve Irwin and support the notion that he was some kind of bushman. Tonight his hair was tied up in a messy bun and he wore a large tooth on a necklace. A lot of girls looked very impressed.

"So when you said, 'I'll get us drinks,' you actually meant, 'I'll search through my trash for a used bottle'? I feel betrayed."

"*Two* used bottles, my friend. It took me all day to track down these babies. Plus I scored this," she said, pulling a silver flask from inside her bra (lucky flask). "Now go get a beverage."

The punch was already a little worse for wear. Several bugs had come to a tragic yet poetic end in it, not to mention the log Muz had floated in its sickly yellow depths to represent his reptilian nemesis. But I didn't care. I sank my empty bottle in and waited for the bubbles to disappear. I took two huge gulps—almost half the bottle—then sank it back into the punch again for a refill. I didn't want to get "salmon eggs" wasted, but I wanted the alcohol to loosen me up a little.

Lola came bounding over to me as I screwed the cap back on my bottle of hooch, her girlfriend, Georgia, at her side.

"Touch me, Henry Page," Georgia said, grabbing my free hand and pressing it to her cheek. This was her standard greeting, which tells you pretty much all you need to know about Georgia McCracken except that she a) was a pocket-sized redhead with a spray of freckles across her pale face and b) somehow had the lilted remnants of an Irish accent despite never having lived in Ireland.

"Hey, G," I said, hugging her loosely because she was so small, I feared a real hug would snap her spine. "How's small-town life treating you?"

"Watch *Swamp People*. It's pretty much a documentary on my life."

"Yikes."

"Oh boy. It's gonna be an interesting night," said Lola, taking a long swig of her drink, then nodding at something behind my shoulder. I turned to spot Murray talking to and clasping the hands of a very unimpressed-looking Indian girl. Sugar Gandhi. "That boy does not know when to quit."

"Shit," I said. "Somebody set their alarm for a one-a.m. emotional breakdown. La, I believe it's your turn to provide support? I handled the last one."

"Fuck" is all Lola said, which meant she knew it was her turn. She took another large swig of her drink, entwined her fingers with Georgia's, and said, "Let's intervene now before he starts singing Bollywood love songs to her again."

"Why? What's more romantic than a little casual racism?" said Georgia as Lola dragged her toward Sugar Gandhi, who was now glaring at *me* like I was somehow accountable for Muz's terrible behavior. I shrugged and tried to look apologetic and then walked back over to Grace. By the time I sunk to the ground next to her, I'd downed another quarter bottle of punch and could feel the strange yet familiar warmth of intoxication radiating from my chest down to my thighs.

"It's going to be a good night," I said. I leaned back against the tree, my shoulder pressing into hers, my words sparkling on the tip of my tongue, my mouth already feeling a size too small for my face.

I was sufficiently drunk by the time we walked to Heslin's, so I don't actually remember how we got there or who carried the bathtub (with Murray in it).

I also don't remember exactly how Grace and I ended up sitting next to each other at a patio table in Heslin's backyard. Some kind of musical chairs occurred. Someone got up to go to the bathroom, someone else got up to go get a drink, someone sat down in someone else's spot, until no one was where they'd started, and Grace Town was next to me. Close to me. So close, our legs were touching. She was at least a bottle and a half of punch down by now, and already more casual and affectionate than I'd ever seen her before. She laughed when people told jokes. She smiled at me. She engaged. Even when no one was talking and she didn't realize anyone was looking at her, there was a light behind her eyes. She sat up straighter. The body language she lacked when she was sober was there in spades when she was tipsy. She looked—despite being moderately dirty and unkempt—quite beautiful.

People noticed her in a way they never had before. People noticed how pretty she was. People noticed that she was *there*. As fucked up as it is to say, alcohol made her come alive.

When we brainstormed the newspaper, we always sat together. Accidental touches were unavoidable at such close range, but when she hadn't been drinking, Grace always pulled back from them. Always sat so close that they would happen, then pulled back from them. Like she wanted me to touch her until it happened, and then when it did, she suddenly changed her mind. But there was none of that tonight. The casual grazes of skin only got more frequent, until I was telling a story and Grace was laughing at me and saying, "Stop, stop, you're embarrassing yourself." Grace put her hand over my mouth in an effort to silence me, and I mock fought her, both of us giggling at the struggle. My hand on her waist, her hand on my knee, our bodies pressed closer together than they had any need to be.

"Henry! It's our song!" she said as a cover of "Someday" started playing. I was surprised she remembered my favorite song. I was even more surprised she referred to it as *our song*. Not *my* song. *Our* song. Grace threaded her fingers through mine and pulled me to my feet and led me to the crowded makeshift dance floor (i.e., the hardwood floor of Heslin's living room). As the beat dropped, she started moving in the most thoroughly un-Grace-like fashion. All I could do was watch. Under the gold lights of the chandelier above, time shifted, a portal opened, and I could suddenly see the girl she'd been before I knew her, the girl from her Facebook profile pictures.

As she danced, she took off the oversized flannel shirt she was wearing and tied it around her waist, leaving her in only a fitted white tank top and jeans. Under all that clothing, there she was, lean and angular and lovely. There was something sharp about her shoulders and collarbones and jawline, like she didn't quite eat enough. And there was something about her sunken eyes and hollow cheekbones and blunt, self-cut hair that meant she would always look at little bit like a heroin junkie.

But the way she moved. God, the way she moved. The way she closed her eyes and bit her lip, like she could *feel* the music pulsing in her blood.

"Henrik, you're not dancing," Grace said when she noticed, and she took my hand in hers again and kind of shook me, as if this would somehow imbue me with the power of rhythm. I wasn't much of a dancer, but I was here with her, and I was drunk, and she was incredibly beautiful, and I wanted so badly to kiss her for the first time while "our song" was playing. So I pulled her against me, and when the beat dropped again and all the people around us screamed in delight, I danced with her.

Grace kept touching me, kept finding excuses to run her fingers over my skin. All I had to do was find the courage to lean in and put my mouth on hers. One moment of extraordinary courage.

"Henry! Grace!" yelled a familiar voice. A second later, Lola was there, hugging the both of us, dancing between us, Georgia at her side. I could've killed her. Then the song was over and the next one began and we were all dancing together, jumping up and down to the beat, me silently mourning what could have been.

Three songs later, Grace took my hand. "I need a drink," she said.

"We'll come with you," Lola said.

I shot La an "I'm going to strangle you later" look, but she didn't see it, so I gritted my teeth and followed the girls off the dance floor back into the yard. What remained of the tub punch was now a suspicious brown color and had one of Murray's shoes floating in it. (I'd seen Muz only once since we arrived at Heslin's, inexplicably dressed in a pirate costume and drinking out of a yard glass with a curly straw. God love him.)

Grace still had the flask of vodka in her bag, so we split it four ways, topped it up with the only available mixer (Barq's Red Creme Soda), and sat down in the dark by the garden to drink.

"Actually, I'm gonna go to the bathroom," Grace said, handing me her cup.

"Oh, me too," Georgia echoed.

As soon as they were out of earshot, I turned to Lola. "I don't mean for this to sound harsh, but please, for the love of all that is holy, you need to fuck off immediately. I think something is happening with Grace."

"I did notice a bit of hand-holding going on."

"Then why the *hell* did you come over?"

"Because she's drunk, and so are you, and I think this is a very bad idea."

"Lola."

"Have you found out who she visits at the cemetery every day? Because the more I think about it, the more messed up it seems."

"Lola."

"Are you falling for *her*, Henry? For the Grace we know? Or for the girl in her Facebook profile picture? Because that's clearly not who she is anymore, as much as you might want it to be."

"*Lola.*"

"Fine! But when this ends with her gouging your heart out through your kneecaps, I won't be your shoulder to cry on."

"Yeah, you will. Because that's what best friends do." I

nodded over Lola's shoulder at Murray and Sugar Gandhi, who were arguing quite animatedly at the bottom of the garden, Muz still dressed as a pirate.

"God." Lola shook her head. *"Men."*

When our respective love interests returned, La stood and kissed Georgia on the cheek and said, "Come, my darling, we must go see a man about a dog."

And then, finally, it was just us. Just us, and the universe.

Grace pulled me to my feet and we wandered, holding hands, through the crowd for a few minutes, waiting for the alcohol to seep back into our bloodstreams and return us to the blissful haze we'd been in thirty minutes ago.

I don't know who led who, or if we both had the same idea, but suddenly we were in the dark corridor that ran up the side of the house. I leaned against the bricks to steady myself, and before I had time to really comprehend what was happening, Grace was on me, her mouth moving against mine, her fingers in my hair. And my first thought was, *Damn. I don't even know what song's playing*, but soon that didn't matter, because Grace Town was kissing me and it was everything I thought it would be. The weeks of *Does she even like me?* melted away because she did, she must, she had to.

My drink was sloshing in one hand but I didn't want to interrupt the kiss, so I wrapped my free arm around her waist and tried to keep the red soda from spilling down her back. We moved against each other like tessellating shapes. I wanted to pick her up and for her to wrap her legs around my hips but I was aware that people could see us and I didn't want to be the couple that practically had sex in public.

The kiss went on for two songs, both of which I didn't know, then Grace broke away and bit her bottom lip and looked at me like she wanted to tell me something, her palms pressed into my chest, but eventually she just said, "I should go home."

"I can walk you, if you'd like."

"Okay."

I grabbed our bags and coats from Heslin's little sister's bedroom (there was a NO SEX IN HERE YOU FUCKING HEATHENS sign taped to the door) while Grace called her parents to let them know she was walking home, like she was trying to make it clear that when we got there, I wasn't coming inside. Which was fine by me, really, because I'd never had sex before and I didn't think being this drunk would be very conducive to giving a great performance, virgin or not. So I walked with her in the cold, not touching her, not holding her hand, the both of us brainstorming inane themes for the newspaper ("school spirit"? "the story so far"? "leave your mark"?) like we hadn't been making out.

When we got to her place, she waved good-bye and said she'd see me on Monday and that was that.

Still drunk enough to be courageous, I messaged her as I wandered toward Murray's house, which was easy enough to break into and way closer than mine.

HENRY PAGE:

> Okay, Dusty Knupps. It's probably pretty obvious by now that I kinda maybe sorta think you're a babe.

GRACE TOWN:

Well, that's good to hear! I wouldn't have chased you if I didn't feel the same way.

> Good to hear, Knupps. Good to hear. I'll keep you posted on stuff and things and whatnot over the weekend.

Haha yeah. Be good to hear about all the stuff and things.

> Excellent. I shall ensure you're well informed. Adieu, Mrs. Knupps. It was a pleasure.

Indeed it was, Mr. Knupps. Indeed it was.

"Muz," I whispered when I got to Murray's house and started tapping at his bedroom window. No one came to answer, so I lifted the window, hauled myself inside, and fell asleep, alone and fully clothed on Murray's bed, thinking of Grace Town and how, if people really were assembled from pieces of the universe, her soul was made of stardust and chaos.

CHAPTER 12

OUR PARENTS HAD become entirely accustomed to coming into our bedrooms in the mornings and not finding their own children there, but someone else's. Murray's dad, Baz (short for Sebastian, not Barry—he was always sure to tell people this when he introduced himself), roused me from sleep with the smell of bacon and coffee. I came to with my brain detached from its tethers. Whenever I moved, it moved, too, smacking around the inside of my skull like an angry jellyfish, stinging as it went.

I carried my thumping head out to the dining room, where Murray's mom and three younger sisters were already sitting around the table.

"Morning, Henry," the girls sang in unison, giggling as they went. They all looked like Muz, all blond perms and blue eyes (minus the seedy teenage 'stache, of course).

"Hush, hell beasts," I said to them as I sank into a dining room chair and laid my forehead gently against the wooden table, which only made them giggle more. "Why is the sunshine so bright?" It seemed to be streaming in from everywhere, searing my vodka- and punch-soaked veins, burning through me like wildfire. "Maybe Dracula wasn't a vampire, just a raging alcoholic who was constantly hungover."

"Now, *that* is a story I would read," said Baz.

"I don't suppose you know where our child is?" said Sonya, Murray's mom. Keeping my head on the cool wood of the table, I checked my phone. There were three messages:

LOLA LEUNG:

> Right on goddamn schedule.

This was followed by a picture of a very drunk Murray, half-conscious and crying violently on Lola's kitchen floor, hugging what appeared to be a plush kangaroo toy.

LOLA LEUNG:

> (I put the kangaroo there for effect, but I'm not going to tell him that when I show him this picture in the morning.)

And then, at 4:03 a.m.:

MUZ FINCH:

> I escaped Lola's despotic rule. Your dad let me in to your house. I'm about to have drunk reconciliation sex in your bed. Hope that's cool!

I closed my eyes and groaned. "That Australian *bastard*."

"Henry," said Baz, nodding to the girls. "Language."

"Oh, sorry. Yeah, Murray's at my place."

"Musical beds again, is it?"

"As always. He originally fell asleep at Lola's. Possibly on the kitchen floor. Possibly with a kangaroo. Your son is a miscreant."

"And that's why we allow him to hang out with you lot. Because you use words like *miscreant* in general conversation," Sonya said, mussing my hair and pouring me a glass of orange juice.

We ate breakfast together in the too-bright sun, and then the girls dragged me into their playroom to watch *Avatar: The Last Airbender* until my parents brought Murray home. I let the girls paint my fingernails with silver glitter in exchange for them covertly fetching me snacks from the kitchen. They tried to braid my hair, but none of them were good enough at it yet to get it to stay.

Finally, Mom and Dad arrived to trade children with Muz's parents. Murray wandered in barefoot, still dressed as a pirate, carrying an empty baking tray and a sign around his neck that read FREE HUGS AND COOKIES.

I didn't ask. I didn't need to.

My folks decided to stick around for lunch, so I lay in Murray's bed for the next hour and a half, slipping in and out of sleep as he tidied his room and told me about how he'd made up with Sugar Gandhi (twice) in my bed. Which I wasn't very happy about, but he pointed out that my sheets were offensive and long overdue for a wash anyway, which was true. And I told him about Grace, about the kiss, about the message she'd sent me afterward. *I wouldn't have chased you if I didn't feel the same way.* About how, all this time, when I thought she'd been indifferent, she'd actually been pursuing me in her own strange, quiet style. It wasn't the sort of thing Murray and I normally talked about, because it wasn't the sort of thing I normally did, but I liked it. It was nice to have something to share for a change.

"Look at us—two fools in love," Muz said as he flopped down on the bed next to me, wrapped his leg over my hips, and nuzzled into my neck like a shaggy dog, as he was wont to do.

I wasn't sure about the love part yet, but the fool part, certainly, was true.

CHAPTER 13

AND THEN THERE was nothing.

I don't know exactly what I expected. I knew a single, drunken kiss didn't mean Grace had to pledge herself to me body and soul, but I at least thought we'd be more, like, *obvious* about our feelings. That, now that I knew she liked me, it would be easier to draw her out of herself on the days when she switched off, easier to be around her even when she pretended she was the only person in the world, easier to accidentally brush her arm and not have her go rigid, like an electric current was twisting through her spine. I thought that after people made out with each other, things kind of fell in place around them. I was, naturally, very wrong.

The week after our first kiss went something like this.

SATURDAY

When I got home from Muz's in the early afternoon, I sent Grace a message (after I'd peeled the sheets off my bed and stuffed them in the washing machine while wearing gloves and a surgical mask).

HENRY PAGE:

Ugh. Woke up feeling like I gargled a dead hamster. I heard Heslin got grounded, poor kid. How is Grakov? Let me know if you wanna hang this weekend.

GRACE TOWN:

I am feeling all right this morning. I will let you know about this weekend. Have a good day.

SUNDAY

Despite what she'd said, Grace Town did *not* let me know about that weekend. I know, because I spent most of the those forty-eight hours waiting for her to message me, but she didn't, so I went to bed at eight p.m. on Sunday night but didn't fall asleep until the sky was turning pale pink with sunrise through the basement windows.

MONDAY

Grace Town walked into the newspaper office in the morning before class, nodded at me, collected a stack of papers off her desk, and left. It was at this point that I became fairly certain that The Kiss (as it would come to be known) had been little more than a hallucination caused by mild methanol poisoning from the punch. I spent the day wanting to go home and research new schools that didn't frown on senior-year transfers.

Unfortunately I had to stay after school to finish (read: begin) my first English assignment for Hink, catch up on my math homework, open my Spanish textbook for the first time, and start thinking about college applications, which is why I was still in the library when I received Grace's message and felt my heart kick up into my neck. It was much, much worse than I thought it would be.

GRACE TOWN:

> Do you want to play touch football Thursday nights? Hink is putting a rec team of teachers and students together "for fitness" and wants to know if you're in? Sounds like everyone else (i.e., all the teachers) is. I won't be playing, but I'm gonna come and cheer you guys on.

I'd been expecting a "Friday night was a mistake" or "I don't want things to be weird" type message, but this? This was torture. On the one hand, joining the teachers' recreational football team had two benefits:

1. Grace Town, obviously. Obligatory social events meant more obligatory time spent together, outside of school and the newspaper office and Grace's car.
2. The chance to prove to my teachers, especially the ones who still thought I was Sadie Page's male

equivalent, that I was neither criminally devious nor psychotically brilliant.

On the other hand, there was one massive downside:

1. Sports.

The cons almost won. The thought of Grace having to witness my fumbled attempts at hand-eye coordination made me cringe. But I couldn't pass up the opportunity to spend more time with her. So I typed:

HENRY PAGE:

> I guess I could use it as an opportunity to get within three feet of Mr. Hotchkiss. In class he makes me sit all the way at the back, but he won't be able to hide from me on the field!

> Do you know what time they're planning on playing? And how is your Monday going?

Game will be at 4 p.m. Thursday each week. Today was okay. I helped Lola with design stuff for the articles we've already got. Do we really want to run that 10,000-word piece on Magic: The Gathering tournaments . . . ?

Oh! Maybe "Magic: The Gathering" could be the overall theme?

Sorry I couldn't be there to help out, assignments and all that.

Didn't I tell you I made "Magic: The Gathering" the theme, like, a week ago? That epic piece of literature is going to be the magnum opus of the Westland Post.

(Although maybe we should trim it to 9,000 words.)

What are you up to tonight?

I just left the office and I'm on my way to hang out with a couple of girls from East River who I used to run track with. Might need a beer or three after attempting to edit Galaxy's grammar.

That beer fridge I suggested might not be such a good idea. I'm probably going to be an alcoholic by the end of the year, no joke.

All the best writers are! Hemingway would be proud. Also . . . shots before football? They do call booze liquid courage for a reason.

Drinking before football is going to be 95% of my strategy.

And the other 5%?

1% pure, unadulterated athletic talent. 4% luck.

It's a bold strategy, Cotton. Let's see if it pays off.

Indeed it is. 60% of the time, it works every time.

TUESDAY

At lunchtime we went to a café near the mall and stood in line together, in silence, because it was a Bad Grace Day and she'd barely said more than a word to me for hours and it's hard to bounce off someone who isn't there. The song over the loudspeaker changed to "Can't Help Falling in Love," the Elvis version, and it was so ridiculously cliché that I had to press my lips together to keep from laughing.

When we reached the counter, I ordered a tea. Grace didn't want anything, but she insisted on paying for my drink, which I let her do, because I liked the way it made me feel. People didn't buy hot beverages for just anybody, right?

In that moment, with Elvis crooning *Take my hand, take my whole life too* over the speaker, tea was so much more than leaves steeped in boiling water. It was a symbol, after half a week of nothingness, that Grace Town was still interested in me, even if she couldn't find the words to say so.

"What part of that outfit, exactly, will help us blend in while we're shadowing her?" I said.

It was Tuesday night, one week since Madison Carlson had

provided us with insider intel, and I was driving toward East River High. Murray was sitting next to me in the passenger seat, wearing a trench coat and a fedora, an unlit cigar wedged between his lips.

"The rain was falling like bullets," said Murray around his cigar, continuing his hard-boiled narration of the evening's events in a fifties American accent. It was not, in fact, raining at all. "I turned to the kid"—Murray turned to me—"and said, 'I hope you know what you're getting yourself into.' He was a good guy, six feet of skin and bones, with a decent head screwed on his shoulders. I didn't have the heart to tell him that the dame he was chasing was like secondhand smoke: beautiful but deadly."

"Secondhand smoke isn't beautiful."

"The kid said something stupid, but I ignored him. 'We're coming up on East River now,' I said as we rounded the corner and the acrid lights of the school came into view. 'Park here or they'll have eyes on us in two shakes of a lamb's tail.'"

"Seriously, if you don't shut up and take that hat off, I'm gonna leave you in the car."

"I couldn't take any more of the kid's whining. I needed a smoke, and badly." Murray struck a match and went to light his cigar, in my mother's car no less. I smacked him across the back of the head.

"Ow, fuck, all right, all right!" he said, shaking the match until the flame flicked out. He took the hat off and left the cigar in the car, and we walked toward the white lights of East

River's track. The wind picked up, carrying with it the clean, crisp smell of fall. Dead leaves crunched under our feet. Streetlights burned in the dimness, but the roads were empty and quiet. I dug my hands into my pockets and speculated as to what the hell Madison Carlson had sent us here to see.

When we reached the track, we found the bleachers deserted, so we hung back in the shadows. Muz nudged me in the ribs and pointed across the field and said, "Over there," which was entirely unnecessary, because she was the only one there, a small figure cast up against a galaxy of fluorescent light.

Grace was dressed in her usual oversized, boyish attire, but there was something different about her tonight. Her hair was pulled back and her face was pink and glazed with sweat and she was bent over, hands on her knees, heaving breaths. After a minute she stood and limped—caneless—back to the starting line, where she knelt. Took a breath. Started running, her limp haphazard, her face set in a grimace that deepened each time her injured leg impacted the red rubber of the track.

"What's she doing?" said Muz as we watched her.

Maybe it was because she was usually so pale and brittle—not fragile, not by a long shot, just hard somehow—but I'd never imagined her as capable of physical exertion. After she'd sprinted about one hundred feet, Grace stopped and screamed and pulled at her hair. She took up her cane from where it'd been cast trackside and hit it across her injured leg again and again and again before sinking to the ground in a sobbing heap. No wonder her limp remained pronounced.

"Fucking Christ," Murray said, pulling another cigar from his trench coat pocket. I didn't stop him when he went to light this one. He took a long draw, like he really was some hard-ass detective from a crime novel.

"Secondhand smoke, in the flesh," he said in his American accent as he breathed out, swirling gray eddies slipping from his lips. "I didn't want to say nothing to the kid, but I thought, as we watched her, that the more he breathed her in, the sicker and sicker he'd get."

WEDNESDAY

"Ask her out," Muz said to me the next afternoon. We'd decided not to tell Lola about seeing Grace at the track because a) she'd point out the obvious—that Grace was deeply emotionally damaged and clearly bad news—and be far too rational about reasons why I should stay away from her, and b) we already felt bad enough about what we'd done, what we'd seen. The memory of it had clung to me all day, sticking to my skin like I'd walked through a spiderweb, so now, like the graveyard, I was trying to repress it entirely. "You're never gonna get in her pants if you mope around like a delicate sunflower all the time. Stop being such a pussy."

"Murray," snapped Lola. "We talked about the 'pussy' thing."

"Oh, shit, right," Muz said, genuinely apologetic. He left his *CoD* game and twisted around on the couch to face where Lola and I were lying in my bed. "Vaginas are pretty gnarly, and in no way was I insinuating that the female reproductive organs are weak. I was using it as it's understood in its colloquial terms, but I realize that this might've been construed as offensive. I shall cease and desist from such usage in the future."

"Thank you."

"Anyway, you gotta do a grand gesture. That's how I bagged Sugar Gandhi."

"Sugar Gandhi almost punched you in the face at Heslin's when you started crying." Lola shook her head and turned to me. "Henry, you need to tell her how you feel. None of this cryptic bullshit. If you want something, you say something. Send her a message right now that says: 'So I liked kissing you and would be super into doing that again sometime. Sound good?'"

"Do you even know what you want from this broad?" Murray said. "Like, do you really wanna start a relationship now when you're going away to college next year anyway? Or are you only after a root?"

"Eloquent as ever, my Australian friend," I said. The trouble was, I *did* know what I wanted from Grace Town. I wanted to sleep with her, sure. I wanted her to be my girlfriend. A few years from now, I wanted to marry her. And then, when we were old, I wanted to drink peppermint tea and read Harry Potter to our grandchildren with her on the veranda of an old house out in the countryside as we watched a summer storm roll toward us. Was that so much to ask?

"Maybe I'm doomed to be alone forever." I pulled out my phone, opened the Notes app, and started writing.

Draft Four

Because it seems like a lot of hassle, liking someone.
Your brain runs hot, the cogs inside your mind jarring
together until all the oil of your thoughts is burned away.
The fire spreads to your chest, where it chars your lungs
and turns your heart to embers. And right when you
think the flames have burned away everything but your
skeleton, the spark skips from your bones to immolate
not only your flesh, but your entire life.

"Jesus, Henry," Lola said, rolling her eyes as she read over my shoulder. "Very dramatic."

"Shut up, dude. You don't know my struggle."

Later in the afternoon, I messaged Grace and used the only excuse I could think of to start a conversation:

HENRY PAGE:

> Is the first touch game tomorrow, do you know? Should I come prepared to kick ass and take names?

GRACE TOWN:

> Yeah, it's at 4 p.m. Start getting angry. I want to see you bring it.

> Oh, I'll bring it. Maybe. Possibly.

> Your confidence is infectious.

Okay, how about: "And I will strike down upon thee with great vengeance and furious anger those who attempt to obstruct and forcefully contact my touch team. And you will know my name is Randy Knupps when I lay my vengeance upon thee." Better? Better.

Well, I'm glad you're on my touch team, Mr. Winnfield.

Say "touch" again. I dare you. I double dare you, motherfucker, say "touch" one more goddamn time!

THURSDAY

The afternoon rolled around far too quickly, as I've learned things you aren't looking forward to tend to do. After last period, I went straight to the guys' locker room and changed into what few pieces of clothing I owned that could pass for "athletic." I'd hit the six-foot mark about a year ago, but my weight had yet to catch up with my height, despite the fact I consumed food like I was a garbage disposal. I looked especially lanky in my gym gear, all limbs, and I hoped Grace wouldn't be too repulsed by my pale, spindly body.

"This is *not* going to end well," I said with a sigh, wishing I'd conned Muz into joining the team so everyone would be so awed by his athletic prowess that they might not notice me slinking away to hide under the bleachers.

"Very fetching, Henrik," Grace said with a suppressed

grin when she saw me in my sports gear. Her limp was distinct again, like some kind of old-school Bond villain, and she winced when she walked. ("My rehab is really pushing me," she'd explained the day before. I'd nodded and pretended not to notice how easy it was for her to lie.)

"I hate you," I said.

The teachers organized friendly recreational games between themselves and teachers from other high schools on a weekly basis, but frequently brought along students to give their team an edge. Hink—who'd never played before and apparently had a competitive streak—thought injecting some young blood would be a good idea, so there were two other students on the team apart from Grace and me. Suki Perkins-Mugnai, who was apparently some kind of touch football whiz kid, and a dude who was repeating senior year for like the third time and who I'd only ever known as "Buck." Buck, who was small and nuggety and had an even seedier teenage mustache than Murray, was, I suspected, only on the team because he looked like a thirty-year-old convicted felon.

"Ready, team?" Hink said when he met us outside his office ten minutes later, dressed in athletic gear, the walking embodiment of Kip Dynamite when he went to meet LaFawnduh at the bus stop. All of us tried very, very hard not to laugh at his sweatband-and-knee-high-socks combo. At least I wouldn't be the most ridiculous-looking person on the field.

Hink walked with us to the football field, where the rest of our teachers were already warming up, stretching and practicing passes.

"God, this is horrifying," Suki said. "No high schooler is ever meant to see their teachers in these kinds of positions."

"If this were a movie," I said, grimacing at the sight of our motley crew, "we'd be the underdogs who overcome great personal shortcomings to win this entire tournament at the end. Like *DodgeBall*."

"Yeah, I somehow don't think dodging wrenches is going to help you much," Grace said. "You guys are screwed."

"Tsk, tsk. Ye of little faith," I said as I copied Hink's stretches without him noticing, which made Suki double over with laughter.

"More like ye of practicality," Grace said. She nodded toward the other end of the field. "*That's* who you're playing."

As it turns out, it was much more like *DodgeBall* than first anticipated, but without the happy ending. Instead of enrolling us in the Beginners or even Intermediate tier of recreational football, Hink had slotted us into the Advanced category, mostly (only) because Suki Perkins-Mugnai had played before and he thought that would be enough to get us through.

The opposing team was composed entirely of gym teachers and lightly injured star athletes from Rockwood High, who all looked remarkably similar to the Mountain That Rides from *Game of Thrones*. They'd been playing (and winning) together for so long that they'd even invested in legit uniforms, black

T-shirts emblazoned with red anatomical hearts being crushed by a hand.

The game went pretty much how I expected it to go. Grace sat on the bleachers, waving a pom-pom attached to her cane to cheer us on as the Gutcrushers lived up to their name. (Our team name, thanks to Hink, was still "Hi, Maria, can we decide on this later and get back to you?") Most of the opposing team were either ex or current football players and frequently forgot the "touch" aspect of the game and went in for tackles instead.

The first time he was thrown the ball, Buck looked at it, looked up at the stampede coming in his direction, said, "Oh hell no," turned around, and bolted. We didn't see him again.

I tried to touch the ball as little as possible and would always feed it through to Suki, who really was the only person who knew what she was doing. She scored our only two touchdowns, both of which the Gutcrushers were extremely unhappy about despite the fact that they were already slaughtering us.

Hink was like a newborn gazelle that hadn't quite yet learned to walk. Beady sprained her ankle after being on the field for seven minutes. My math teacher, Mr. Hotchkiss, seemed to hate me more during the game than he did in class, which was the exact opposite of my motivation to be there. And then, when the hell was nearly over and poor Suki looked close to death from carrying our entire team against a horde of wildebeests, I accidentally found myself with the ball and no one to pass it to.

The impact made the horizon shift sideways in a violent tilt. One moment I was standing, panicking about what to do with the stupid ball, the next I was on the ground, unable to breathe.

"Sorry, dude, momentum," said the giant who'd plowed me over as he grabbed my arm and pulled me off the ground, which I suppose was meant to be friendly, but since I was winded, all I could do was flop my free hand in his general direction. "You guys should probably think about dropping down to Intermediate. Or Beginners."

Grace was, naturally, cackling her evil laugh as I stumbled toward the bleachers, sure at least some of my ribs were broken. I kept stealing glances at her as I staggered across the field, but there wasn't even a shadow of the manic stranger she'd been at the track Tuesday night.

"Never. Ever. Again" were the first words I said to her once I'd regained the ability to speak.

After the Gutcrushers were through macerating us, Hink took us all out to dinner to apologize for what, in the end, had amounted to little more than a ritual sacrifice: sixteen touchdowns to two. What made the hell worth it, though, was sitting next to Grace at dinner. She was in one of the better moods I'd ever seen her in, playful as she teased me for being unable to eat my sushi with chopsticks, and wondering aloud if we'd ever see Buck again or if he was pulling a Forrest Gump and still running.

Hotchkiss even remarked that I wasn't doing as well as

Sadie had in math class and I really needed to start handing in my homework if I wanted to scrape a pass, so that was nice. Maybe he was finally starting to get the message that we weren't the same person and I wasn't likely to light firecrackers under his desk.

In the end, we made a pact to go to our graves without ever playing recreational football again, so the bruises and mild concussion were *almost* worth it for several more hours with Grace on a Good Day.

FRIDAY

We met in the library in the morning before homeroom, me with the pagination folded and tucked under my arm, her with a thermos and two delicate teacups with *Alice in Wonderland* illustrations on them and little tags on the handle that read *Drink me*. Lola had finally lost it and demanded that we pick a theme so she could start designing the front cover and main articles. We'd done as much as we could do with the Magic: The Gathering piece, several photo pages, and Galaxy Nguyen's enthusiastic weekly recaps of the year so far. It was almost getting to crunch time.

I followed Grace silently through the stacks, far deeper into the bowels of the library than we usually went, both of us too sleepy to talk.

There were no chairs or tables set up back here, so we sat cross-legged on the carpet, the pagination on the floor between us. Grace poured us tea—caramel and vanilla, she told me, nowhere near caffeinated enough to dezombify me at this ungodly hour—and then we went about silently numbering the little boxes, 1 to 30, each one representing a page in what would eventually become a full-fledged, tabloid-sized newspaper. Laid bare before us, it became clear that all of the usable content we'd accumulated so far only filled up about a third of the available space, even if we included the nine-thousand-word Magic: The Gathering feature story.

Fuck.

At first it was strictly business. We sat apart from each other, Grace straight-backed and straight-faced, doodling in ideas. *Possibly controversial sex ed feature?* she wrote. *Cliché spotlight on up-and-coming athlete/high school jock?* As the hour passed and we both woke up, it became clear that today would be a Good Grace Day. She shuffled closer to me. Rested her head on my shoulder while she worked, like it was the most casual thing in the world, like we'd been this intimate one hundred times before.

I distinctly remember thinking, *God, she's so confusing.* Because she was. A week of barely anything, and now this, her (uncharacteristically) clean and brushed hair spilling down my back, her elbow resting on my knee, her fingers tracing small circles on my shoe. The smell of her, warm and heady and somehow stale, rising from her skin and filling up my head with rabid possibility. It felt almost like we were together.

There was no work to be done after that. I kept my pencil in my hand but I didn't make another mark on the paper. I didn't want to move too much, lest Grace think I was uncomfortable. So I rested my head against hers and breathed quietly and steadily while she scribbled on the pagination, apparently unaware of the proximity of our bodies. We stayed like this for some time, until the bell rang, and Grace sat up slowly, yawning, as if waking from a dream.

But it was the look she gave me when she turned to me, the same look I'd seen on her face after The Kiss, that really had me confused. It was a brief moment of confusion, of disbelief almost, like she'd been expecting to find someone else next to her and not me.

How to reconcile that look? What did it mean? Or was I imagining things?

"Lift this afternoon?" she said as she composed herself and folded the pagination and handed it to me.

"Yeah," I said. "That'd be great."

Grace just nodded before she stood and left, as indifferent as always.

I decided to skip my first two classes, because today was reckoning day. It had to be. I couldn't make it through another weekend, let alone another week, unsure if she felt about me how I felt about her. So I went to our office and turned off all the lights and sat under my desk. While I was there, curled up in the fetal position, I wrote her a message, like Lola told me to, but it didn't feel big enough somehow. It didn't feel grand enough. If by some miracle we ended up together, I wanted the story of us to begin with something extraordinary, not just a Facebook chat.

In the end, I settled on an appropriately Henryesque PowerPoint presentation entitled "Why You Should Date Me," based on an extremely persuasive one I'd seen on Imgur. It wasn't the sort of thing I ever would have done before meeting Grace, but I thought about the conversation we'd had that night at the secret fishpond, about cosmic redemption. How Grace had talked about bravery and a blank slate at the end of time, about doing what you could while your atoms were in such a pattern that produced consciousness. In that moment, writing that PowerPoint, I thought I finally understood why she didn't mind oblivion. How it could make you fearless, knowing that the universe had your back, in the end. Redemption for all the stupid shit you'd done. Total absolution of your sins.

It didn't matter if she said yes or no. Not in the end.

So I wrote my PowerPoint while sitting under my desk. I barely even noticed when Lola came in, and she apparently didn't find me being curled up on the floor under the furniture strange enough to question me about it, so I carried on silently until it was done. And then it *was* done. It was playful and silly and hopefully funny enough to make her laugh.

Why You Should Date Me

An Informative PowerPoint Presentation
by Henry Page

Central Arguments

- You are attracted to males (I hope—it wouldn't be the first time I've been wrong).

- I happen to be a male.

- I enjoyed making out with you. So much so that I would like to do it on a regular basis.

- As you once so wisely said: #YOLO

Benefits of Dating Me

- I pronounce GIF correctly.

- Star Wars movie marathons with pizza and ice cream.

- I would allow you to make out with me whenever you wanted.

- My references are out of control.

- I never skimp on guacamole at Taco Bell.

- You would be dating me.

- Please.

What You're In For

A Breakdown of Henry Isaac Page

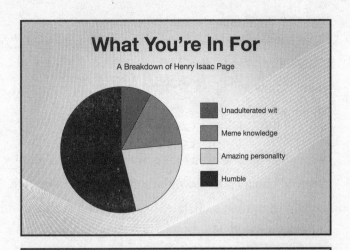

- Unadulterated wit
- Meme knowledge
- Amazing personality
- Humble

Pros and Cons of Dating Me

PROS	CONS
I can cook both cupcakes and mini pizzas.	Neither of them are very good.
I make romantic PowerPoints.	This potentially constitutes sexual harassment.
I have an extensive collection of Pokémon cards and *Doctor Who* merchandise.	Your parents might disapprove of you dating a bad boy.
I won't abandon you like your grade school boyfriend did. (What a dick.)	That could be interpreted as stalking.
Ricky Martin Knupps II would have a more stable childhood if we made this official.	**No more cons. Pros wins!**

Celebrity Testimonial

"As an entirely reliable narrator, you can take my word
for it that Henry Page is a special and unique snowflake.
In Tyler we trust."
—famous reliable narrator Tyler Durden

I read it and reread it and reread it, thinking, *Should I show her? Am I* really *going to show her?*

Then "Someday" by the Strokes came on Lola's Spotify.

My song for Grace.

Our song.

"I didn't know you liked the Strokes," I said to Lola.

"Hmm?" Lola spun slowly around in her chair. "Oh, I don't really know their stuff, but I heard Grace listening to this the other day and I liked it."

Screw it, I thought as I opened Facebook and typed:

HENRY PAGE:

> Grakov. Meet me in the auditorium during last period. Say it's for the newspaper to get out of class. I have something to show you.

GRACE TOWN:

> Henrik. How devious. I shall see you there.

I blinked several times and turned off my computer, then stayed in the office for the rest of the day. Principal Valentine walked past at one point and spotted me, my forehead pressed flat against my desk, and said, "Page. Aren't you supposed to be in class?"

To which I replied, without sitting up, "My teenage

hormones have rendered me too emotionally fragile to be in a learning environment right now."

Valentine was silent for a few seconds, and then she simply said, "Carry on."

So I did.

CHAPTER 14

I'M GOING TO *have to kill myself,* I thought as I paced back and forth onstage in the auditorium later that afternoon. I really couldn't see any way around it. My plan, clearly, was spectacularly stupid, and I couldn't imagine living with the humiliation of being turned down, universal redemption or not.

Grace was late, which made me panic and think she wasn't coming, which actually would've been a good thing. I considered bailing, but then the door at the back of the auditorium creaked open and she was moving down the center aisle between rows and rows of seats, leaning heavily on her cane. She looked so small in the vast, empty space, her long shadow cast up behind her. Like a miniature figurine in a diorama.

"What's this?" she said when I jumped off the stage and jogged up the aisle to meet her.

"A grand gesture I'm going to regret in about five minutes."

"Oh."

I clicked the power button for the projector and the title slide glowed to life on the screen.

"You're a ridiculous human being," Grace said, but it was playful, and she smiled, and then she limped to the front row of seats with me by her side and put down her bag and took a seat. "Well, let's get the regret train rolling, then."

Grace watched it from between her fingers like it was a horror movie, and said things like, "I'm so embarrassed for you right now," as she laughed. I clicked the *Next* button again and again until the *Pros and Cons of Dating Me* slide popped up and I watched her eyes flick from side to side as she read, her grin growing wider. But when she reached the second-to-last Pro (*I won't abandon you like your grade school boyfriend did.*), Grace immediately went cold.

"Stop," she said, her voice strong and clear, but I didn't have time to stop because she was already on her feet, her backpack already slung over her shoulders as she reeled toward the closest exit. It was *Groundhog Day* of the first afternoon I'd followed her from Hink's office: I grabbed my things and went after her, but she was fast, her movements wild as she raced across the school grounds.

"Wait!" I said, but she didn't wait, didn't stop, not until I caught up to her and put my hand on my shoulder, at which point she sank to the ground right near the bus stop. It was like freaking Obi-Wan in *A New Hope*—she seemed to fold into a pile of clothes, her body gone.

"This is not going at all how I envisioned it," I said as I sat next to her, running my hands through my hair, and Grace was kind of laugh-sobbing then, something between a manic cackle and hyperventilation.

"He was driving," she said between breaths. "Dom was driving. I messed up my leg, but he . . . he . . ." Grace couldn't say the words, but I didn't need her to. My insides shriveled, my stomach and lungs compacting to the size of pennies. I'd had asthma as a kid. That thick feeling in your throat, the way the spot behind your sternum turns to concrete and each breath becomes a battle.

It all made sudden, shocking sense. The graveyard. The clothes. The car. The track. The abandoned train station. Jesus Christ, even the Strokes.

It hadn't been her music I'd been listening to. It'd been his. *Our song.* Fuck. Our song wasn't even our song, it was *their* song. I had the sudden urge to vomit Julian Casablancas out of my bloodstream.

Grace buried her head against my shoulder, more for stability than anything else, like she might actually sink into the earth if she didn't. "That's why I transferred. I needed a fresh start, away from all the places we'd been together. I was trying to keep my shit together and then all of a sudden there you were, and I didn't plan to like you and I didn't plan to kiss you and I didn't plan for . . . I didn't want to be the girl with the dead boyfriend, I just wanted . . . I wanted . . ."

"Jesus. Grace. I don't even know what to say. *Jesus.*" My face was on fire. Murray and Lola were standing in the bus line, watching us with frowns on their faces, and I really wanted to get on the bus and get out of there and go home and start researching methods of suicide. Self-immolation seemed preferable at this point in time. I held up my hand to them and mouthed, *Wait for me.*

Grace lifted her heavy head from my shoulder, her breathing still ragged.

"I understand if you don't want—" I started, but then she had me by the collar and was kissing me like I was oxygen and she was drowning, so I let her draw all the breath from my lips to save herself.

I somehow knew, in that moment, that Grace Town was a jagged piece of glass that I'd cut myself on again and again if I let myself get involved with her. That the way forward would be pockmarked by sadness and grief and jealousy.

I thought about Pablo Neruda's poem, still folded where I'd nestled it in my wallet the first day she'd given it to me. I thought about loving her in secret, between the shadow and the soul. Maybe I should do that. Maybe that was where my feelings for Grace Town belonged, in the darkness, never to be realized.

But I'd never had a crush on a girl before, not like this, anyway, and as selfish as it sounds, I worried that I might never again. What if my family had some long-forgotten voodoo curse on them so that the firstborn male could only be attracted to someone every seventeen years? Dad's older brother, Uncle Michael, had never (as far as I was aware) had a serious girlfriend. (He did have a live-in "housemate" named Albert who seemed to come to a lot of family gatherings, but I digress.) If the spark of attraction only came along every seventeen years for me, I'd be thirty-four before I found another girl I liked. And if *she* didn't work out, the next one wouldn't come along until I was fifty-one. That seemed like a long time to wait to have your first relationship.

Grace liked me. We worked well together. And I wanted her. God, I wanted her. But was I really willing to throw all caution to the wind and get involved with someone who was still clearly very deep in mourning?

Then a teacher said, "Leave room for Jesus," over a megaphone. (Our school had a "no loving, no shoving" policy in place in an attempt to curb teen pregnancy and fights. Students were supposed to retain a two-foot no-touching radius at all times.) Grace broke away from me and scrabbled to her feet and all of the kids were on the bus and the driver was honking the horn and Murray was yelling at me to "get a bloody move on, you drongo!" I thought Grace might offer me a lift home so we'd have more time to talk, but she didn't, so I just said, "I want you anyway." And then I turned and ran shakily to the bus, sucking in breaths through my mouth like I'd done as a child before the inhaler kicked in.

As the bus pulled out of the school grounds, it drove past her, already limping toward the road. She was running the fingers of her free hand through her hair, her head drooped toward the ground like she'd recently been told some terrible, tragic news. And I thought, as a sting of misery murmured through my veins, that I'd never seen a human being look quite so sad as Grace Town did in that moment.

CHAPTER 15

THERE WAS NO MENTION, the following Monday, of the events that transpired the Friday before. In fact, I don't believe it was ever mentioned again. I'd decided, over the weekend, not to solidly make up my mind about how to move forward until I saw Grace again in the flesh. I was still uncertain, leaning more toward saying "let's just be friends," because it was stupidly complicated and rocky and I didn't know if I could deal with that.

It was senior year. Between school, the newspaper, deciding which colleges to apply to (hint: any one that would take me), and maintaining the slim resemblance of a social life, my existence was already busy and knotted enough.

And then, of course, I'd Googled the crash. It had taken a while to find the article, because Grace's name was never used, and I didn't know her boyfriend's full name. When I found it, I didn't want to read it. It felt like getting a shitty mark back on an essay and seeing a wall of text from the teacher about everything you'd done wrong, everything you couldn't change now, so what was the point?

Still, I skimmed it, picked up quotes here and there, tried to read as little as possible because the words stung me like barbs.

Classes at East River High School were suspended on Wednesday after a junior died and a second was severely injured—

Skipped to next paragraph.

The unnamed passenger, a 17-year-old girl believed to be the driver's girlfriend, remained in critical condition Friday with major injuries to her—

Skipped to next paragraph.

The car skidded off the road and flipped several times before impacting a tree near—

Skipped to next paragraph.

It's believed that the 17-year-old driver, Dominic Sawyer, died on impact, while the passenger was rushed to—

Skipped to next paragraph.

"The car is just destroyed," said the officer. "There's nothing left—

Skipped to next paragraph.

At East River, school counselors are on hand today to provide support to students and—

Skipped to next paragraph.

Jeffers said Sawyer "was one of the kindest students I'd ever taught. Brilliant at everything and—

Skipped to next paragraph.

Plans for a memorial service for the popular East River student are—

Closed website.

By the time I reached my afternoon drama class, I'd all but decided that we couldn't be together. We couldn't make it work. Grace was too broken. Too weird. How could you move on from that? What she needed was a friend, not a boyfriend. I could be that for her. I could be a good friend. God knows she needed one. So I sat where I normally sat in the black-walled drama room, across from the door, close to the stage, waiting for her to arrive. Surely it wasn't too late to nip it in the bud. Feelings could be suppressed if you tried hard enough, right?

Grace got there late, as she always did, and Mrs. Beady didn't say anything, because she never did.

Nothing about her had changed, specifically. Her hair was still a mess. Her skin was still sallow. She still had guys'—her dead boyfriend Dom's—clothes on. She still walked with a limp that was in no way attractive. But the moment our eyes met across the room and her hard expression softened at the sight of me, I knew.

I knew I wanted to try.

So she was grieving and broken and it would almost definitely end in one or both of us getting destroyed. But some things were worth fighting for, right?

CHAPTER 16

BECAUSE I'M A COWARD, I didn't ask her about him. Maybe it would have been the best thing for both of us to sit down and for her to talk about him and cry about him and tell me that she still regularly visited his grave.

There were things I was curious about, of course. How long had they dated? How long had they known each other? Had they slept together?

Had she loved him?

But Grace didn't belong to me. She wasn't my girlfriend. I'd only kissed her twice. In fact, she'd asked me not to tell anyone about us, to keep it on the down-low, at least until she knew for sure what she wanted, because it was generally considered poor taste to date someone so soon after your significant other had died. I tried my best not to feel hurt that she wanted to keep me a secret, because, well, fair enough.

So it didn't feel like my place to ask about him, and I think, deep down, I kind of didn't want to know. The Grace I'd fallen for hadn't been a girl in mourning for someone else; she'd been a mystery to be unraveled, and part of me wanted to keep it that way.

The trick to dating, I figured, was to have some kind of activity to do. Going to the movies seemed kind of lame and antisocial, but there was a new Liam Neeson action flick out, and we had the whole Liam-Neeson-improvisational-comedy in-joke thing going, so I decided to message her on Monday afternoon to see what she was doing.

HENRY PAGE:

Are you busy tonight?

GRACE TOWN:

Nothing at the moment. What are you up to?

Was thinking of going to see that new Liam Neeson flick. There will no doubt be much improvisational comedy involved. I mean, I'm pretty sure it has the same plot line as all of Liam Neeson's other movies, but I'm okay with that.

Where and what time?

Well, I would normally suggest the theater near my place, but Regal is probably going to be easier if you're busing it like us peasants. 7:45 p.m.

Yeah, I may have to. But that sounds good. Liam Neeson vs. the world. My money's on the big man.

No one messes with Neeson! Meet you there at like 7:30 p.m.?

Sounds good, Henrik Page. See you then.

Grace was waiting outside the theater when I arrived, hunched over her phone, unkempt as ever.

"Hey," I said when she looked up and saw me. Was I supposed to kiss her? We'd already kissed before, but did that mean I was allowed to kiss her whenever I wanted to now? Were we allowed to be affectionate in public places, or did that break the down-low rule?

"Henry Page," Grace said. Why had I still not kissed her? "Shall we get our tickets?"

"Sounds like a plan."

Normally, on Good Grace Days, conversation between us flowed pretty easily. There were still awkward silences sometimes, when I couldn't rack my brain for words to save my life, but tonight felt different. There was a new tension that'd never been there before, because this was a *date* date (wasn't it?). Something had shifted between us. Attraction had been acknowledged, and it somehow made everything more difficult.

When the lights went down, I tried to decide if I should hold her hand. I'd held hands with Lola at the movies once, during the week that'd ultimately culminated with the kiss that had determined her homosexuality for her once and for all. I really hoped this would end differently.

It took until all the trailers and ads for the concession stand were over for the skin of our fingers to finally meet, slow-moving magnets drawn together in the dark.

We held hands the entire movie, Grace tracing slow circles on my skin with her fingertips. Occasionally she'd lift my hand to her lips and kiss me. I stared at the screen for two hours, vaguely aware that Liam Neeson was kicking someone's ass, but if you'd asked me afterward what the movie had been about, I would've had very sketchy details about the plot at best.

After it was finished, we walked back to the bus stop together, both of us with our hands tucked into our pockets because it was almost November and too cold to have them out. Or maybe it wasn't because of the cold. Maybe it was because our relationship (was it even a relationship?) was supposed to be a secret. It was fine to make out at dark parties and hold hands in dark movie theaters, but out in the open, out where other people could see us, Grace and I were still only friends.

"Liam Neeson," Grace said when we slowed at the bus stop. "What a badass."

"I know, right."

"Best comedian in the world."

"Too bad all his jokes are about AIDS."

"What are you talking about? AIDS is comedy gold. Oh, look, it's your bus."

Damn. Already? I'd been hoping Grace's bus would show up first. That, while we waited, we'd sit on the low stone wall that surrounded the city park and talk and laugh and make out.

"Rats. Well, bye," I said. Smooth, Page. So smooth.

I leaned in. Kissed her quickly. Pressed my forehead against hers for a second, hoping this small gesture would convey what I couldn't say aloud: *I like you very much.*

Then I turned and went, unsure if anything I'd done all night had been right. The caustic lights of the bus stripped away the haze of darkness I'd been in for the last few hours, and the whole situation suddenly looked far uglier. I stared out the window the entire trip home, my phone clutched in my hand, wondering if I was supposed to message her and tell her what a great time I'd had and how much I liked her. But it felt tacky somehow. Like a cheap shot at her dead boyfriend, still not fully decomposed in his grave.

And I realized then that this would never be a normal love story, if there is such a thing. Even if neither of us wanted to talk about him, Dom would always be there, a ghostly presence neither of us could escape. I'd felt him in the theater, wedged between us. I could feel him now, his half-rotten body in the empty bus seat across the aisle from me. He was shaking his head and saying, "Dating my girlfriend while my eyeballs putrefy? Dick move, bro."

But it could get easier. Grace could get better. She could

go back to the girl she'd been before, in time. The girl I caught glimpses of sometimes.

My phone buzzed in my hand.

GRACE TOWN:

I've been inspired by Mr. Neeson to take up the position of voluntary undercover bus marshal. No suspicious action yet. I'll keep you updated.

HENRY PAGE:

I still think the kid being the terrorist would've been an awesome plot twist.

Yes. Definitely.

I'm still of the opinion that Neeson should play Qui-Gon Jinn in all of his movies from now on.

It would be a lot easier to be a bus marshal if I could use the Force.

Wait, let me try.

Well?

No luck.

I've been trying for years. One day. One day.

There's always the dark side.

I'm rather partial to the dark side. I once had a dream that Bellatrix Lestrange was my girlfriend, so there's that. She wasn't really a very good girlfriend. Far too fixated on killing Harry Potter. We fought a lot.

You're so needy.

All I wanted was a little attention, but no, she was always hanging out with Voldemort and his Death Eaters, plotting genocides and killing children.

The poor woman obviously had some issues she needed help with and you were too self-centered to notice. Henry Isaac Page, you disappoint me.

I suppose I could've been a little more supportive . . . Maybe told her occasionally what a good job she was doing persecuting Mudbloods. If the dream ever reoccurs, I'll be sure to be more enthusiastic about her interests. Like murdering teenage boys and being obsessed with Dark Lords. Maybe we can make it into a couple's activity. The couple that slays together stays together.

I wish you the best. Also, confession time (don't hate me): I've never read Harry Potter. Or seen the movies. So I only have the vaguest idea of what you're babbling on about.

WHAT. THE. ACTUAL. FUCK?

Yeah.

WHAT KIND OF CHILDHOOD DID YOU HAVE? WERE YOUR PARENTS NAZIS?

Not quite. I never went in much for fantasy. Give me Death Stars and AT-ATs over wands and robes any day.

I just . . . I don't know how I feel about you anymore . . .

Harry Potter's the deal breaker?

We must all face the choice between what is right and what is easy, Grace. Reading Harry Potter is what is right.

That's some kind of quote, right? Who said that? The Dumbledude?

HOW DARE YOU STAND WHERE HE STOOD.

Yeah, I have no idea what you're talking about anymore.

I'm home in record time!

That's good. I'm gonna crash. I was going to send you a very romantic GIF from Anchorman 2 but you have to earn that kind of thing and you've really lost a lot of brownie points with this whole Harry Potter sacrilege.

Awesome. Thanks for the invite! Catch you tomorrow.

Night night.

CHAPTER 17

THE FIRST THING I did when I woke up in the morning was message her.

HENRY PAGE:

> Wanna come over for dinner tonight, Town? I'mma woo you with my culinary expertise.

GRACE TOWN:

> Yo, Page, I'mma let you cook for me, but my momma has the best culinary skills of all time.

> (That was a yes by the way.)

> (Also, my mother can't cook.)

> Grand. See you in drama.

I considered tacking an *x* onto the end of the message, but I didn't quite know if we were at that level yet, and the thought of the *x* not being reciprocated was enough to discourage me from typing the *x*, so I didn't. I stayed in bed, slipping in and out of sleep, until Mom yelled, "Henry, are you alive?" down the stairs and I had to drag myself away from my comfortable tangle of sheets and begrudgingly dress for the day.

Upstairs, my parents were performing their usual morning routine: Mom was already dressed in a light blue suit, her pale hair pinned up in curls, ready for a day at the gallery. Dad was swaddled in an absurdly fluffy white bathrobe, black-rimmed glasses balancing on the end of his nose. They sat at opposite ends of the table, as far away from each other as possible, reading the morning news on their separate iPads.

"Mother. Father. I have news," I announced.

Dad looked up from an article about one of the Kardashians. "You've been conscripted to the war? What decade are you speaking from?"

"Ugh, fine: Home-Daddy, Mama P., I got a live tweet coming at you. Better?"

"Oh God, go back to World War Two, please," said Mom.

"What's up, kid?" Dad said.

"Can I cook dinner tonight?"

"Darling, the only thing you know how to make is mini pizzas," said Mom.

"I know. I'm going to cook mini pizzas for everyone, if you

don't mind buying the ingredients. Also." I cleared my throat. "There's a girl coming over."

"Do you have a group assignment at school?" Mom asked.

"Is she tutoring you?" Dad said.

"Are you selling her something?"

"Did you lure her here under false pretenses?"

"Does she think you come from old money?"

"Are you blackmailing her?"

"Is she a heavy drug user?"

I rolled my eyes. "Oh, ha-ha, you're both *very* funny."

"We think so," said Mom as Dad air-high-fived her. (Okay, so I take back what I said about them being cool.)

"Well, who is she?" Dad asked.

"Her name is Grace. We're, um, editing the newspaper together."

"Oh, Henry. Have you never heard the saying 'don't shit where you eat'?"

"Justin, that's disgusting," Mom said.

"I'm not shitting anywhere," I said.

"Well," Dad said, "I suppose this would be the point when we'd normally say, 'No sex, drugs, or rock 'n' roll under our roof,' but we raised your sister here, so I'm ninety-nine percent certain all of that's already happened."

"I *did* find a baggie of white powder in the elk's mouth the other day," I said, stroking my chin.

"My point exactly," Dad said.

Mom stood and cleared her plate and kissed the side of my head as she made her way to the sink. "We'll buy the ingredients. You cook. And I *am* going to say, 'No sex, drugs, or rock 'n' roll under our roof,' even if your father won't."

I patted her on the back. "That's not going to stop me from doing lines of coke off a hooker while listening to Led Zeppelin, but hey, at least you tried."

She shook her head. "God, sometimes I don't know where we went so, so wrong with you two."

Mom and Dad were in the kitchen unpacking the dinner ingredients when Grace and I arrived, both of them dressed in full *Star Trek* uniforms, Vulcan ears and all.

"No," I said when I saw them. "Dear God, *no*."

It'd already been an odd sort of afternoon. We'd performed our usual routine of walking to Grace's, but as we'd turned onto her street, Grace had let out a long, thin breath and pushed her palm into my chest. We were still a far way off from her house, but Grace had sensed a disturbance in the Force—a small car with paneling in three different colors was parked in her driveway next to her Hyundai.

"Stay here," she'd whispered.

"Who is that?" I'd said.

"Stay here if you want a lift."

It wasn't lost on me how close it sounded to *Stay here if you want to live.*

So I sat in the gutter and watched Grace as she limped

wildly down the street and into her sad gray house. She was gone for a long time, maybe forty-five minutes, long enough that I thought I'd better either call the cops or start walking home, before a woman with bleached-blond hair slammed the front door open and stalked across the lawn to the car. She backed the shabby vehicle so quickly and violently out of the driveway that she hit a trash can on the opposite side of the road before smoking the tires as she took off.

"Was that your mom?" I'd said when Grace finally emerged with her car keys another ten minutes later, her jaw clenched, her lips a hard line.

"No. Yes. It doesn't matter."

"You look like her."

"I look like a forty-five-year-old alcoholic slash casual meth user?"

"Jesus, Grace, I didn't—"

"I *know* you didn't. It's fine. Just drive."

"Do you live with your dad?"

Grace was silent.

"I don't know anything about you and you won't even tell me when I ask."

"You know my favorite song and my favorite color."

"We aren't in kindergarten. I want to know real things about you. I want to know the shit stuff too."

"There's more beauty in mystery."

"I don't want you to be a mystery."

"Yes, Henry. You do."

And maybe the thing that stung the most was that Grace was right. My best friends and I had never had to deal with unstable parents or broken homes. Lola, Murray, and I were the blessed three. The most gut-wrenching fight any of us had had with our families was when La was eleven and she'd run away from home (all the way to my house). During her weekly English lesson at the YMCA, Lola's pint-sized Haitian mother, Widelene, had proudly announced to the class that the loose skin on your elbow was called "the weenus"—a fact taught to her by her preteen daughter, who was in a lot of trouble from her dad when he found out. Lola and I had hid under my bed eating Reese's Peanut Butter Cups and looking at pictures of boobs on Sadie's laptop. Which, in retrospect, left no excuse for me not guessing that Lola had a penchant for the ladies *way* sooner.

Grace and I hadn't spoken for the entire drive to my house. And now here were my parents trying to embarrass me, and I wanted to be pissed at them, but neither of them was an alcoholic or a casual meth user, and I'd never taken the time to be truly appreciative of that fact before, so when Dad said, "Live long and prosper," and did the Vulcan salute, I held up my hands in surrender and said weakly: "Please. Stop."

Grace's lips were pulled into a tight line, her attempt at a smile, but her eyes were glassy and she had the thousand-yard stare of a battle-weary general who disapproves of everyone's bullshit. Jesus. This was gonna be fun.

I cleared my throat and continued. "Grace, parentals. Parentals, Grace."

While Grace was shaking my mom's hand, Dad said, "Henry, catch," and because I'd obviously developed lightning-fast reflexes from that one game of touch football, I caught what he threw me without a second thought. Which turned out to be a box of Trojan condoms. "Just in case. I don't want you to have to endure the hell of an unexpected pregnancy like we had to. The pregnancy I'm referring to, of course, is yours. We wanted Sadie."

"You know, I tell people that you're cool and then you consistently manage to make me look like a delusional liar."

"You tell people we're cool?" said Mom. "Well, beam me up, Scotty!"

"We don't need his approval," said Dad. "I already know we're the most illogical Vulcans in town."

"Oh my good God. Grace, please, move away from them slowly."

"Later, gators," said Dad as I took Grace's hand and dragged her away from them.

"It was nice to meet you," Grace said over her shoulder.

"No, no, it was not nice, don't lie to them."

"No copulation in the house, please," Mom yelled after us in a sweet voice. Then, much quieter, "Why does no one tell you that being a parent is so much fun?"

I poked my tongue out at her as I closed the basement door.

"I'm *so* sorry about my parents," I said.

"Don't be sorry. Not about that."

"Do you want to talk about your mom or—"

"Highly presumptuous of you," Grace said as she took the box of condoms out of my hands while I walked down the stairs with her, one step at a time. "I was thinking . . . maybe I could stay over after the Halloween party this weekend?" Grace shook the box of condoms. "These might come in handy."

"Um . . . uh . . ."

"This is the point where you say something smooth to seduce me."

"If you were a carrot, you'd be a good carrot?"

Grace burst out laughing and chucked the condoms across the room. "Well, I guess we won't be needing those."

I picked them up and put them on my bedside table. "Let's not rule anything out," I said.

Grace sat on the side of my bed and pulled me down next to her and kissed me. "I'm serious. About Halloween. If you want me to stay, I'll stay."

"I'm not really good at this whole subtle-seduction thing, so I'm gonna come right out and say it: I assume you're alluding to sexual intercourse?"

Grace rolled her eyes. "Yes, Henrik. Well done."

"I see. Well, that sounds fine by me."

"Excellent."

"You're a . . . I mean, you and . . . *him*?" He was rarely referred to by name. "I assume you're not . . . ?"

"I'm not a virgin, no."

"Okay. Just checking."

"And have you . . . ?"

"I am, uh . . . I mean, I haven't . . . made the beast with two backs."

Grace collapsed into laughter, burying her face into my chest. Man, I was doing well tonight. "It's even harder for you to talk about sex than it is for you to talk about yourself."

"What can I say, I'm a gentleman."

"No, you're a weirdo. Sex is a basic human function. Do you have trouble talking about breathing or blinking?"

"My respiratory function is extremely private information. Wait, where are you going?" I said, tugging Grace's wrist as she made to stand up.

"I haven't finished judging your room yet."

"Always with the judging," I said as she stood and started to wander in a slow circle around the basement.

"You can tell a lot about a person from their bedroom, don't you think? Bedrooms are like crime scenes. So many clues to be uncovered."

"What's your bedroom like?"

"Maybe you'll find out one day. For now, let me use my *CSI*-level investigative skills to determine exactly who you are."

"Well?" I said after a few minutes of listening to her hum the *CSI* theme tune. "Who am I?"

Grace cleared her throat. "Judging by the decor and the decades-old electronics," she said, sliding on my sunglasses and doing a fairly convincing impression of Horatio Caine, "I conclude that this is some kind of conspiracy theorist's bunker and you probably believe the president is a reptilian shapeshifter."

"That's crazy talk. The *royal family* are reptilian shapeshifters. The president is your plain old run-of-the-mill warlock."

"Oh, of course. My apologies. What's this, though?" Grace gestured to the small antique display cabinet that my great-grandfather had kept his absinthe collection and drinking paraphernalia in before it was outlawed in the Netherlands, at which point he'd promptly moved the cabinet and his entire family to the States.

A plaque in the shape of a banner had been nailed to the top. *Matigheid is voor de døden*, it read. *Moderation is for the dead*. Johannes van de Vliert, true to his life philosophy, died at the age of forty-seven from alcoholic hepatitis. He was far and away my favorite ancestor.

"Only the best thing in this room. Apart from you, of course."

"It's a display cabinet . . . full of broken junk . . ."

"It's not junk!" I sprang off the bed and went over to her and the cabinet, which I'd been filling with various treasures since I was in elementary school. "Grakov Town, you filthy casual. It's a cabinet of curiosities. The bowls here are my favorite. I read about this technique called Kintsukuroi in an art book in middle school. Have you heard of it?" Grace shook her head. "So basically it's this old-school Japanese art form where they mend broken pottery with seams of gold. Like, they glue all the shattered pieces back together, and when it's done, it's covered in these webs of gold veins. They do it because they believe that some things are more beautiful when they've been broken."

Grace picked up one of the Kintsukuroi pieces. I had eleven in total now, some of them gifts from Lola over the years, some from Mom after art acquisition trips to Japan, some purchased on eBay or Craigslist with my allowance. There were other things in the cabinet as well, all of them broken or crooked or wrong somehow. A silver bangle that Sadie had been given as a gift, the joint warped. A can of Coke with a misprinted label.

"It's a shame people can't be melded back together with gold seams," Grace said, turning the bowl over in her hands. I wasn't sure if she was talking about herself or her mother or some other person in her life, and I probably never would, because Grace Town liked being a mystery. And then, realizing the lighthearted nature of a minute before was gone, weighed down now by something much heavier, she put the bowl back and said, "You know this is only slightly less creepy than collecting Cabbage Patch Kids, right?"

"You know nothing, Grace Town. The ladies love Kintsukuroi."

Grace tried and failed to fake a smile. "Can we make dinner? I'm starved."

"Sure," I said. "Sure."

Grace helped me prepare the mini pizzas. Well, sort of. The kitchen seemed like an alien place she'd never set foot in before, and I had to direct her on how to assist. *Would you mind cutting the tomatoes? You can grate some cheese if you'd like.* After every small job, she'd stand out of the way and watch me quietly, awkwardly waiting for her next instruction.

While the pizzas were in the oven, we ventured back downstairs and lay on my bed, not touching, the both of us staring at the ceiling.

"What do you want from this?" I said, overcome by a sudden rush of courage, because I was genuinely curious. What *did* she want from me? What did she hope to gain from all this?

Grace didn't look at me. "I don't know. What do you want?"

"You know what I want."

"I'm not sure I do."

"I want you."

She smiled a little then, but she never said, "I want you too."

At dinner, Grace was odd around my parents, the way she was around almost everyone except me, all of the warmth drained out of her. She spoke only when spoken to and didn't laugh or smile at the appropriate times. She ate little and spoke less.

By the time I walked her to the door at eleven p.m. and watched her disappear into the darkness toward the graveyard, I was almost glad to see her go, worried that my parents would find the first girl I'd ever brought home to be lacking somehow.

When I came back inside, Mom and Dad were in the kitchen, stacking the dishwasher together. I sat quietly at the breakfast bar, waiting for their assessment, which I knew would come whether I wanted to hear it or not.

"She's very brooding," Mom said after a while. "Beautiful, but very brooding."

"Do you think?" I said, puzzled. *Brooding* is the way I'd describe vampires, not Grace. "I hadn't noticed."

"Pretty smile, though, when she *does* smile. Strange girl."

"Strangeness is a necessary ingredient in beauty," Dad said, threading his arms around my mother's waist. Mom nodded but pulled away from him, and as I watched them for the next ten minutes, watched as they moved around the kitchen but never touched, were never drawn to each other, I realized it'd been a long time since I'd seen them kiss or hold hands or slow dance together when they thought no one was watching, like they used to when I was a kid.

A long, long time.

For the next three days, hardly an hour went by when Grace and I didn't see each other. In the mornings before school we sat in the office and worked on the newspaper and teased each other endlessly. We brought in a badminton kit and had silly framed family pictures of us with Ricky Martin Knupps II on our desks. At lunch we'd go to McDonald's together, or read each other passages from books in the library (me: always Harry Potter, her: always poetry), or walk around the outermost boundary of the school grounds and kick the last of the leaf piles and brainstorm bullshit newspaper themes, neither of us realizing that we hadn't actually eaten anything until the bell rang.

And then in the evenings, when school and work were done, we'd follow the routine that was now our ritual: We'd walk to her house and I'd wait outside while she fetched her keys, and she'd make me drive myself home in her car. And that's where everything would change. The moment the sun set, it was like Grace became a different person, like the sunshine fueled her somehow and without it she powered down, empty. On Thursday she came inside and sat uncomfortably in the basement, clinging to Lola like she was a life preserver, barely speaking to Murray, and rarely engaging in any sort of group conversation. On her own, Grace could be effervescent, illuminating the entire room with her intelligence and wit. Around others she seemed to lose her luster.

"I swear I used to be good at this stuff," she said to me after Muz left, by this time convinced that Grace hated him. "At socializing, I mean. I used to do it all the time."

"I guess it must be harder. Without him. Right?" It was one of the rare instances that either of us acknowledged that there had been someone before me who wasn't here now.

Grace shook her head. "Not harder, no. I just forget to do it. I slip into my head and keep falling deeper into the abyss. I forget the world exists."

Which is the point when I probably should've said, "That sounds remarkably like some kind of mental illness that you should seek therapy and medication to help treat," but I didn't, because I didn't want Grace to be sick or broken or depressed. I wanted her to brush her hair and wash her clothes and to be whole and full and happy.

So I pretended she was.

And slowly, hour by hour, the countdown to All Hallows' Eve ticked away, until it finally arrived. My street turned into an annex of the cemetery, tombstones, cobwebs, and skeletons strewn everywhere. By midday on Saturday, it looked like some sort of kitsch apocalypse had exploded in our front yard. Sadie brought Ryan over to carve pumpkins on the lawn, but all I could think about was the party happening that night. Or rather what was happening *after* the party, which I felt wholly underprepared for.

"Dude, what the hell are you doing to that pumpkin?" Sadie said as she surveyed my handiwork. Sadie, with her piercings and dreads and leather jacket, looked maniacal with a carving knife in one hand and a pumpkin wedged between her knees. My pumpkin was a little soft and my knife was a little blunt, which combined to make it look like the face had been carved using a sawed-off shotgun at close range. "It's worse than Ryan's and he doesn't even have fine motor skills yet. No offense, Ryan."

"It's a surrealist interpretation of the traditional jack-o'-lantern, thank you very much."

"If it could speak, it would simply whisper, 'Kill me,' before vomiting seeds and pulp everywhere."

I sighed and put my carving knife down. "Suds, I know it's unethical, but do you think you could score me some Valium from the hospital?"

"Pray tell, what do you need Valium for?"

"Grace is kinda coming over tonight, after the party. Sleeping over, actually. For the first time."

"Oh. *Oh.* My baby's growing up so fast!"

"Get off me, She-Devil," I said, trying to push Sadie away as she squashed my ribs in a bear hug, her pumpkin rolling across the grass. "Ugh, I shouldn't have told you."

"Don't stress too much, man. People have been banging for millions of years. You got condoms?"

I grimaced. "Yeah."

"You know how to use 'em?"

"Christ, Sadie. Yes."

"And you want to have sex with this girl?"

"She's a consenting human female and I'm a teenage boy. That's an irrelevant question."

"No, it's not. Look, you don't need to love someone to lose your virginity to them, but you should know them and trust them and feel comfortable with them and really, really *want* to sleep with them."

"Well, yeah. I guess. I mean, yeah. I want to be with her."

"And it's a stupid cliché question, but do you feel ready? I mean, sex is not a big deal, but it's not *not* a big deal, you know?"

"I think I feel ready?" I didn't mean for it to sound so much like a question.

"Okay, good. That's all that matters. Everything else is biology. Now give me that poor pumpkin before you make it any worse."

Grace came to my house in the evening to do my makeup, a small yet ominous overnight bag in her hands.

"It still cool if I stay here tonight?" she said when she caught me staring at it.

"Yeah. Yeah, of course." It wasn't that I didn't want to have sex with her. I'd been thinking about having sex since I was about twelve years old.

"Good," she said as she pulled a palette of face paint and a thirty-ounce bottle of fake blood out of her bag. "Now, do you want to be a zombie or a car crash victim? Because they're the only special effects makeup I'm good at."

My eyes flicked down to where her cane was resting across my bed. "Uh . . . I don't . . ."

"That was a joke, Henry."

"Oh . . ." I forced out a nervous *ha* sound. Making light of the horrific car accident that killed your boyfriend. Hilarious. "Zombie, I guess."

For the next hour I sat on the edge of my bed while Grace moved around me, holding herself away from me in her usual rigid marionette fashion while she applied liquid latex wounds and decomposing special effects to my face. Which I know is not the most romantic of situations, but it felt almost clinical, the way she went about touching me as little as possible.

I expected her to go as something entirely weird, like a meme or an obscure literary character or a figure from an eighteenth-century impressionist artwork. But when she went upstairs to get dressed and do her makeup while I shredded an old T-shirt and drenched myself in fake blood, she came back down in a sexy vampire costume, a single trickle of red seeping from the corner of her mouth.

It was the first time I'd seen her in clothes that were made to fit a feminine figure, and it was shocking. Her legs were long and toned, encased in dark stockings, her breasts and waist accentuated by a black lace corset that gave her the kind of shape I'd never imagined a high school girl as capable of having. Her blond hair was brushed and curled and pinned back by black netting that covered her smoky eyes, and she'd even tied a red ribbon around her cane.

She was darkly beautiful, a femme fatale, a heroin junkie risen from the dead—and I could hardly recognize her.

"I didn't really think much about a costume, so I recycled this from last year," she said, shrugging. "It's lame."

"No. I approve wholeheartedly."

"Really? 'Cause you look a little . . . shocked?"

"I guess I didn't expect . . . It doesn't seem like something you'd wear, that's all. Not the you that I know, anyway. I was expecting something, I don't know, weird or something that I'd have to ask you twenty questions to get. You look sexy as hell, though."

"Grace this time last year was pretty different from the Grace I am now."

I looked at her for a little longer and then nodded.

"Say it, Henry."

"Say what?"

"Whatever it is that's going on in that mysterious brain of yours. I can see the cogs furiously turning behind your eyes, but all you do is nod. So say it."

"It's just . . . I wonder sometimes . . . Man, I'm no good at this drafting business . . . If the person you were . . . What if that's who you are? I mean, I don't know her at all, I don't know anything about her. I see her in you sometimes, I get these flashes of this girl you used to be, but . . . Was she an act and you're more yourself now, or is the Grace I know an act until you feel comfortable being yourself again?"

"People change. There's no way you're the same person you were when you were sixteen."

"Yeah, but I didn't change schools and start wearing a dead guy's clothes."

There was a beat of silence. "So you know," she said slowly, staring at me, unblinking. "The truth outs."

"I'm sorry, I shouldn't have—"

"I know who you want me to be, Henry. It isn't hard to see."

"What does that—"

"You look at me differently sometimes. You think I don't notice, but I do. There are times when you really like me, and others when you don't so much. But I can't pretend to be all better because that's what you want."

"Grace, it's nothing like that, not at—"

"Look, let's not talk about it tonight, okay?"

"I want *you*, all the time."

"I know you think that. But sometimes I don't know which version of me you want. The one I am. The one I was. Or the Kintsukuroi dream girl you think I'll be a couple of months from now."

"*You* were the one who said people can't be melded back together with gold seams."

"That's exactly my point," she said as she turned and started climbing, step by painful step, back up the stairs.

I typed my fifth draft of "Why Henry Page Is Single" as I followed her, dripping blood all over the floor as I went.

Draft Five
Because apparently you still have to chase girls who
can't even run.

CHAPTER 18

THE FIRST HALF of the party, for the most part, was a lot like Heslin's. We went to the football field to drink, not from a bathtub this time, but from—I'm not even kidding—an industrial rainwater tank. (The bathtub had ended up on Heslin's roof. No one had claimed responsibility yet, but I very strongly suspected Murray.) The concoction this time was red-tinged and suspiciously frothy, like someone had cleaned the tank with dishwashing liquid and not rinsed it out before they'd sloshed in ten boxes of cheap wine. Still, it didn't taste as poisonous as the last batch, and after two bottlefuls I was fairly intoxicated, and so was Grace, thank God, because we both seemed to be much nicer people when we were drunk.

We slipped away from the group and made our way to a friend of a friend of someone's cousin who graduated three years ago's house, where the party was going down in the basement. We got there earlier than everyone else and Grace found us a suitably dark and secluded corner where we weren't likely to be spotted making out, but all I could think about was the sex we were supposed to be having later, so I just kept drinking.

The music grew louder and the basement slowly filled up with zombies and witches and pirates and sexy iterations of entirely unsexy things, like the Teenage Mutant Ninja Turtles, a papier-mâché planet Pluto in a bikini, and Madison Carlson—for reasons I will never understand—as a slutty corncob.

Grace leaned in and kissed me quickly, then went back to watching costumed people cram into the space.

"I'm going to stop going to the graveyard," she said quietly, her words ever so slightly slurred. "That's something I've never told you. I visit him almost every day, at the place where he's buried. I'm going to stop, though. For you."

I was taken aback. I'd come to accept Dom's ghostly presence as a fact of life, a condition of dating Grace Town. She would always dress like him. She would always smell like him. She would always visit his grave. But here she was, giving up a small piece of him already.

"I'd like that," I said quickly, without thinking, because now that she'd offered it, I realized it *was* something I wanted. I wanted her to stop spending so much time with her dead boyfriend, lying on the grass above his decomposing corpse, crying tears that seeped into the earth to rest upon his coffin.

"And I don't want you to feel like I'm, like, settling for you or whatever," she continued, still staring straight ahead. "I've never gotten along with anyone the way I get along with you."

I had to resist the temptation, in that moment, to ask her if

Dom and I were standing side by side, both whole, both alive, which one of us she would choose. Because I knew, still, that it would be him. For a long time, it would be him. Maybe always. And I felt the tear in my heart rip open a little bit more. Here she was, doing her best to declare her feelings to me, and all it did was make the hurt pierce a little deeper.

"You've been drinking. I don't want you to make any decisions tonight. Wait until you're sober. Think it over. I want you to be sure." *I want you to be sure that you can let him go.*

Grace turned to me and looked at me for a long time, her focus moving from one of my eyes to the other and then back again every few seconds.

"What?" I said after a while.

"Most guys would be assholes about all this. You've been so cool."

"Why would I be an asshole?" I was forcing myself to be cooler about it than I actually felt, but I couldn't say that—being a dick would only make her run in the other direction. "You've been up-front about everything since the beginning." *Except the car crash and dead boyfriend and the graveyard and the clothes, that is.*

She did the eye thing again twice more, then closed hers and leaned in and kissed me. I watched her the whole time to make sure she didn't open her eyes, like this was some kind of indicator of whether she really meant what she was saying. Grace kept her eyes closed, and when I could feel the kiss coming to an end, I jammed mine shut as she pulled away. And

I thought, *How could anyone kiss anyone like that and not mean it?*

"How long do we have to wait here before we go back to your place?" Grace said.

My heart kicked into a gallop. Oh yes. The losing of the virginity. I'd momentarily forgotten about it.

"I want to see everyone first. Hang out for a bit. Wait until my parents are asleep."

What I really wanted—what I didn't tell Grace that I wanted—was for people to see us together, to catch us, to accuse us of being more than friends with sly smiles on their faces. I wanted our relationship to have solid tethers outside of us, like the more people who knew about us, the more reasons she'd have to stay. We were in a Schrödinger's cat relationship, neither dead nor alive because we had not been observed. And maybe it was better that way. Maybe it was better to be unobserved, to be in flux, because there was every chance that being observed would kill us. I knew it was dangerous. After all, if nobody knew, then nobody would know if it didn't work out. My heartache would be private. But it was a gamble I was willing to take.

So, as the room grew loud with chatter, I kissed her. We talked and drank and flirted, Grace becoming more light and open with each sip of alcohol, and I kissed her, hoping that someone we knew would see, would point, would shout our names.

And eventually, an hour or so later, someone did.

"I knew it!" shouted Heslin, and some great coil of tension that had been sprung tightly inside of me all night was released. We had been seen. We had been observed. There was someone outside of us who could testify that we were real. That we had been here. "I fucking *knew* it!"

"Shh," I hissed at Heslin, because even though I wanted him to know, I didn't want Grace to know I wanted him to know.

Grace pulled back from me immediately and stood up and said, "You ready to go? I'm gonna go get my things."

I nodded and watched her weave her way through the costumed crowd to get her coat.

Heslin was still grinning at me. "How long have you been banging her for?"

"Please don't tell anyone, we're trying to keep it quiet." It didn't seem necessary to inform him that I had not, as of yet, banged her at all.

"Your secret's safe with me," said Heslin as he leaned down to muss my hair. We rarely spoke at school, but apparently this insider knowledge of my almost sex life somehow warranted a closer bond.

"I should go find her," I said as I stood up.

"*Yeah*, you should," said Heslin, clapping me on the back.

So our quantum superposition was over. Grace Town and I were either dead or alive, no long both simultaneously.

I wasn't sure, yet, which one it would turn out to be.

• • •

We walked home together, drunkenly, in the dark. In my semi-intoxicated state, knowing what we were going to do, I finally had the courage to do the things I wanted to do to her. I pushed her up against a tall chain-link fence covered in creeping vines and kissed her, more hungrily than I ever had before. I kissed her down her neck, across her collarbone, ran my hands over her hips, her thighs. Grace responded with gasps, ran her fingers through my hair, grabbed tufts of it, pulled herself against me. She sank her fake teeth into my neck, enough to hurt but not to break the skin.

"Take me home, Henry Page," she said, fake blood still smudged at the edges of her lips. And then she turned and started walking into the darkness, and I followed her, of course, my hands around her waist, kissing her all the way there. We got downstairs without waking the parentals, thank God, and then it was time to have The Sex.

We sat on my bed together and wiped away all of our makeup first. I peeled off my shirt and cleaned all the dry blood from my chest, wondering if I looked anything like how he'd looked after the accident, and if that's what she was thinking about, or if she was thinking about me. And then we sat for a minute after that, in silence, and I contemplated turning the lamp off, because maybe it would be easier in the dark.

But Grace knew what she was doing. She'd done this before. She sidled over to me and kissed me and then she was undoing the back of her corset.

"Holy shit," I said quietly when she took it off, because she was exquisite, and all my hesitation evaporated at the sight of her bare breasts.

We kissed some more, and then I rolled down her stockings, my fingertips grazing her scar tissue. There were two large, red rectangles cut from her upper thighs.

"From where they harvested the skin grafts," she said as I touched them. "The first one didn't take well, so they had to come back for more." I pulled her stockings all the way off and threw them across the room. The worst of the scarring was on her calf, where skin and muscle had been gouged away, covered with a mesh of skin that made the flesh look like a plucked bird. This leg was about half the size of the other, thin and raw and delicate looking. Fresh bruises and welts bloomed across the unmarred flesh, a keepsake from her latest expedition to East River's track.

It was amazing that she could walk at all.

"They've changed the pins once already. In a few years they might even take them out. I'm not sure. Maybe they'll eventually put Humpty Dumpty back together again."

I leaned down and kissed the angry red skin of her calf. "You're perfect."

And then it began.

It wasn't super romantic. There was no music playing or candles burning. It wasn't like any of those rom-coms that show brief touches of skin and hands clasping crisp white sheets. It wasn't even like the porn I'd seen. It was sweatier, quieter, more intense, more awkward. It was just me, and her, and no space in between us.

I'd spent a good part of my morning Googling "how to be good at sex," which turned out not to be particularly helpful in the moment. I forgot everything that AskMen.com had informed me and instead went with what felt right.

And then it was over. The V card had expired. There were no extravagant gasps or anything like that, but it can't have been too bad, because she said, "That was a thousand times better than I thought it would be," and I wasn't sure if I should be pleased because it'd been decent or offended that she'd been expecting it to be bad. Grace rested her head on my shoulder and I kissed her forehead and we lay together, naked in the dark, neither of us talking and neither of us able to fall asleep.

Eventually, when she thought I'd drifted off, Grace Town started to cry. I felt her trembling against me as she tried to control her breathing, felt her warm tears on my skin as they fell onto my chest. She sobbed only once, and then she wiped her eyes and her breathing calmed and she whispered, "I miss you," and then, steadily, steadily, she dropped away into sleep.

I stayed awake for an hour more, staring at the ceiling as her tears evaporated from my skin, trying to decide if I wanted to vomit because I was drunk or because the girl I'd lost my virginity to had probably been thinking about her dead boyfriend the whole time.

CHAPTER 19

WHEN I WOKE in the morning, Grace was already up, re-encasing her skin beneath layers of Dom's clothes. A butterfly for a night, returned to her cocoon. I pretended to be asleep as I watched her gather her vampire costume in a plastic bag and stuff it in the trash can next to my desk. She left without saying good-bye.

That night, I messaged her.

HENRY PAGE:

> Evening, Town. So, one night this week, I'm thinking I want to see the new Pixar movie. It's rated PG for mild animated violence and crude humor—I have a feeling I'm going to love it. You down?

I sent the message at 7:58 p.m. Grace saw it immediately, started typing back, then deleted whatever she was going to say. Ten minutes passed, then ten minutes more, still with no reply. Was I not allowed to ask her out, even though we'd slept together? Had I overstepped the unspoken boundaries of our relationship (or whatever it was)?

I ate dinner. Checked my phone. No reply.

She's changed her mind, she's changed her mind, she's changed her mind.

Had a shower. Checked my phone. No reply.

She's changed her mind, she's changed her mind, she's changed her mind.

Attempted my math homework. Checked my phone. No reply.

Oh God, oh God, oh God. She's changed her mind, she's changed her mind, she's changed her mind.

I went to bed feeling like someone had opened a black umbrella inside my chest. My lungs were pushed up under my collarbones and beneath that was a gaping hole where my insides used to be. Finally, at 11:59 p.m., right as I was slipping into unconsciousness, Grace messaged back.

GRACE TOWN:

Pixar! Sure I want to see that. Lock it in. Night!

The insane rush of endorphins that flooded my system the moment my phone vibrated and her name popped up on screen was worrying. I'd never been addicted to anything before, but I thought maybe this is what it felt like to be a junkie in desperate need of a hit.

"Edward Cullen, you poor, miserable bastard," I said as I locked my phone screen and stared at the ceiling. "I should not have judged you so harshly."

After school on Monday, Grace and I decided to keep walking past her house and catch a bus into the city, where a fall beer and food festival had been set up in the park. I had homework to do, and essays to work on, and the newspaper probably could've used some serious attention, but Grace was happy and she'd brushed her hair and there was no way I was going to miss out on spending time with this version of her.

In the park, the space between the trees had been transformed into a shantytown of little white canopies, a different flavor of food and/or beer nestled beneath each one. It was a hipster's delight: pallet furniture, antique teakettles hanging by twine from every tree branch, a decorate-your-own-hula-hoop station. The Plastic Stapler's Revenge had even managed to get themselves hired for a gig, and their warbled acoustic tunes (none of which, sadly, were about avenging stationery) carried across the park.

"What shall we feast upon, Town?" I said, but the end of my question was lost to the shout of another.

"Grace?!" said an unknown male voice.

We both turned to find its source: a tall, not-unattractive blond guy with a bunch of tall, not-unattractive male friends.

"Lyndon!" Grace said, and then she was darting through the crowd toward him and he swept her off her feet/cane when she reached him, and I was thinking, as I followed her with my hands in my pockets, about how much I suddenly despised the name Lyndon and anyone attached to it.

I stood by Grace's side for a solid five minutes while she chatted with him, before Lyndon's eyes slid to me and Grace remembered I existed. "Oh, sorry! This is Henry. We work together at the school newspaper. Henry, this is Lyndon, my cousin."

I shook his hand, thinking maybe Lyndon wasn't such a pretentious name after all. Whatever monster had been scratching away inside my chest since he'd shouted her name slunk back to its cage.

Holy shit, I thought as I surveyed his features and found that, yes, they did look alike, were definitely related. *Am I the jealous type?* I suppose it's one of those things you can't really know about yourself until you're faced with it. Like you can't really know if you're brave and heroic until something terrible happens and you're forced into action. I'd always thought I'd be the fearless type, calm and controlled and Sully Sullenberger–esque. Last off the plane, go down with the ship, that kind of thing. But now I wasn't so sure.

I thought about Tyler Durden, about him saying, "How much can you know about yourself if you've never been in a fight?" But how much can you know about yourself if you've never liked anyone before? I'd never felt so removed from myself as I did at that moment. Whose body was I walking around in? Whose brain was inside my skull? How could I *be* me, live inside my flesh, and still have no idea who I was?

Grace and I had come to the festival planning to get food, but Lyndon and his friends were all in their mid-twenties, so we gave them money and they bought us spiced cider and mulled wine. We all sat together under a tree, the hundreds of string lights illuminating the park growing muddled as the alcohol made its way to my head. We shared dishes from all the different food vendors—hot-and-sour soup from the Thai tent, honey-glazed mystery meat from the red-lantern-lit Chinese place, transparent rice paper rolls dipped in thick, sweet sauce from the Vietnamese vendor.

By the time Dad messaged me at nine p.m. saying *Here*, my stomach was full and my eyelids were heavy.

I sat up from where I'd been lying in the grass, staring at the fairy lights twinkling in the branches above me, and said good-bye to Grace, who looked outrageously beautiful in the golden light. I was keenly aware that Lyndon was watching us, so I made my farewell as casual as possible, despite the fact that we usually kissed good-bye. I even called her "dude."

"I've gotta jet, dude. I'll see you tomorrow," I said. Then I said good-bye to everyone else and strolled off into the festival crowd, hands in my pockets. I looked back once. Grace was staring after me. I expected her to look away, but she didn't, and I wasn't sure what that meant. If I was supposed to go back to her or not. But her cousin was there and we weren't together and whatever we were, whatever this was, the world wasn't supposed to know about us. I worried that if I *did* go back and kiss her like I wanted to that it would be the wrong thing, that it would make her angry. So I turned my head and kept walking, consumed by the crowd, certain that Sully Sullenberger would've gone back and swept her off her feet and that I was almost definitely a jealous coward.

My phone buzzed on the car trip home, while Dad told me about his day and I tried very hard not to sound like I'd been drinking.

GRACE TOWN:

So saying good-bye sucked.
You still up for the movies this week?

HENRY PAGE:

I didn't know if it was cool for me to kiss you in front of your cousin or not, so I kind of panicked and bailed. Or if we're still doing the whole "keep it on the down-low" thing or not . . . So yeah, sorry. But movies fo sho. Thursday night, 7:30 p.m. The theater near my place. We can chill in my room after school or get dinner or something beforehand.

Sounds good. I don't really know what's going on.

We're hopeless, you and me. I'm amazed that Hink put us in decision-making positions.

· · ·

On Wednesday, I woke up to Grace calling me at six a.m.

"What's wrong? Are you okay?" I said, jolting upright as soon as I saw her name on my screen. It should've been a sign, how constantly worried I was about her. It should've been a sign, because I knew she was depressed and reckless and there was always that voice in the back of my head that was scared her grief would get the better of her. Not that I ever thought she'd hurt herself or anything like that. It was more like I thought she might spontaneously dissolve on purpose, her atoms scattered away on the breeze.

"Chill out. I can't sleep, that's all. Do you have anything important to do at school today?"

I had an (unfinished) (FML) English assignment due, I had a newspaper progress meeting with Hink, and Hotchkiss had been asking after my math homework for a week, but they seemed far less important than spending time with Grace, so I lied and said, "No."

"Good, 'cause I'm outside your house. We're going to have an adventure."

"You're here?"

There was a tap at the basement window. Grace was crouching on the other side of the grimy glass, looking tired, still dressed in the same clothes she'd been wearing yesterday.

When Mom came downstairs to wake me an hour later, I pretended to feel sick while Grace hid under my bed. After the Birthgiver had gone to work, I begged Dad to let me spend the day with Grace while already knowing he'd rat me out to Mom as soon as he could. He finally, reluctantly agreed, on the condition that he was allowed to play *GTA V* in my room all day, and I was forbidden from telling anyone.

I was shocked to find Grace's car parked in its usual spot outside my house.

"*You* drove here?" I said.

"Surprise."

"First time since . . . ?"

"Yeah. I don't know why. I woke up in the middle of the night and decided it was time. After all, I'm never gonna make it into *Fast and Furious 11* if I don't get back into drifting."

I smiled and Grace said, "Henry. Don't look at me like that."

"Like what?"

"Like you can see the gold veins forming before your eyes," she said, but it was playful, not accusing. "I'm still not a bowl."

"Not a bowl. Duly noted."

We drove north to the outskirts of the city, and then through the national park for over an hour, slowing at all the lookouts but never stopping. Out here on the coast, it barely looked like fall. The slips of beach visible through the forest were bleach white, and although most of the trees were stripped of their leaves, there were evergreens among them, palms and shrubs. We drove with the windows down despite the cold, my face numb and my ears ringing with the speed.

Eventually the open coastline was swallowed by a forest, still as colorful as a jewel box despite the approaching cold.

The traffic signs said things to the effect of SLOW DOWN, WINDING ROAD AHEAD, but Grace ignored them. In fact, she cranked the music so loud that she couldn't hear me even if I'd been screaming, and then she sped up. My knuckles blanched of color at every hairpin twist in the road as I scrabbled desperately to keep myself from being thrown around the front seat. Grace braked, accelerated, smoked the tires, drifted around each bend. And then, instead of slowing down and readying herself for the next one, she'd speed up in between turns.

I held on and prayed to deities I didn't believe in that I wouldn't die today. Not like this. Not like him. Over and over again, visions of crashes replayed in my head. The impossibly hard crunch of a car slamming into a tree, crumpling around it like a paper fan. A body—mine—wrenched from the vehicle, tossed through the windshield, a rag doll of blood and bone. Skin sloughing off against asphalt. Limbs snapping, the splintered ends of bones piercing through skin.

Grace was a decent driver, if not maniacal. I trusted that she had control of the car, but at these speeds, her reaction time would be negligible. All it would take was an animal on the road, an overcorrection, a pothole. And then, still, there was the lingering voice at the back of my head, the one that reminded me over and over again to worry about her safety.

I'd never felt so close to death before. Never been so afraid of my own mortality as I was in a car with her at the wheel.

Did things like this matter to her at all? Grace saw the world as little more than a temporarily ordered pattern of atoms. Dying only meant that the atoms briefly allotted to your human form were to be redispersed elsewhere.

Finally, finally, she brought the car to a stop at a lookout and turned the music off. She grinned at me and stepped out into the brisk coastal breeze. It was an odd kind of day. The sun beat down warmly, but the wind carried in a chill from the ocean.

"What the hell was that about?" I said as I slammed my door closed. My legs and hands were physically shaking, and not from the cold. I tried not to let her see how unnerved I was, because a small part of me thought that maybe, just maybe, she was trying to screw with my head on purpose. I sat down on the barrier fence that separated the lookout from the wilderness beyond it and rested my elbows on my knees, trying to steady my breath. Grace sat down next to me—sometimes the way she positioned herself around me felt as platonic as a sister—her scarf half covering her face.

"I used to drive along this road all the time, even before I got my license," she said, her words muffled. "I know it like the back of my hand. Actually, I know it better than the back of my hand. I could draw it from memory. I don't really know the back of my hand at all. I wonder why people say that?"

"You can't fucking drive like that after nearly dying in a car accident."

"I wasn't the one who veered off the road, if you want to know. That was Dom. I loved this drive before he died. I should be able to love it again."

The bitterness in her voice. Grace had never spoken of Dom in any negative light before, but here she was, blaming him for the crash that killed him. I suppose it made sense for her to be mad.

"I just . . . You can't be with him, okay? You can't follow him where he went, as much as you might want to. So stop trying."

"Shit, Henry. I didn't think—"

"That's exactly what I mean. You don't *think*. You're taking hairpin turns so fast, your tires are burning. That whole thing was not okay."

"I just wanted to feel like myself again." When I didn't say anything, Grace stood. "C'mon. There's a restaurant about ten minutes from here, tucked away in the trees. Let me buy you lunch to apologize."

And with those words, the near-death horror of the last half hour melted away, replaced by the giddy feeling I got when Grace did the occasional nice thing that made me think she was falling for me too. Which was really messed up.

The restaurant was set on a cliff overlooking the seaside. She bought me lunch, like she said she would, and we ate outside together on the grass, basking in the sunshine.

Lola messaged me as we were eating.

LOLA LEUNG:

Where in the name of sweet baby Jesus are you?

Ugh, you're so needy. National park. It's too nice for classrooms.

Get your ass to school right now or I swear I will rat you out to Hink for your wantonness.

Who uses "wantonness" in general conversation?

You better be brainstorming a fucking awesome theme for this stupid newspaper. I'm not even joking anymore, Henry.

Don't make me save you from yourself. I hate being the reluctant hero. It's why I don't wear a mask and fight crime on the streets of Gotham every night.

ORGANIZE YOUR SHIT.

Dude, I'm all over it.

You better be, or I'm going to put one of the Kardashians on the cover. Or maybe ALL of the Kardashians.

I need the newspaper for my college applications as well. Don't forget that, dickbag.

Sorry, La. We'll pull ourselves together soon.

Good, because I've got Widelene Leung on my side, and she will get up in your grill if you wrong me. She knows where you live.

Noted.

When the food was done, Grace and I lay together under the vast blue sky, neither of us talking until she said, "I'll be back soon." I watched her as she stood and limped to the garden at the edge of the cliff and picked the last of the fall flowers. Then she walked back up the softly sloping hill of grass toward the restaurant, the small bunch of yellow blooms grasped in one hand, her cane in the other.

She was only gone for ten minutes. I thought nothing of it. Just another quirk of Grace Town.

On Thursday afternoon we stayed back late at the newspaper, then caught a bus to the little boutique movie theater near my house. We ate hot dogs for dinner before the movie. Grace spilled ketchup down the front of her oversized Ramones T-shirt but made no attempt to sponge it off.

"I'll pretend I have a stab wound," she said as she licked ketchup off her fingers.

I stared at her lips and thought about her naked.

Inside the theater, we did what we always did in the dark. We pretended like we were together. She kissed me, once, before the movie started, and then she ran her fingers in soft circles around my palm. Like a palmist, uncertain of the future, trying to divine her destiny from the wrinkles that cut through my skin.

I don't know what she read there. Maybe nothing at all.

We walked home together when the movie was over, each of us with our hands by our sides. Eventually, Grace grabbed mine with a sigh. It didn't feel like a victory. It felt like I'd failed a test.

We walked back to my place, her hand in mine, and for the first time, I felt like we were really a couple. That this was really, actually going somewhere.

My God, I thought as we walked, *I'm really falling for her.*

Don't be stupid, said another voice in my head. *You can't fall for someone after knowing them for two months.*

Jack and Rose were in love after, like, four days, I argued.

You really wanna use Titanic *as proof this is gonna end well?* the voice said.

Damn it.

"Well, thanks for inviting me, kid," she said when we reached my house.

"Anytime, Town."

Then she kissed me halfheartedly on the garden path that led to my front door, her body warm against mine despite the cold.

I'm going to marry her, I thought as I watched her walk home, and I smiled to myself, because for the first time since The Kiss, I felt like I knew something in this world for certain.

CHAPTER 20

A WEEK PASSED. It was a good week, full of Good Grace Days. We were productive. Our junior writers submitted content for the newspaper that wasn't about cats. Lola had designed almost half the pages. Our Magic: The Gathering feature article had been edited down to five thousand words. I attempted some math homework. I didn't necessarily understand any of it, but there was an attempt nonetheless.

Grace and I also had sex again. She didn't cry this time, so that was nice.

Things were starting to look up.

On Thursday night she came to my house for dinner. We were sitting on my bed in the basement, laughing and teasing each other while Mom and Dad cooked dinner. I wondered if tonight would be the night we'd finally make it official. *Are you my girlfriend now?* I practiced it over and over again in my head, practiced the point I'd slip it into the conversation. And then, of course, once she'd said yes, there would be the public aspect of it.

I imagined what people would say when we changed our Facebook relationship statuses. I mean, not that I *needed* that. But it was nice to fantasize about. The people who'd known from the start—Lola, Murray—would comment things like *Ugh, God, FINALLY* and *You're punching above your weight, mate*. The people who'd had no idea would be shocked. I thought about the *Um . . . WHAT?*s and the comments from Grace's friends who didn't know me. *So happy for you, Grace. So, so glad you've found someone.*

We were—for reasons I can't remember now—curled around each other, both silently reading Matthew Broderick's Wikipedia page together on my iPhone. I was twirling a thread of her hair through my fingers as we read, baffled that I ever could've thought of her as anything other than obscenely beautiful. That first day I'd seen her in drama class, it was like she'd been jet-lagged—the way people looked after flying from one side of the world to the other, like they weren't just exhausted and dirty, but like every cell in their body was literally out of alignment with their surroundings. Now I liked that Grace's atoms buzzed at a different frequency.

Thinking about her atoms got me thinking about her skin, which got me thinking about her skin without any clothes on, which gave me a sudden gust of courage. I said, quite slowly: "So, regarding the whole *situation* . . ."

The change in Grace was sudden but palpable. She drew

back from where she had been nestled into my shoulder. Stopped reading about Matthew Broderick. Stopped smiling. And I thought, *Oh, shit. Oh, shit. Not again. Please don't let me have been wrong* again.

"Yeah," she said. But she knew why she was here, didn't she? She knew what I wanted. She'd known since the beginning how I felt. How could she turn so cold so quickly?

"I guess I want to know where we're at with that."

"I don't really know what to tell you."

"Last time we talked about this, you said you were gonna stop going to the cemetery."

"Did I?"

"Yeah. At the Halloween party. You were kinda drunk, I guess."

"I'm sorry. I always think stupid stuff when I've been drinking. I shouldn't have said that to you."

"So you . . . you're not going to stop?"

"Henry."

"I hate talking about this as much as you do."

"I can still feel him. He's in my bones. When I fall asleep, I can feel the warmth of his fingers on my skin."

"I'm not asking you to let him go."

"Then what do you want from me? I'm giving you all I've got."

"I want, when someone asks us if we're dating, to be able to say yes. I don't want to have to hide it from my friends. I want people to know that we're together. I want to be able to hold your hand and kiss you in public without worrying if I'm allowed to. I want this to be real." Grace didn't say anything, just stared at the ceiling, until I eventually said, "What do you want to do?"

"Maybe . . ." There was a long pause as she breathed in and out several times, her eyes darting from side to side as she tried to find the words to say. "Maybe we should slow down. I mean, we fell into this so quickly. If we wind things back a bit, maybe it won't feel so wrong."

"I feel *wrong* to you?"

"That's not what I meant. I meant . . . I'm not ready, to be better. Not yet."

"I don't care. I want *you*, exactly as you are."

"No, you don't. You want *her*. You're dating me on the hope that I'll one day become that girl. You've fallen for an idea, not an actual person, and it kills me when I see you looking at me but seeing someone else."

"That's bullshit."

"Is it, though?"

"God, I hate this. I hate this whole thing so much. I want *you*, Grace Town. I've wanted *you* since the beginning."

I pulled her on top of me so she was sitting on my hips and she leaned down and kissed me the way she did, the way that made me sure she was in love with me even though I knew that she wasn't and probably never would be. I opened my eyes and watched her, like I did sometimes, to make sure the kiss was real. Grace drew away from me with her eyes still closed, the smallest of smiles playing on her lips. And it took until then for me to realize that she wasn't kissing me, not ever, not really, at least not in her head.

Maybe we were both in love with ideas.

Grace's eyes flickered open slowly to find me staring at her. She looked momentarily confused, like she'd genuinely forgotten for a split second that she wasn't kissing Dom. Then a heaviness settled over her features, and she lifted herself off me and got out of bed.

"I should jet," she said, slinging her bag over her shoulder without looking at me.

"I thought we were gonna do schoolwork."

"It's not like I'm going to pass any of my classes anyway."

"We haven't had dinner yet."

"I'm not really hungry. I'll see you later."

I didn't say good-bye.

After half an hour of letting the acid ball inside my chest slowly gnaw at the flesh of my trachea, I got up and dragged myself to the shower. I stood under the hot stream and tried to cup water in my fingers but it kept running through the gaps and it was all very metaphorical and it hurt like hell because I knew, *I knew* I was losing her. And it wasn't something I could fix.

Human beings could not be mended with gold seams.

I pressed my forehead against the cool white tiles of the shower wall. My head pounded like I was going to cry, but my eyes were dry. *Right girl, wrong time,* I thought, even though I knew that was a delusion, because Grace would never be the right girl. But damn, I still wanted her so badly. I still needed her so deeply. My whole body ached at the thought of losing her and I suddenly felt like a real dick for judging the breakups of my friends so harshly. Is this what Murray felt like all the time because of Sugar Gandhi? Did he feel her sear across his very skin, hotter than boiling water?

There had to be, *had to be* a way to make her love me.

My eyes jolted open, my brain overcome by the kind of sudden epiphanic moment that can only be provoked by a long, hot shower. I turned the water off quickly and wrapped a towel around my pink-seared ass and stumbled, still dripping wet, downstairs into the hovel that was my basement bedroom, frantic that it might not be there. But it was, tucked neatly into the large bottom drawer of my desk, as though the space had been made for it.

A typewriter in duck-egg blue, a manual Olivetti Lettera 32. The same model that Cormac McCarthy used. I'd bought it off eBay three years earlier for thirty-five dollars after reading *The Road* and deciding that novels written on typewriters were vastly superior to novels written on computers (but still probably not as good as novels written by hand). I had not, as of yet, written anything more than *All work and no play makes Henry a dull boy* over and over again on both sides of a page to make sure the ribbon was working. After that it'd sat on my desk for six months next to the dying iMac, until the sight of the two of them together made me feel so guilty for writing on neither that I shoved the typewriter in the bottom drawer and hadn't thought of it since.

In the top drawer of my desk was a ream of thick, canary-colored cotton typewriter paper, swiped from the set of *The Great Gatsby* by Murray the last time he'd visited Sydney. When held up to the light, the faintest hint of a translucent damask pattern was visible in the top corner. It was among the more beautiful things I owned.

Dear Grakov, I wrote, my fingers punching the keys in a storm of mechanical sounds.

I would write Grace Town a letter. I would say all of the things I struggled to say out loud. I knew she preferred spoken drafts, but she'd never read my work, and maybe after she had, she'd understand why I preferred writing to talking.

I sent her a Snapchat of those first two words, *Dear Grakov,* and captioned it "Get ready to have your mind blown." And then I wrote.

```
Dear Grakov,
    For the last few months I've lived my
life according to a simple truth: that, in
the end, nothing we do here really matters.
Some people fear oblivion. Some people
are scared by the idea that their lives
are meaningless. You taught me to find it
beautiful. You taught me to let it give me
courage.
```

The courage, for instance, to show a girl a PowerPoint presentation about dating me, knowing that if she said no, any proof of my embarrassment would one day be eaten up by the universe. It was you who taught me that oblivion is our reward for being human, that the very fabric of reality itself is kind enough to ensure that all our sins and silliness will be stripped away.

It's that same courage that I'm using to write you this letter, laying bare for you exactly how I feel. You're special, Grace Town. You're beautiful. You shine. I never get tired of looking at you, or being around you. Before you, I'd never been able to imagine wanting someone in my life the way that I want you. From the first day you made me drive myself home, there was chemistry unlike I'd ever felt for anyone before.

That's not the kind of thing you walk away from, even if the situation is difficult. Even if it's so messed up, you begin to believe you might be in The Truman Show because, goddamn, someone must be plotting this crap. I know you know this, because if you didn't, one or both of us would've left by now, or we wouldn't have started. Because some things are worth fighting for.

There's still the problem of him, of course. I know you still love him, and I can understand that.

I'd never ask you to choose between us. I'd never give you an ultimatum, or a time frame, or hold you accountable if you couldn't let him go. Firstly, because to do so would be unreasonable and only make you resent me. Secondly, because I don't believe I should have to. I know who I am. I know my worth. I hope that you can see it as well.

So, Grace Town, that's how I feel. I wish I could be this eloquent when we talk, but I'm a writer at heart. I'm wasted on the spoken word, but there's a small piece of my soul in this letter. To surmise: I am here, I am game, I am staying, and I want you.

It's the end of the Earth and the death of the universe that give me the insane courage to say that I am yours, if you want me.

All that's left now is for you to decide

what you want. No mean feat, I'm aware, but
something that must be done regardless.

Catch you on the
flip side, kid.

Henrik

I reread the letter a dozen times, then folded it, put it in an envelope, and handwrote her name across the front. Then I put it and the typewriter back into the dark drawer of my desk and sat and waited for her to Snapchat me back. She didn't, even though I knew she'd opened it, so I messaged her.

HENRY PAGE:

> Just hit Safari on my phone and it opened to the Wikipedia page of Matthew Broderick. Good thing I'm not in public.

GRACE TOWN:

> Matthew Broderick is never something to be ashamed of. What's this letter you're writing? Doesn't look like an English essay to me.

> I'll have you know I'm seriously contemplating the implications of capitalism on postmodern feminist literature at the moment, so there.

The letter is about ALL OF THE STUFF AND THINGS. Also, it's written on paper from The Great Gatsby film set, 'cause I'm fancy like that.

The stuff and things, huh . . . Sounds interesting. As for you being fancy . . .

No comment.

THE GREAT GATSBY, TOWN. You're getting a letter written on paper that has been in the presence of Leo DiCaprio. It probably has some of his skin cells on it. HIS SKIN CELLS.

How'd you even get your hands on that? I thought you were exaggerating? Plus that doesn't make you fancy, it makes the paper fancy.

Nope, it really is from the Gatsby set. Muz knew a guy who knew a guy who let him into the set warehouse and said he could have whatever we wanted 'cause they'd finished filming. I wanted him to take a car, but alas, apparently that was dreaming a little too large. So you see, I'm at least 85% fancy by association.

Well la-di-da, Page. Us plebs bow down to you and your shiny script paper. We are not worthy.

> Don't worry, you're at least 15% classy by association with me. You might even gain a temporary percentage point or two after you touch the Gatsby paper.

> Cool. Well. I'll read it tomorrow after school, I guess.

"Mr. Page," said Hink at the end of the next day's English lesson. I was sitting at my usual desk in the front row, between La and a girl named Mackenzie who'd once asked me if *very* was spelled with one or two *r*'s. "A word, if you will."

"Sure."

I stayed at my desk as the rest of the class filed out to lunch, trying to guess if Hink was going to chew me out for a) not doing the homework assignment, b) staring at the dandruff dusting his shoulders and imagining them as Sea-Monkeys trapped in a tar pit for the entirety of the lesson, or c) both.

Once the classroom was empty, Hink walked around to the front of his desk and sat on it with his legs crossed, his hands resting on his knee. I wondered if, in the bizarro world of Alistair Hink, this was supposed to be a sign of intimidation. "Do you want to explain to me where your essay is?"

"Essay?"

"The one that was due last week. The one that you failed to hand in."

"Oh." *Shit.* That *essay.* The one I'd eschewed in favor of nearly getting killed in a national park and writing a stupid grandiose love letter.

"What's going on with you, Henry? You're missing newspaper meetings, you haven't done any of the required reading or homework assignments for class this week, and now this. I had a chat with Mrs. Beady and Señor Sanchez and some of your other teachers as well, and everyone is concerned. Mr. Hotchkiss says you're frequently distracted in math."

God, Hotchkiss, what a dick. "That's nothing out of the ordinary, to be honest."

"I know we expect a lot from you. Maybe more than we expect of most other students. So if things are getting to be too much—if everything is piling up and you can't handle it—you need to tell me. We can find ways to help you."

"It's fine, really. I'm fine."

"Miss Leung came to see me yesterday. She subtly implied that the newspaper might be suffering due to a misguided relationship between you and Miss Town."

Damn it. She actually did it. "I doubt Lola 'subtly implied' anything."

"Well, yes, her exact words were 'they're destroying the very fabric of this publication with their wantonness,' but I thought it best left unsaid. She actually said 'wantonness' so much that I had to Google it after she'd left to check it was a real word. 'Their wantonness, Mr. Hink, their wantonness. They're ruining everything with their wantonness!'"

"Please stop saying *wantonness*."

"You and Grace have missed or rescheduled every meeting I've planned to discuss the newspaper. Without a theme or enough content, Lola can't finish the design on time. I'm starting to get worried."

"I'll get it under control. I promise."

"Good. Because if the two of you can't get it sorted out by the end of the month, I'm going to have to replace you as editor."

"But . . . I worked my ass off for two years."

"You did. But that doesn't mean you get to *stop* working your ass off now. Now go adjust your attitude. And for God's sake, butter Hotchkiss up a little bit, won't you?"

"Judas," I hissed when I walked into the newspaper office after school and found Lola lazing on the sex couch, reading a dictionary.

"Which would imply that you're Jesus?" she said. "Ego much?"

"I can't believe you went to Hink. Also, did you know we had an essay due last week? I totally spaced on that one."

"I *told* you I was going to rat you out if you didn't get your act together." Lola stood and walked over to me and grabbed my shoulders. "I know you're the captain of a sinking ship and you're determined to go down with it. That's admirable as fuck, but when this baby goes belly-up, I'm going to be on a goddamn lifeboat."

"Who's Grace in this analogy?"

"Those dudes on the *Titanic* who played violin until the very end."

"Strangely accurate."

La picked up the dictionary and smacked it into my chest. "*Pick* a theme. Just close your eyes and open it up to any page and point at something. It's my birthday *tomorrow* and all I want from you is. One. Goddamn. Word."

Grace came in then and looked from Lola to me to the dictionary aggressively forced into my chest. "A strange tableau," she said as she put her bag down and leaned on her cane and waited.

"Lola's forcing me to pick a theme for the paper." I took the dictionary from her and scrunched my eyes closed and did as she instructed. "*Fail*," I read. "Verb. Definition one: 'To be unsuccessful.' Definition two: 'To be less than expected.' Sounds about right."

"I don't know if you did that on purpose or not, but that's actually a good theme, so damn well use it. You," said Lola, letting go of me and digging her talons into Grace's shoulders instead. "Life is a crapfest and you're having a really, really tough time, but you *can't* go down with the ship. Get in a lifeboat. Shape up or ship out." Lola did the "I'm watching you" gesture to Grace and me in turn, then grabbed her backpack and stalked out of the office, grumbling something under her breath that sounded very much like "wantonness."

"Well, that was incredibly surreal," Grace said. "What was all that about lifeboats?"

"Hink's pissed because we've done jack on the newspaper."

"Have we?"

"Christ, Grace, I need help with this. You're supposed to be assistant editor, so why don't you assist me with editing?"

"What is there to edit? We've done everything we can do without a theme. Why don't you just make it 'failure'?"

"Because I can't handle that amount of irony."

Then she looked pissed and I wanted to kiss her to make her (and maybe myself) feel better, but I was afraid that if I tried, she'd pull away from me, and I didn't want to be saddled with that feeling all afternoon, so I didn't.

"I'm gonna go," she said. "I have stuff to do this afternoon."

"Wait a sec," I said, and I turned and jogged over to my backpack to retrieve the letter from where it had been lodged in my copy of *84, Charing Cross Road* all day. I hadn't forgotten it. Not for a single moment. It'd hung over me like a small storm cloud. I'd waited for the right moment all day, hoping an insane rush of courage would wash over me.

"Oh yeah. This. *The Letter*," she said, taking the envelope from me and folding it and putting it into her bag. And I knew. I knew that this moment would either be our last as we'd been or our first as something more. A beginning or an ending. It couldn't be anything in between. I said I'd never make her choose between us and now I was because I couldn't stand it anymore. She loved him; she still loves him. I knew that.

But wasn't I worth something too?

"Can you read it now?" I said.

"You want me to read it in *front* of you?"

"Uh . . . yeah?"

"Can't you say it? Everything that's in the letter is inside of you right now. I don't want the filtered version. I don't want the pretty words, the final draft. I want you to say something raw. Something real."

"I can read it out to you, if you'd like."

"That is not what I said."

"Come on, at least let me skim it, remember what I wrote."

"You don't remember how you feel?"

"Of course I do, I just don't know how to put it into words."

"Try."

"You're . . . You're special."

Grace sighed. "I'm a beautiful and unique snowflake? I complete you?"

"No! It says . . . Look, everything's in there, okay? It's all in there, everything I want you to know. You just have to read it."

Grace didn't read it. She simply said, "I'll see you tomorrow night for Lola's thing," and pulled the door open and walked out. It all felt so strangely, ominously final. I tried to remember the last kiss we'd shared, many hours ago now, but I couldn't recall the specifics of it, which upset me, because I knew it might very well be our last.

I stepped out into the hall and watched her limp across the

linoleum-clad floor toward the door, breaking every few steps to rest her leg.

After she'd left my house last night, she must've gone to the East River track to push her injury until it hurt her again. Maybe it was something like cutting. Maybe slowing down the healing process was the only thing that made her feel in control. Maybe the injury was the last thing that tied her to the accident, and therefore to Dom, and she wasn't ready to let it go yet.

Or maybe she just hated herself so much, she thought she deserved to be in pain.

Finally, Grace made it to the exit and the door swung closed behind her and she disappeared into the school grounds. She didn't look back once.

As if, one way or another, she'd already made up her mind.

Lola's birthday was the next day. Georgia drove in from her hometown and arrived at my place as the sun was rising. Lola's parents, Han and Widelene, let us into their house, and the four of us quietly went about blowing up and filling the hallway, living room, and kitchen with about two hundred–odd balloons. We were all giddy by the end of it, our heads spinning from lack of oxygen, but it was worth it to hear La say, "What the hell?" in her raspy, half-asleep voice, then start giggling like a maniac.

"Happy birthday!" we shouted in unison as she wandered

into the kitchen in her very un-Lola pink nightdress, her hand held over her mouth, an impressively large cowlick giving her a Mohawk.

After she'd showered and changed, we picked up Muz and all went to breakfast together in the city. Georgia gave Lola a cactus. ("That's romantic as *fuck*," was her reaction upon unwrapping it. "Taking our relationship to the next level.") Muz gave her a set of oil paints in a bamboo box, and I got her a skeleton cat candle, one of those ones that burn down to bones when all the wax is gone.

Lola and I both highly believed in the value of metaphorical gifts, so while everyone else saw a demonic-looking cat skeleton dripping wax on the packaging, Lola saw the message: Our friendship is like this feline-shaped candle—burn away all the shit, and you and me are still solid underneath. Always.

"Henry, you magnificent creature," she said, pressing her forehead to my temple. "What grand deed did I do in a past life to deserve the fortune of living next to you in this one?"

"You two are so cute, sometimes I wish you weren't a raging lesbian so you could get married and generally live an adorable life together," Georgia said. "I mean, I'm glad you *are* a raging lesbian, but I digress."

I started thinking about what kind of gift to give Grace for her birthday at the end of the month. None of the usual presents boyfriends bought for their girlfriends would do, because a) Grace Town was not my girlfriend and b) I was fairly certain she would've dry retched at the sight of flowers, chocolate, or jewelry. It didn't have to be something grand; it only needed to mean something.

But what do you give a girl whose mind is like the universe, when the brain inside your own head is stuck firmly on planet Earth?

Draft Six
Because you're worth nothing less than stardust, but all I can give you is dirt.

CHAPTER 21

DAD DROPPED ME OFF at Grace's place on Saturday evening as the sky split and rain began to fall. I ran for shelter under the tall elm tree that stood in front of her house. As I got there, my hair already dripping, my phone buzzed in my hand.

GRACE TOWN:

I'm running 10 minutes late. Stay on the lawn.
Don't go inside.

I looked up at the sad, gloomy house with its drawn curtains and overgrown garden and thought back to how Murray had wondered if Grace was some kind of supernatural creature. A vampire. A fallen angel. There were definitely secrets inside these walls that she didn't want me to know, but what kind of secrets were they?

The door cracked open and a small, balding man appeared

from the shadows. The same man who always came by in the afternoons to pick up Grace's car.

"Henry Page?" he said, squinting at me in the low light. "Is that you?"

"Uh, yes," I said quietly. And then, louder, "Yes, I'm Henry Page."

"Oh, wonderful. Yes, wonderful. Come inside, come inside. My name is Martin."

An irrational pang of fear shot through me. *Stay on the lawn. Don't go inside.* What if Grace's message hadn't been a request so much as a warning? What if Martin was a werewolf or something? And then, under the irrational fear was the real fear. Of betraying Grace. Whatever was in this house, she didn't want me to see it yet. Or maybe ever.

"Uh . . . I don't mind staying out here. Grace will be home in a few minutes."

"Don't be silly, the rain is getting heavier. Come in and get warm." Martin beckoned me with one hand, his other pressed against the screen door to keep it open. So I went. Mostly because it was cold and dark and raining, but a little bit because I wanted to know what she was keeping from me. I thought again of Sully Sullenberger, how he would never do what I was doing, how I was falling further and further from his white-mustachioed grace.

"Shut up, Sullenberger," I muttered to myself.

"Henry," said Martin, shaking my hand. "We've heard a lot about you."

"Good things, I hope." Which was the cliché thing you were supposed to say when people said that to you. But it gave me a little thrill. For someone so close to Grace to know that I existed.

"Mostly, mostly," he said with a chuckle. "Please, make yourself at home. You can wait in Dom's room, if you like," he said, and then he faltered. "Well, Grace's room now, I suppose."

"I'm sorry? Dom. Lived. Here?" I said it in this weird staccato way, a pause between each word as my brain tried to process the meaning attached to the sentence.

Martin frowned. "Lived here? Grace has told you that we're not her parents, hasn't she?"

"Um . . . no. I kind of assumed you were her dad."

"No, no. My name is Martin *Sawyer*. Dominic was our son. We had Grace move in with us about a month before the crash. I'm sure she's told you all about her troubles with her mother? After Dom was gone, Mary and I insisted she stay with us. They were together for so long, so many years. Grace is practically our daughter."

"Grace . . . lives . . . in Dom's room?"

"I thought she would've told you this."

"Uh." I shook my head, licked my lips, and looked around for the first time. The walls were this off-cream color, almost pale orange, and all the furniture was made of dark wood. The stairs were carpeted, worn bare in patches with age, and on the wall were dozens of photographs. Smiling graduation portraits and faded wedding snaps and he was in all of them, Dominic, over and over again.

The closest photo of him was with Grace seated atop his broad shoulders, his hands resting on her uninjured calves. It was the first time I'd seen a picture of him. The sight of him stung me like venom. Dom was broad and built and classically handsome. The exact opposite of me. In the picture with Grace, he was wearing a football jersey and grinning widely. Grace had her head tipped back in laughter, shrieking with delight inside his football helmet, her fingers in his hair.

I felt bile bubble up from somewhere in the black, destroyed remains of my gut. Not jealousy. Not anxiety. Just sadness.

"Dom was our youngest," said Martin, leading me away from the torture wall. "Bit of a gap between him and Renee. The older two had already moved out by the time of the crash. It's been nice having Grace here. I don't know if I could handle the silence."

"I'm so sorry. I had no idea this was his house."

"There's nothing to be sorry for, kid. You've been a good friend to her. You and your girlfriend, Lola. We appreciate everything you've done for her."

"My. Girlfriend. Lola?" I said, again in staccato, and Martin was looking at me then like I was a little bit slow. Grace had been lying to him. Had been lying about what we were. But then again, why wouldn't she? How exactly would you tell your dead boyfriend's dad that you were sleeping with someone else? "Yeah. My girlfriend, Lola. We love Grace."

Martin nodded to a door at the end of the hall. "You can wait in there. Grace will be here soon. I'll send her to find you."

"Thanks." I waited for Martin to leave and then opened the door slowly, with one hand, hesitant to step over the threshold into his tomb. The air was heavy and smelled distinctly like Grace.

No.

Like Dom.

I wanted to vomit. Or take a scalding-hot shower. Or vomit while taking a scalding-hot shower. But my curiosity was still stronger, so instead I turned on the light and stepped inside.

It was a fairly typical teenage boy's room, filled with the same sort of clutter and haphazard order as my own. The checked duvet was crumpled and unmade at the foot of the bed. There was a bookcase filled with the likes of Harry Potter and The Lord of the Rings. An acoustic guitar resting on a chair. A record player with stacks of old vinyl. A globe. A skateboard. A backpack. A desk and a laptop and sports magazines and trophies from his childhood. A chalkboard and a canvas with a portrait of Mozart on it and trinkets from far-away lands. On the dresser was Dom's jewelry—an assortment of long leather necklaces with anchors and crosses and skulls—and his deodorant.

We wore the same scent.

A snapshot of a lifetime, boiled down to the size of a bedroom. I stood there for a few minutes, taking in the stillness of the place. Here he was, laid out before me, everything he'd been, everything he was.

I wondered if Grace felt close to death in this room, like I did, or if she felt close to life. And I marveled at the unfairness of it all. How a person could be so tethered to this world one moment, and gone from it the next.

I wandered into the walk-in wardrobe and pulled the cord for the light. Here was more of his tomb. All of his clothes. A pressed suit, probably in preparation for prom. A football jersey from the East River team. Half a dozen pairs of shoes. Unlabeled boxes on the overhead shelves.

The gray band shirt Grace had worn to the movies was folded on the shelf. There was a dark smudge where she'd spilled the ketchup, almost as if she'd sponged it off instead of . . .

Then it dawned on me.

"Oh God . . . ," I whispered as I picked the shirt up. The stain had been sponged away, but the shirt hadn't been washed. The fabric still smelled of Grace. Of Dom. Of me.

Grace didn't wash Dom's clothes. She didn't wash his sheets. There was always that musty, boyish smell that hung on her wherever she went. I'd assumed it was a natural quirk, or that she had lackluster hygiene practices, but standing in her dead boyfriend's closet was a great way to provoke an epiphany.

Grace lived in him. Every hour of every day, he was there with her. The scent of him on her skin. Grace was the ghost, not Dom. Two people had died that day, but one of them still had a body.

I looked around the room again, trying to find any sign of something that belonged to her. There was nothing of Grace here except for an envelope on the dresser that bore her name. The letter I'd written her, still unopened. There was no girls' clothing, no girls' shoes, no makeup, none of the things you'd find in your sister's or mother's or friends' bedrooms.

She wore his clothes and his deodorant and she slept in his tangled sheets every night. Whoever she had been—the bright, beautiful girl in her Facebook profile picture—that person was gone now, replaced by this Dom impostor.

You can tell a lot about a person from their bedroom, she'd said to me once. What was there for me to discern from this room apart from the fact that Grace Town did not exist at all?

"So now you know," said Grace quietly.

I spun around to find her staring at me from the door frame, Dom's shirt still crumpled up in my shaking fingers. Looking at her then, it was easy to understand that she wasn't of the corporeal realm. Her skin was as translucent as perfumed paper, and her blond hair fell in ashen curtains to settle blunt and dead about her shoulders. There were whispers of bruises beneath the skin of her eyes, like she cried so much it made her bleed. Grace was a lost soul, a ghost adrift, the human embodiment of secondhand smoke.

I wanted to touch her. I couldn't remember if she'd ever felt warm beneath my fingertips, or if she'd always been spun from something more ethereal than skin. "Grace, I'm so sorry. I shouldn't have—"

"I moved in a month before the accident," she said, taking the dirty shirt from me and folding it and placing it back on its shelf in the wardrobe. She smoothed the fabric out with her hands, then placed her forehead against the shelf, her eyes closed. "The Sawyers had been trying to get me here for years. I finally worked up the guts to run away from my mom. It was the best worst day of my life."

"That's awful. Grace . . . I don't . . . I don't know what to say. I don't know how to help you."

Grace looked up at me. "I'm not broken, Henry. I'm not a piece of pottery out of your cabinet. I don't need to be fixed."

"I know that. I didn't mean that. But—you can tell a lot about a person from their bedroom, remember?" It went so much deeper than she'd ever been willing to tell me. Grace hadn't only lost him in the physical sense—she'd lost the promise he held as well. It wouldn't just be his corpse that would haunt us, but the ghost of the life they could've had together. He knew everything about her, all the bad, all the good, and I was only allowed the occasional glimpse. All the potential energy Dom had held had been dispersed back into the universe when he died, and she was scrabbling to hold on to it. "So what does your bedroom look like?"

"*That's* what you want to know? I don't have one, okay? My 'bedroom' before I moved in here was a couch in my mother's husband's basement."

"Sometimes I feel like you don't exist."

"Get out."

"You keep everything from me. You don't tell me anything."

"Get out, get out, get out!"

Then Martin Sawyer was at the door. He looked from Grace to me and back again and said, "Henry," and I said, "I'm going." I stalked out of the house, down the hallway filled with pictures of him that greeted her, smiling, every morning and every night. I was hurt and angry and stupidly, stupidly jealous, which was dumb, because worms were probably eating his eyeballs right now, or maybe they were done with his eyeballs and had moved onto his brain, or his heart, or his testicles, and that wasn't exactly my idea of a good time. He couldn't love her anymore and he still got to keep her and it all just seemed so desperately unfair to everyone involved.

I was sitting in the gutter outside her house when my phone rang. Murray. I smudged a tear from my eye and answered. "Yeah, I know, I'm on my—"

"Hello, Henry. It's Maddy."

"Who?"

"Madison Carlson. From school."

"Oh . . . Why are you calling me from Murray's phone?"

"I think I broke Murray."

"I can't deal with this right now. I have to get to Lola's party."

"No, seriously, he's lying facedown in the grass and he hasn't moved for, like, twenty minutes and Lola's gone."

"What did you do to him?"

"Well, he asked me if I'd heard anything more from Seeta, so I told him about her new boyfriend, and then he kind of sank to his knees and laid down and refused to get up. I think he might be dead. I can't deal with a dead body, Henry."

"Christ. Send me a drop pin of your location. I'll come and get him."

"We're at the football field. Everyone's gone. You need to get here ASAP."

I didn't get there ASAP. I hung up and wandered slowly from Grace's house to the school, hoping Murray would grow up before I got there so I could go home and die in peace. While I walked, I messaged La and told her I might not make it to her party because Murray had been injured at the pregame.

When I got there, I almost didn't spot them because it was dark and Madison was lying down as well, using Murray's lower back as a pillow.

"I thought I might as well get comfortable while I waited for you," she said.

"Sugar Gandhi really has a new boyfriend?" I said.

"If you're referring to Seeta, a) yes and b) that is incredibly racist."

"How bad is he?"

"Watch this." Madison stood and proceeded to kick Murray in the legs, to which he didn't react.

"Jesus, woman, stop. Don't kick a man when he's down." I poked him in the neck to make sure he was still warm, which he was. "Muz, buddy?" When he didn't respond, I instructed Madison to grab his legs as I took him by the shoulders and turned him over. Murray's eyes were open, staring unblinkingly at the night sky. I squeezed his cheeks together until he had fish lips.

"How you doing, man?" I said.

"Oh, hey, Henry. I didn't see you there," he said without looking at me, his cheeks still squished together.

"You wanna maybe sit up?"

"Oh no, I'm gonna lie here until I decompose and carrion birds pick apart my innards."

"I don't think the groundskeepers are gonna let that fly."

"Drag me under the grandstand, then. Bury me next to Ricky Martin Knupps."

"Is he high?" Madison asked. "Did you take something, Murray?"

"No, we buried a fish under the bleachers," I explained. "It's a long story."

"Racist fish murderers. Nice."

Then someone shouted my name from across the field and a small, dark body sprinted toward us through the night. Lola skidded on the grass to Muz's side and took his head in her hands and turned it this way and that as she pushed his hair back and inspected him for injuries. "What happened? Do you have a concussion? Should I call an ambulance?" she said frantically.

"Not unless the docs can fix broken hearts," Murray said.

Lola looked up at Madison and me, frowning.

"Seeta Ganguly," Madison said in explanation, "has a boyfriend."

"He's not even Indian!" Murray wailed. "His name's Taylor Messenger! Her parents don't care who she dates!"

"Your message," La said, narrowing her eyes at me, "said he was hurt."

"I said he *might* be hurt. Besides," I said, gesturing to Murray's slumped form, "heartbroken is a kind of hurt."

"The fucking pair of you." Lola smacked the back of Murray's head as she stood. "I'm sick to goddamn death of all this hormonal teenage *bullshit*. You." Lola jabbed her finger in my direction. "You will get your shit together. You will hand your essays in when they're due. You will *stop* obsessing about a girl who never asked you to love her."

I nodded without speaking.

"And you," Lola said, turning on Murray with even more ferocity. "It's been months. Frankly I find your behavior deplorable. Leave her alone. You're better than this."

Murray started crying then, and proceeded to vomit in his own lap.

"Can we go to your party now?" said Madison.

"No! No parties for any of you! Get up off the ground right now, Murray Finch, or so help me God . . ." Sobbing and covered in vomit that smelled strongly of tequila, Muz fumbled his way to his feet. La pushed his hair out of his eyes, not unkindly.

"We're going to get some Burger King, we're all going to sober up, and then we're going to Henry's house to do something productive with our lives."

An hour and two Burger King meals later, I was sitting cross-legged beneath the elk head in my basement, twirling a cold onion ring around my finger. I had a dictionary in my lap, Lola was using a random word generator on the iMac, and Murray was browsing Urban Dictionary on his phone. Madison Carlson, who'd silently followed us back to my house (quite likely in fear of Lola's wrath if she tried to escape), was asleep in my bed. Which is not a place I ever imagined I would see teen goddess Madison Carlson. I tried not to notice the way her black jeans clung to the curves of her hips, or the way her hair fanned out across my sheets, or the way she smelled of vanilla and soft spices, the very antithesis of everything that was Grace Town.

"Survey says . . . *costumed*," Lola said, who'd decided the best use of our Saturday night was to try and salvage the newspaper, which I already knew at this point was beyond salvaging, because it was too late to put together anything decent. "That could actually work. You could do articles about the masks we wear as high schoolers and other kinds of deep shit."

"No, shh, this is way better," Muz said. "You should make the theme 'species dysphoria.' A feeling that one is in the body of the wrong species. We could finally address my transspecies desire to become a dragon. Think of the possible articles: 'Six

Degrees of Smaug.' 'Puff the Magic Dragon Gives First Post-Rehab Interview.' 'Falkor the Luck Dragon: How the Story Finally Ended.'"

"Don't trivialize transspeciesism," Lola said.

"Don't doubt me being dragon kin."

Then Murray started crying again, so we stopped trying to save the newspaper I'd probably singlehandedly destroyed with my wantonness and put our energy into half inflating an air mattress, which we slept on together, the three of us curled around each other.

"Sorry we ruined your birthday, La," I whispered to her, but she pressed her fingers to my lips and shook her head.

And I thought, even though the pain of wanting a girl who didn't exist had burrowed into my bones and infected the soft tissue of my lungs, that things could definitely be a lot worse.

CHAPTER 22

THE NEXT TWO WEEKS melted together in a blur of catching up on schoolwork, missing newspaper meetings with Hink, changing weather, and absence. The absence of orange leaves, for one, as fall went from "pumpkin spice everything" to "my entire Facebook newsfeed is one giant Ned Stark meme."

And second, the absence of Grace Town.

"Where's that weird girlfriend of yours? Haven't seen her around here for a while," said Sadie one afternoon as Murray, Lola, Madison Carlson (a strange new development), and I walked in the front door. La quickly did the "cut it out" hand motion across her neck, but it was too late. "Oh, shit." Sadie bit her lip. "Sorry, kid. Did you and Grace break up?"

"We don't use the *G*-word anymore," Murray said. "Please refer to her henceforth as She-Who-Must-Not-Be-Named."

"Grace would've had to have been my girlfriend for us to break up," I told Sadie as I unraveled the scarf from around my neck and hung it up.

"Dude, it's *She-Who-Must-Not-Be-Named*," Murray said. "Christ. Get it right."

"What happened?" Sadie said.

The problem was, I wasn't really sure what'd happened. I knew I'd screwed up big-time by going into Dom's house, but I hadn't expected Grace to evaporate. I wanted to apologize to her, to pull her aside and say all the things I hadn't been able to say out loud, but Grace had stopped appearing outside my locker after school. Grace had stopped appearing, period.

The few times she bothered to turn up for class, our teachers, too, seemed determined to keep us apart.

"Hey," I whispered to her in the second week, when she finally returned to drama and reclaimed her perch at the back of the room. "I've missed you."

"Henry, pay attention, please," Mrs. Beady said. "You can't afford to miss learning about Bertolt Brecht's dramatic theory." Beady pointed to where the rest of the class was sitting at the foot of the stage. "Over here."

"Can I talk to you after school?" I whispered as I stood. Grace Town looked at me but said nothing, and after school she was already gone.

I drove past her house sometimes when Mom let me borrow the car, but her Hyundai was never in the drive. I rode my bike by the cemetery in the afternoons, hoping to catch her laying flowers at Dom's grave, but—although fresh blooms appeared almost every day—I never saw her there. There was evidence of her everywhere. Sometimes I'd catch a glimpse of the back of her head in the cafeteria, or find that someone had fed Ricky Martin Knupps II when I forgot, or *Seen 5:50 p.m.*, *Seen 11:34 a.m.*, *Seen 8:05 p.m.* would appear under the messages I sent her asking where she was, but she was never there. Not really. Not ever.

Grace Town had become the ghost she wanted to be, and the absence of her—the gouge wound she left behind when she ripped herself from my life—made my breath catch.

"Was she real?" I asked Lola one afternoon. We were sitting out on the football field with a flask of hot chocolate, watching thin clouds slip overhead. "Or did I make her up?"

"Christ, you're so melodramatic," she said, flicking hot chocolate at me.

It was the smell, more than anything, that killed my soul bit by bit. The scent of her in my sheets, on my clothes, hanging heavily in the newspaper office. It made something inside me crumple in an explosive decompression every time I could smell her close by but not see her. There was a momentary temptation, no more than the space of a heartbeat, where I'd considered never washing anything I owned again, just to savor what I had left of her. But then, no. God no. Dom's room, Dom's tomb—I couldn't. So I stripped my bedding. Washed all my clothes. Avoided the office (and Mr. Hink) at all costs.

The bus was almost as bad. I'd only caught it a couple of times in the last few months, and hadn't been expecting to catch it that first afternoon Grace failed to materialize outside my locker. It was loud and cramped and smelled like a time before her; smelled like her absence. There was no seat for me anymore, so I had to sit with a freshman girl at the front, who glared at me the entire way to my stop.

I shrugged at Sadie. "I probably fucked everything up."

"Language, Henry," said Dad from the kitchen. He was cooking tacos with Ryan, who was sitting on his shoulders and pulling at Dad's hair to direct him like the rat from *Ratatouille*.

"Can't you fix it?" Sadie said.

"I don't think so. I think she's gone."

The four of us went down to the basement. Ever since the night Madison Carlson had slept at my house, Murray had started ironing his clothes and attempting to comb his wild hair, which made him look like he was getting ready to sit for his yearbook photo sometime in the mid-eighties. He was playing (and losing to) Madison in *Mario Kart* when all of our phones dinged at once. Lola checked hers first. Her face fell and her eyes darted up to meet mine.

The notification was from Grace Town, to attend her birthday party at the Thanksgiving fair on Saturday. A hundred or so people had been invited, most of them from East River. La launched out of her chair, but I pressed "Going" before she could snatch my phone out of my hands.

Lola sighed and shook her head. "There's a storm coming," she said, even though my weather app predicted little more than light rain.

CHAPTER 23

THE END OF NOVEMBER brought with it an influx of eccentric relatives who came from all the far-flung corners of the country to a) attend the annual Thanksgiving weekend craft fair, b) eat all our food, and c) make my life a living hell.

Normally the parasites got free run of the house at Thanksgiving, meaning they usually set up their camp in the basement and kicked me out to sleep upstairs, but seeing as it was senior year and I had so much studying to do, the parasites had (much to their disgust) been relegated to sleeping in Sadie's old bedroom and on air mattresses in the living room.

The visitors included:

- My grandmother on Dad's side, Erica Page, a terrifying woman who'd supposedly been a spy during the Cold War and had a shady past she refused to talk about.

- Grandma's boyfriend, Harold, a meek, pleasant landscape architect who'd been following Erica around saying little more than "yes, dear" for the last decade.
- Dad's brother, Michael.
- Uncle Michael's "housemate," Albert.
- Mom's sister, Juliette, and three of her five children, all of whom were named after fictional animals. Pongo, Duchess, and Otis were supposedly still too young to be left at home alone (even though Pongo was almost my age). Bagheera and Aslan had purposefully chosen colleges on the opposite side of the country to make the facilitation of easy travel impossible. Aunty Jules still couldn't understand why they never came home for the holidays, even after they legally changed their names to Bradley and Asher.
- Lola's aunt and uncle, Wing and Richard, who were inexplicably staying at our house this year instead of at Lola's. Plus their two kids, Sarah and Brodie.

Thanksgiving dinner went how most Thanksgiving dinners go in the Page household (or any household, for that matter). Albert left in tears after Uncle Michael introduced him to Lola's relatives as his "long-term housemate." Aunt Juliette overcooked the turkey and also decided that halfway through the main meal was the perfect time to ask Pongo if he'd ever smoked pot. And Granny Page, when giving a demonstration of what she'd been learning at her local YMCA, managed to knock Brodie momentarily unconscious with a Wiffle Ball bat.

But the cops weren't called and Uncle Nick, Juliette's ex, didn't show up at our house and break his restraining order this year, so it was pretty much a resounding success.

Black Friday brought with it another Page family tradition: going to stores at five a.m. in an attempt to satisfy all our most intense capitalist cravings in one day. Unfortunately, this was also the tradition of almost every other family in town. We all nearly got trampled in a small stampede, there'd been an altercation with pepper spray that left our eyes burning, Brodie had gone missing for several hours, and there were news reports that someone had been stabbed in a department store, but I got a GoPro and an animatronic Yoda for 85 percent off, so yay consumerism, I guess.

By Friday night, I'd taken to barricading myself in the basement to escape the upstairs carnage and questions from my aunt and grandmother about why I looked so glum.

"I see his skinny jeans and his long hair," I overheard Grandma telling my parents. "He's been indoctrinated into an emo circle, that's the problem. I read all about them on the computers at the YMCA."

"Oh no," said Mom. "He's actually practicing Satanism." Which shut Grandma up pretty quick.

Then it was Saturday. Cold. Dark. Miserable. Appropriate for Grace's birthday. Time for the oncoming storm: the Thanksgiving fair.

Although the craft fair had originally been designed to showcase livestock and fall produce, it had—since its inception some seventy years before—been a favorite annual social event of teens across the city. Something about the crisp, cool air, the twinkling carnival lights, and the scent of deep-fried food provided the perfect atmosphere for reckless teenage abandon.

I spent most of the day getting ready. Normally I didn't give much of a crap about how I looked, but tonight . . . Tonight it seemed important to look as attractive as possible. I got my hair cut short. I bought a new jacket—gray marl—new black skinny jeans, and a new black scarf. I didn't wear my dad's old clothes, but the expensive wool coat my parents had given me as an early Christmas present. I shined my shoes. I combed and parted and slicked down my new hair. I plucked a wayward strand from my eyebrow. By the evening, I looked like a different Henry. An older Henry, from an age long past.

I wrapped the present I'd bought for Grace as I waited for Lola and the others to arrive. In the end, I'd settled on a book as her gift, a kids' book called *You Are Stardust* by Elin Kelsey. It wasn't exactly metaphorical; the paper didn't represent the fragility of life or our relationship or anything like that. It was just something I thought she'd like.

I enclosed it in brown paper, a tradition started with Murray years ago after he'd watched *The Sound of Music* for the first time. We never gave each other cards. Instead we drew on the wrapping paper, sometimes deep and meaningful quotes, sometimes random patterns, sometimes Abe Lincoln riding a velociraptor into battle. It varied. (For instance, this year Lola's had been the Magic: The Gathering symbols. She was not impressed.)

I thought about poetry at first, some romantic or moving quote, but it didn't fit. So I sketched Walter White in black pencil, the same rough image the Salamanca cousins used in *Breaking Bad*, and wrote "Happy Heisenbirthday, bitch" underneath.

"Holy," said a voice from the stairs. I turned to find Lola in her usual ASOS garb, looking like she'd time traveled here from the late nineties. "Henry, you look *hot*. Like, *super* hot. I don't normally find the male species attractive, but *damn*."

"Your tone of absolute surprise is not good for my self-confidence."

"Do a little turn for me, sugar tits."

"How dare you treat me like an object," I said, but I stood and turned for her and she whistled.

"You're a dapper young lady-killer."

Then Georgia and Muz arrived and brought Pongo downstairs and we started playing Never Have I Ever with vodka shots, but by sunset my nerves were still getting the better of me, so I snuck a bottle of red wine from my parents' liquor cabinet and took it back to the basement and drank a glass. When that did nothing to calm my nerves, I drank another glass, and a third, until it was time to go and almost the whole bottle was gone. By the time we got there and the cool, pink-tinged light of sunset was settling over the fairground, we were all swaying, drunk not only on booze but on the magical possibility of the night ahead.

La interlocked her arm with mine as we made our way into the fairground. "Are you ready for this?" she said.

"No."

"What do you think she'll be like?"

"I can never predict what she's going to do. All her East River friends are going to be here, so I assume I'll say hello and happy birthday and that'll be it. That's all I want to do, really. Let's just have fun, La. You and me against the world. Screw the rest."

"Sounds like a mighty fine plan, darling."

I didn't know where Grace would be, only that she'd be here somewhere, surrounded by people I wouldn't recognize. The five of us made our way through the crowds toward the Ferris wheel, its multicolored baskets shining like hard candies in the evening light. The speakers of an antique carousel crackled out Glenn Miller's "Moonlight Serenade" while an old couple danced in line for fries at a food truck.

And as the music played, I saw her through the crowd. The people parted around us as if they could feel me staring at her.

Grace Town was not Grace Town.

She was dressed in a red coat with red lipstick on her lips. Her hair was washed and curled and honey blond and fell around her face in soft waves. There was color in her skin, like she'd been out in the sun all weekend. Blush on her cheeks, even, like she'd made a real effort with her appearance. I could see what Lola meant when she said Grace looked like Edie Sedgwick. They both had that femme-fatale, might've-just-overdosed-on-heroin-and-been-brought-back-to-life-by-adrenaline look. She was set alight, shining, the stars that died to give her all the atoms that made her glowing from beyond the grave. I'd never seen anything so excruciatingly, heart-breakingly beautiful.

Grace was surrounded, as I knew she would be. I'd seen glimpses of the girl she'd been before—the type of girl who could fill a fairground with friends—but here was proof, in the flesh. Grace saw me staring then, and she smiled and beckoned me over.

"Henry," whispered Lola, squeezing my arm. "Don't."

"Look at her, Lola."

"I *am* looking. All I see is bait." I said nothing, but because La was my best friend, and because we'd known each other all our lives, she sighed and let me go. "Be careful."

Grace and I walked toward each other through the crowd, our steps slower than the people bustling around us. Time seemed to slow, too, as if it were coated in honey, thick and sweet and golden.

"Look at you," I said to her, and she smiled tiredly, the way she did.

"It's been a long time," she said, smoothing out the red woolen fabric of her coat. I could tell from her lightness, the way her voice sounded so sweet and carefree, that she, too, was already drunk. "I hardly feel myself in these clothes."

I ran my fingers across her cold cheek and Grace smiled and kissed my palm. "You're beautiful," I said. "I missed you."

"We can fix that."

Then she took my hand and led me away from my friends and her friends. I'd expected to spend the evening at a distance from her, stealing glances across the fairground, maybe having a brief conversation. Now my hand was in hers, our fingers entwined, like they had been that one night we'd walked home from the movies together. The night I'd been sure we would be together.

It was like a montage out of a film, everything seen as if through a filter. We wandered the fairground for hours, me with my arm around her waist, and she didn't even seem to care that people would see us. That night, Grace was not Grace; she was effervescent, lighthearted, a character out of a book. We competed against each other at bumper cars. Fed each other cotton candy. At the top of the Ferris wheel, we took swigs of straight vodka from her flask. The city, sprawled out in the distance, looked small from up there, a collection of toy buildings in a tilt-shift photograph. I even won her a prize at the laughing clowns. And I lapped it up, every moment of it, thinking that this was how things would be from now on.

Grace took my hand again—God, why was it so easy for her to touch me when she'd been drinking?—and led me away from the crowds, down toward the empty field next to the Ferris wheel, where it was quieter and there were fewer people.

"I've changed my mind," she said when we came to a stop.

My chest and face immediately started burning. My ears felt like they were on fire. For weeks I'd been working toward this moment, certain that it would never come, and now it was here and instead of feeling elated, I felt like I was going to vomit. I wanted so badly to stick to my guns, to make her feel bad for the weeks of hell she'd put me through when she chose her dead boyfriend over me.

You chose somebody else, I said in my head, for the hundredth time. *How am I ever supposed to get over that?*

But because she was beautiful and I wanted her so badly and here she was, finally saying the thing I desperately wanted her to say, I just said, "Grace, I really don't . . ." My voice trailed off and she started talking over the top of me and with every beautiful word that dripped from her mouth like poison, I grew sicker and sicker, like Murray had said I would, and wanted her more and more.

"I've never met anyone like you. I need you to know that," she said. "I loved Dom, I really did, but there's something between us that there never was with him."

"Grace."

"I mean it, Henry. The way we get along, the chemistry we have. Dom and I were never like this. You're so special. The way we are together . . . After him, I never thought I'd give a shit about anyone again. I didn't *want* to give a shit about anyone again. But there you were. And I was afraid, because it was so soon after, but we work, Henry. God, I want you so badly, all the time."

"I don't want to hear these things when you've been drinking. I want you to say them to me when you're sober."

"I could see us together. Really together. I want to do this."

"I want you to say these things to me tomorrow when you wake up. I want you to be sure."

"And the way you handled seeing his room. I thought it would be shit, but the way you handled yourself made me want you more."

"Are you even going to remember saying these things tomorrow?"

"I need to know if you're going to go away for college."

"I don't know. Probably."

"Because if we're going to do this, you need to stay. I'm not ready to leave. So I need to know if you're going or not."

"Grace . . . I don't know yet. I haven't decided."

"I know I'm being forward, and I'm sorry."

"It's fine. I mean, I was pretty forward from the beginning."

"But that's how it *should* be with feelings. People should be forward. I'm jealous that you can say exactly how you feel about me."

"I never can. Only sometimes. Only with you."

"Do you still want me?"

"Nothing has changed for me," I said, the last of my resolve crumbling. Because how could I blame her for still loving him. Because she was still shaky, still uncertain, and I wasn't.

I wasn't.

I never would be.

And I wasn't in any kind of position to play hard to get. I was afraid that if I did, Grace would walk away. I leaned against the wall, the fingers of my left hand in my hair, my eyes burning but dry. I couldn't look at her.

"Tell me how you feel about me," Grace said, her head on my shoulder, her chest pressed against mine.

"Grace."

"I want to hear it again."

"This isn't fair."

"I know. But I miss hearing it, so I want you to say it anyway."

"I've never felt about anyone the way I feel about you."

"More."

Then Lola was there. La. A devil and an angel rolled into one. "There you two are!" she said, pulling Grace off me, detaching the source of poison. "Grace, darling, a *smoking* hot babe named Piper is looking for you."

Grace looked at me. "Come find me," she said, leaning in to kiss my cheek. And then she was gone and I was sinking to the ground, my head in my hands, Lola at my side.

"I think I'm going to have a psychotic break."

"That *goddamn* girl. Women, I swear. We should leave, right now."

But of course we didn't. Grace was my drug of choice, and tonight the dealer was giving out hits for free. I'd stay until I overdosed.

So La and I went back to the fair. We got Grace's cousin

to buy us drinks. And later in the night she found me again, and again she was her usual drunk self: flirty, chatty, giggling. She fawned over me. Ran her fingers through my hair. And I let her. Like an absolute idiot, I sat there and I let her do that to me and I let people see us together, all of her friends, and I felt my chest constricting but she'd said such nice things. Such pretty things. I thought that maybe we would be together after all. Because people don't just do that to other people. People didn't seek out people and then profess their feelings for them if they didn't really mean it, right?

"You need to go crazy, Henry," Grace said suddenly. She was sitting on my lap, her lips against my temple. "You just need to go and fuck lots of girls. So I can hate you. It would be so much easier to hate you."

"*What* are you talking about?"

"This is so *fucked*. This whole thing is so *fucked*." Her words were slurred, her posture slumped. Grace was drunk. Like actually, legitimately drunk. I'd seen her tipsy before, but never wasted. "I need to go to the bathroom."

"Okay," I said as she climbed off me and stumbled toward the bathroom, where I assumed she would vomit and sit and cry for a while. And maybe I should've got up and followed her, but I didn't. I sat at the table by myself for twenty minutes, eating a corn dog, then I went to find one of her friends—Piper or whatever her name was—to go in after her and make sure she was still alive (she was).

Piper came out ten minutes later and found me in the

crowd, plucking yellow ducks out of a duck pond game with Lola. "Can you take her home?" she said. "She says she'll only come out if you take her home."

"Look . . . I don't know if that's such a good idea."

"She said she still cares about you, Henry."

I know she still cares about me, I felt like saying. *I had to hear all about it for the last two hours.*

"Yeah, okay, whatever. Bring her out. I'll make sure she gets home safe."

La and I stood together near the fairground exit, waiting for Piper to extract Grace from the bathroom. She stumbled out another ten minutes later, mascara smudged around her eyes, her lips and eyes swollen from crying. I crossed my arms and watched as Piper sat her down in the grass and went to a cotton candy vendor to get her water. It wasn't fair that some people could still be beautiful even when they were drunken messes.

"Henry Page," Grace said to me flatly when Piper finally managed to get her up and walking. "Take me home."

"Come on, we'll get you out of here," said Lola, slinging Grace's arm around her neck.

I didn't want to take her home. I didn't want her to come back to my place and take off her clothes and lie naked in my bed. It didn't seem fair. That she could choose to have me any-time she wanted.

It started drizzling out on the street, which seemed to revive Grace somehow. She peeled herself away from Lola and started turning in unsteady circles, sprinkles of water clinging to her hair and coat. Her cane was gone, abandoned at some point during the night, but she seemed more agile without it. Like she didn't really need it, just kept it for security, the same way she kept his clothes.

"I used to be a ballet dancer," she said, extending her hands above her head as she moved. "I used to dance. I don't think I ever told you that. Just another thing I can't do anymore."

Lola held my hand, her head on my shoulder, as we both watched Grace dance in the rain, because you couldn't not watch. You couldn't not be enraptured by that. It was something close to reverie.

After a minute, Grace curtsied, smiling. Lola clapped.

"Oh, dear, Henrik doesn't look happy with me," Grace said to Lola, grinning. "I've been very mean to him. I probably deserve it."

"I think you should have this back," I said, taking "I do not love you" out of its home in my wallet, where it had festered for months, a poem that had been a prophecy from the beginning.

Grace took it from me and laughed and slung her arms around my neck. "I don't want it back, my darling Henry. I gave this to you."

"You're never going to be my girlfriend, are you?" I said flatly. Lola was standing right there next to us, but I was drunker than I realized, so I didn't care. I didn't care if she heard.

"Jesus Christ," Grace said, wrenching herself away from me. "Do you ever think about anything else? What do you want from me?"

"I want you to be with me." Ugh, so needy.

"I *am* with you. Literally. Right now. We are together."

"You know what I mean."

"Why'd you have to write me that stupid letter? Why couldn't we just keep doing what we were doing? I hate to go all Hollywood cliché on you, but *why* do we have to put a label on it?"

"Oh my God. Do you realize how ridiculous you sound?"

La, by this point, was making a very good show of looking like something on her phone was intensely interesting.

"Me? What about you? What do you *want*? You want to make it Facebook official so all your friends and family can like it?" She tore the poem in half and in half and in half again and let the pieces fall to the dampened sidewalk. "You can't project your fantasies onto people and expect them to play the part, Henry. People aren't empty vessels for you to fill up with your daydreams."

"Come to Burger King with us," Lola said, sliding between us, putting her hands on Grace's waist. "Get something to eat. Come back to Henry's or mine and sleep it off."

"If I go to Burger King, I will vomit on everyone there," Grace said as she grasped Lola's shoulder to steady herself. She looked back at me, blinking as she tried to focus her vision, her pale hair falling over her face. "I wanted to see how you'd react.

If I forced myself to be her for a night. Kintsukuroi Grace, all stitched up with gold seams. You've never looked at me like that before, when you saw me through the crowd. I think you have feelings for someone who doesn't exist."

Then Grace let go of Lola's shoulder and threw up on the sidewalk and kind of disintegrated into a heap on the ground. It took us five minutes to get her back on her feet, and another five minutes to convince the Uber driver we'd requested that he wouldn't need to call an old priest and a young priest if he drove her home.

"Thanks for looking after me and stuff," she said as she slid into the backseat.

"That's okay," I said. "Just . . . get home safe."

Then she said, "I love you, Dom," right as I was swinging the car door closed. And in the moment that it thumped shut, I felt my heart tear a little bit more. The last thread that had been holding me together ripped away. I couldn't breathe as I watched the Uber pull into traffic and ferry her away. I didn't want to breathe anymore. I wanted to lie down on the sidewalk and be swallowed by the concrete.

"Did she say what I think she said?" said Lola, who was collecting the torn pieces of Pablo Neruda off the ground and putting them in her bag. I'd been really hoping she hadn't heard.

"Yeah," I said, staring after the car with my hands in my pockets, not entirely sure how I was still alive.

"Look, don't let it fuck you up. Falling for her was always gonna be a really shit time. Grace does love you, okay? In her own way. If you'd been first, if you'd been before him, she'd realize that what she feels for you *is* a kind of love. It's just that what they had . . ."

"Was bigger? Was better?"

"People are perfect when all that's left of them is memory. You're never gonna measure up to a dead dude."

"Thanks for the honesty." I shook my head. "When she's sober, she's so hot and cold. It's only when she's drunk that she makes me think she wants me."

"That's when people are most truthful, though, right? When all the inhibition kinda melts away and people say what they really feel."

"Like that they love their dead ex-boyfriend?"

"C'mon. You know what I mean."

"Yeah. I mean, you can't just go around kissing people and taking their virginity if you're not in love with them, right?"

"Exactly. It would be unconscionable." Lola swung her arm around my shoulder and kissed my cheek. "I did love you when I kissed you, you know? I still do. Very much."

"Thanks, La. Love you too."

"Excellent. Now, let's go track down some Burger King. I am fucking *famished*."

When we got home, I didn't go inside. I went to the backyard, into the shed where Dad did all his carpentry work. I found gasoline. I set up the fire pit my parents used when they were entertaining people in the colder months. I started a fire. One by one, I tore out the pages of *You Are Stardust* and fed them to the flames.

I didn't think of it as destroying the book; I thought of it as setting its atoms free.

Lola and Georgia came over at lunchtime on Sunday (uninvited, naturally, each carrying handfuls of food they'd swiped from the kitchen upstairs).

"I'm thinking of a four-letter word that starts with an *s* and ends with a *t* and has an *l* in it," La announced, spilling her contraband across my bed.

"*Salt?*" I said.

"*Slut*, you miserable addict. *Slut.*"

"My heart hurts, La."

"Good. You *deserve* to be in pain," she said as she crawled under the covers of my bed and hooked her legs through mine.

"Lola, we can't flaunt our secret love affair in front of your girlfriend!" I said dramatically, taking her face in my hands.

"You can have her," said Georgia as she turned on my TV and PlayStation and made her herself comfortable on my couch. "She's hungover and whiny and generally being a pain in the ass. Did you hear about her admirer from last night? Samuel? Apparently he asked Murray for her number."

"*Pfft.* As if that's news," said Lola. "Men fall at my feet *all* the time." She unwrapped a candy cane, handed it to me, then unwrapped another one and started sucking on it. "Have you heard from She-Who-Must-Not-Be-Named?"

"Yeah. I texted her this morning."

"*Henry.*"

"I know, I know."

"And?"

"And it was like it always is. She said she was drunk and stupid and sorry, and by this point I should know better than to listen to her."

"Fuck. You didn't get angry at her for going all Mr. Darcy on you and pledging her undying love out of nowhere? And *then* going *Exorcist* and vomiting on my shoes?"

"No."

Lola shuffled closer and patted my head. "You'll be okay."

"I know."

La and I fell asleep to the sound of Georgia crushing skulls in *BioShock Infinite*.

CHAPTER 24

ON THE FIRST FRIDAY in December, I was unceremoniously hauled out of Mr. Hotchkiss's math class by Mr. Hink (who I'm sure thoroughly enjoyed the opportunity to disrupt calculus). We walked in silence to Principal Valentine's office, where Lola was already seated in front of her desk. Spread out in front of her were thirty tabloid-sized pages, half of them blank.

"Care to explain this, Page?" said Valentine.

I'd been waiting for this meeting for a while. I just hadn't been able to muster the energy to care. Grace had been absent from school for the entire week after Thanksgiving, and despite Lola's insistence that I needed to organize my shit or she was going to go directly to Valentine, I hadn't done anything, because I couldn't even force myself to walk into the newspaper office. "It looks like an unpolished printout of the paper."

"I asked Lola for a printout this morning of everything you've finished so far," said Hink. "This is what she gave me."

Wantonness, mouthed Lola.

Traitor, I mouthed back. "Look, we *do* have more than that. There's this whole massive feature story on Magic: The Gathering, and we've got a few other articles almost ready to go. We can have them to Lola in the next few days."

"It's too late for that," said La. "That's what I've been trying to tell you. I can't do three months' worth of design in a couple of days."

"You go to print on Monday, Mr. Page. If it were solely my decision, I'd fire you from your position effective immediately, but Mr. Hink still has faith that you can slap something together. The printing has already been paid for, and let me tell you, never in its thirty-five years has the *Westland Post* not gone to print. You will not be the exception. Do you understand?"

"Yes."

"You are excused from class for the remainder of the day. Get your writers, get into your office, and get. The. Paper. *Done.*"

"Yes," I said again. Lola marched me to the office then, and she called the classrooms of all the junior writers, and in the afternoon Hink and Principal Valentine came in to supervise and picked the theme "time of your life" for us to focus on. Even though it would be the worst issue ever produced in the already fairly unimpressive history of the *Westland Post*, I thought maybe, just maybe, I'd get my shit together long enough to get the damn newspaper to print. That is until I checked my phone and found two things:

1. A message from my mother that read:

BIRTHGIVER:

> We're at Grace's house. Come straight here
> when you get this. Call if you need a ride.

Which made exactly zero sense.
And:

2. A voice message from an unknown number. I
   checked it quickly, still unsure as to why my mother
   was at my kind-of-ex-girlfriend's house.

"Henry," said a familiar voice through the phone, albeit
panicked and teary. The speaker had been crying. It took a second for me to recognize him, to understand why the sound of
him upset made my gut drop like a stone. "It's Martin Sawyer,
Dominic's dad. Could you give me a call as soon as you get this,
please? We just, uh." He sobbed. "It's an emergency. It's . . . I
don't know if Grace has told you, but it's Dom's birthday today—his first birthday since he left us—and she's . . . she's . . ." I
didn't hear the rest of the message.

"Grace," I said. "Something's happened to Grace."

Principal Valentine looked up from where she was reading
on the sex couch. "I'm well aware that Miss Town is currently
unaccounted for, but the matter is being handled by her family
and the police."

"You *knew*?" I said, in a tone I'd never used to address an adult before. "You knew and you didn't tell us?"

"Your print deadline is Monday. You have less than seventy-two hours left to do months of work."

"I have to go," I said, grabbing my backpack. "I have to find her."

"Henry, if you leave this office, I'll have no choice but to dismiss you from your position as editor."

I was already sprinting. Lola shouted after me, but I couldn't open my mouth because I thought I might be sick.

Grace Town was dead.

I knew it, I knew it, I knew it, deep down in some forgotten corner of the soul where it was possible to know things without knowing how. I ran like I hadn't been able to run in that stupid touch football game she dragged me to. Which, apparently, still wasn't as fast as Lola.

"Henry, wait!" she said.

"Lola, go back."

"Like hell I'm going back." Which seemed like a good enough argument to me, so we ran together, and as we did, I thought, *That coward. She's gone and killed herself and left me here without her.* If I ever had any doubts about whether I really, truly loved her or not, they were all dissolved by the excruciating ten minutes we spent sprinting to her house, knowing, knowing, knowing the news I'd get when I arrived.

There was a police car in the drive. The front door was splayed open in an unsettling manner, the way it is on detective shows when something terrible has happened inside. I stumbled in. There was a cop standing at the top of the stairs and worried-looking adults everywhere, two of whom were my parents. Gasping, my hands on my knees, I looked to the two of them and said, quite flatly, "Is . . . she . . . dead?" My words caused a middle-aged blond woman whom I'd never met before to burst into tears.

Mom came over and hugged me then and said, "No, no, no, no, no," over and over again in that soothing voice moms use to calm their kids after nightmares. Dad went to comfort the bawling woman, who, at second glance, was very clearly Grace Town's alcoholic mother. They had the same thin, hollow features that made them look like drug addicts in the wrong light but at the same time very beautiful. With her bright blond hair and smudged makeup and big doe eyes, she looked even more like a femme fatale than Grace herself did.

"What's going on?" I said when I caught my breath and managed to detach myself from my mother. "Where's Grace? Why are you here?"

"Grace is missing. She left the house around dawn without her phone and hasn't come back. Martin came around to our place looking for you, thinking you might know where she is. We gave him your number and then came back here to wait for you. We've only been here for an hour."

"The police car . . . I thought . . . You should've pulled me out of school as soon as you knew she was gone."

"I'm sure she's fine," said Dad.

Martin came over then, running his fingers through his hair. I'd never seen a human being look quite so haggard. He spoke to Grace's mother, whose name I never learned. "The police think we should look for her at all her usual hangouts first. I know her and Dom were thinking about going away for his birthday up to the lake house, so Mary and I will drive up there now. I'm going to call some of her East River friends, get them to check out the library where she wrote and the café where she always got breakfast and maybe the houseboat down at the marina."

All these places. All these places I never knew she'd been, she'd liked. Grace on a houseboat? Doing what? Having another existential crisis? Thinking about stardust and atoms and the meaninglessness of life? But no. Probably not. Probably sunbathing on a spring afternoon, Dom at her side, party music in the background, both of them sipping sweet wine, smiling their salad-eating smiles. Probably that. Probably Facebook Grace, the girl I'd never known.

Might never know, now.

Then came the question I'd been dreading. Martin turned to me. "Henry, can you think of anywhere she might be?" I desperately racked my brain for places I'd seen her. Grace in our fishbowl office. Grace in the black-walled drama room. Grace in my basement bedroom, curled up in my sheets, wearing only one of my T-shirts.

"Uh . . . maybe . . . uh . . . Have you checked the cemetery? Or the track?"

Martin nodded, but looked disappointed. "We went to both of those places this morning. And the crash site, up in the national park."

"They crashed in the national park?"

"They were on their way to a restaurant up there for lunch," said Martin. My chest constricted the same way it had when the Gutcrusher pulverized me during touch football. Grace had taken me on a date to the place where he died. Had collected flowers from the garden bed and left me alone next to the seaside while she wandered off to lay flowers at his roadside memorial. Jesus. "We can look again this afternoon, though, I suppose. Anywhere else?" I shook my head, keenly aware that Grace's mother had stopped crying and was now staring at me, unblinking, the same way her daughter often did, the way that makes you feel like your skin is made of glass and every secret you've ever kept is engraved in script upon your bones. "Okay, well, if you think of anywhere she might be, let us know. Sorry, I better go make these phone calls."

And then came the worst part.

The waiting.

Waiting as people were assigned locations to go out and look for her. Waiting as more police arrived and said comforting things in between asking questions that hinted at their thinly veiled belief that she'd probably killed herself. Waiting as we drove aimlessly around the suburbs, slowing the car to a crawl as we passed anyone who might be a teenage girl, looking like sexual predators out on the prowl. Waiting at home after the sun went down and the cops told us to get some rest, that Grace would show up "one way or another," which was a fucked-up thing to say. Waiting, fully clothed in my bed, as the clock ticked past midnight and I'd still heard nothing. Waiting with nothing to do except imagine her body somewhere, plunged underwater like Ophelia or Virginia Woolf, because that's how Grace would do it, if she did it, something dramatic and literary that would get people talking about the tragic but poetic nature of death. I was almost tempted to run upstairs and make sure she hadn't put her head in my oven, Plath style. Then I started to think about how Manic Pixie Dream Girls committed suicide. Did they ride their Dutch bicycles on photographic train tracks until a midnight express came along to clean them up? Did they drown themselves in their secret fishponds?

The fishpond.

I sat bolt upright then, because I was *such. A. Fucking. Idiot.* "I know where she is," I said out loud. Dead or alive, I knew she would be there.

There was no time, no reason to wake my parents—I shrugged on a jacket, snatched the keys off the dining room table, and sprinted out to the car. I drove into the city. Climbed the cast-iron fence. Sprained my goddamn ankle rolling off the hedge. Hobbled down to the abandoned train station. Picked the lock to get inside. Ran down the spiral staircase that twisted into the basement.

And there she was, in the dark, waist deep in the still water.

Alive. Gloriously, miraculously alive. My insides melted away in relief until I was a shell spun from glass. My legs almost gave way beneath me.

"Grace!" I yelled as I half sprinted, half slid down the stairs. "Grace!"

Grace turned to face me. Although there was no light except from the moon, I could see trails of tears falling down her face. Her palms were resting flat against the surface of the water and she was breathing these short, sharp breaths that sent plumes of white in front of her lips. I slowed for a moment, sure that I was dreaming, because she looked like something out of a myth. There was a wreath of pale flowers woven into her hair, and she was dressed in white, all in white, like a wedding dress.

Here was Ophelia, in the flesh.

I ran into the water until I couldn't run any more, then I waded out to where she was and took off my coat and draped it around her shoulders, because she was shaking.

"C'mon, we have to get you out of the water," I said, but she didn't move, wouldn't move. Grace looked at me, tears in her eyes. And then the world imploded. It was like she split open, finally, and let the pain pour out. She was crying, bawling, these huge, violent sobs rolling over and over her, almost too much for her body to handle. She collapsed against me, her full weight in my arms, and I swear I could *feel* her grief radiating outward. I breathed it in with each breath until the pressure of it leaked out of her.

"Why'd he have to die, Henry?" she said over and over again through her sobs. "Why'd he have to die? Why couldn't it have been me?"

"I'm so sorry." I crushed her against me and held her tight because I didn't know what else to say or do. "I'm so, so sorry."

And it went on and on like this until my teeth were chattering and I couldn't really feel my legs.

Then, just like that, Grace stopped crying, as though she'd had a certain amount of tears in her inventory and they'd been exhausted. She pulled herself out of my arms and waded back toward the stairs without looking at me, my coat trailing in the water behind her. When she reached the first rung, she climbed and sat, shuddering, with her feet still in the icy water. I followed her, of course, because I'd have followed her anywhere. That night, if she'd walked the other way, into the cold depths of the basement, I'd have followed her there too.

I sat next to her, cross-legged, and tried not to show how cold I was, because I wanted to be with her, just us, alone, before I had to take her back. I leaned over and fished my phone out of my coat's breast pocket and called Martin. He answered after one ring.

"Please, God, tell me she's alive," he said.

"I found her. She's fine. I'm bringing her home."

"Oh, thank God, thank God, thank God. Bring her back to us."

"I will. We'll see you soon. She's fine. She's safe. Can you please let my parents know she's safe and I'm okay and I'll be home soon?"

"Yes, of course. Thank you. Thank you so much."

I hung up.

"Everyone was pretty worried about you," I said quietly.

"You know I was on suicide watch the first month after he died? Everyone assumed I'd try and off myself once he was gone. Like, I couldn't even mourn in peace without people banging on the bathroom door to make sure I hadn't slit my wrists. Dom would never think that of me. Dom was the only one who knew me."

I couldn't look at her. A few hours ago, I'd been sure Grace was dead. That she'd killed herself. I was one of them. The people who didn't know her soul. Not like him.

"I wasn't depressed. I'm still not depressed. I'm fucking angry."

"I want to tell you about him," she said through softly chattering teeth.

"Grace . . . you don't have to." I couldn't say what I really wanted to say. *Please don't. Dear God, please don't tell me about him. Haven't you broken me enough?*

"I know. But I've been unfair to you. You deserve to know the truth."

"The truth?"

"I met him when I was nine years old. God, there are so many things from your childhood that melt away into a haze, but the day I met him . . . It was early fall, so it was cool, but everything was still green. My dad was already dead and my mom hadn't been home for three days and there was no food left in the house. I called my uncle and he picked me up but he wasn't much better with kids than his sister, so he dumped me with this woman he worked with. Mary. I remember on the car ride over there that he told me she had a son around my age, but I hated boys. They were always mean to me at school, when I went. These weird, foreign creatures, you know?

"Anyway, when we got there, Dom was jumping on a trampoline in the backyard. I remember thinking that he was the most beautiful boy I'd ever seen, which was strange, because I'd never thought of boys that way before. I was this incredibly shy kid, but he wasn't. He jumped straight off the trampoline when he saw me and asked me to come and play *Mario Kart* with him. I'd never played before—I'd never even *seen* a gaming console before—so he had to teach me, but he was super patient and he let me win. It was one of the best days of my childhood. We played video games and then, once the sun had set, we held hands while we watched cartoons on a laptop in his tree house. I loved him. I loved his family. I hadn't known, before them, that people like that even existed. I'd decided, by the end of the night, that I was going to marry him."

I laughed softly despite myself and so did Grace.

"Kids, right?" she said, wiping a tear from her eye. "Except he fell in love with me, too, and instead of fading as we got older, it only got more real. Dom was the first boy I held hands with. The first boy I kissed. My first and only everything, until you."

"I didn't . . . think about that."

"I can't put into words what it is to love someone like that. Or lose someone like that. Which is part of the reason why I don't write anymore. Because words fail. A lot of people say they don't know what they've got until it's gone, but I knew. I knew. I knew every day that we were together that what we had was extraordinary. And I was so afraid, every day, that I would lose him, lose them all. I used to worry so much about his safety, worry that they'd finally get sick of dealing with my messed-up family, but they never did. And I used to question how two people could be so lucky. How could the universe justify bringing us together when we were only nine? How could it ever be fair that what everyone was looking for was handed to us on a silver platter when we were too young to even know that we wanted it?

"I guess, now, I know. All the love that's meant to last a lifetime I spent in the space of eight years. We were supposed to grow up together. Go to college together. Travel the world together. When he died, it felt like my future died with him. Dom wasn't perfect. I mean, I *know* that. He was meticulous about some things and sloppy about others. He picked his fingernails when he was nervous or watching sports, and it used to drive me crazy. Katherine Heigl was his favorite actress and he made me watch all her movies. He liked Carl Sagan way too much. But my God, Henry, his soul was *so* extraordinary. The things he would have done with his life . . . You would've liked him a lot. You would've been friends."

In that moment, I felt the terrible weight of the unfairness of it all. Grace Town did not believe in souls for the rest of humanity, but for Dom, she was willing to make an exception.

"I was in the hospital when they held his funeral," she continued. "They waited for as long as they could, but I was too sick and they had to, you know? So they asked me to write something. Something that someone could read out, like a eulogy, because everyone knew I was a writer and they always told me how beautiful my words were. But I didn't do it. I made out like I was in too much pain and I didn't do it and I haven't written anything since. I don't think I'll be able to write anything again until I *make* myself write it."

"Why didn't you write it?"

"It was my fault. I've never told anyone that before, but it was. It was my fault that we crashed and it's my fault that he died."

"It was nobody's fault. It was an accident."

"That's why I haven't told anyone. Because I know you'll all say the same thing. Survivor's guilt and all that. But I was teasing him. Distracting him. He told me to stop but I didn't, and the next thing I knew, we were in the wrong lane. You know the whole cliché of your life flashing before your eyes the split second before you die?"

"Yeah."

"It's bullshit. I saw the car coming and I felt him swerve and I knew in that fraction of a heartbeat that we were both going to die. And the only thought my brain had time to generate was, *Well, this is shit.* Literally. My last thought could potentially have been a curse word. I didn't think about my life or my family or my friends or even about him. It makes me wonder what he was thinking, you know? Maybe the same thing."

"He was probably thinking about you."

"He didn't die right away. When it was in the news, all the articles said he'd died instantly, on impact, but he didn't. It took a minute. We were there in the car, upside down, both of us bleeding, and he was trying to talk. It wasn't like in the movies. He didn't die whispering 'I love you' or anything like that. He was in pain and he was panicking and he was trying to breathe, but he couldn't. And there was nothing I could do. Nothing I could do except watch him go.

"You know what I did on the day of his funeral? I watched *Cosmos*, the Neil deGrasse Tyson one, in its entirety. Thirteen hours of it. He'd been trying to get me to watch it for months, and I'd kept calling him a nerd for being so into space. It was the only way I knew how to mourn him. To be awed by the universe and remember that even though his consciousness was gone, every single molecule of him was still here." She took my face in her hands and pressed her damp forehead to mine. "I wish you could see the world the way I see the world. See that death is the reward for having lived."

"Please don't talk like that. You scare me when you talk like that."

"I don't mean it in any suicidal sense," she said, and she was whispering even quieter now, like she was telling me a terrible secret. "You know how you sometimes have the most exhausting day and you can't wait to get home and fall into bed and sleep for hours? I feel that way about life. There are people out there who read books about vampires and they crave immortality, but sometimes I'm *so* thankful that at the end of it all, we get to sleep forever. No more pain. No more exhaustion. Death is the reward for having lived."

"We need to get you home," I said, and this time she did not protest. Instead, Grace reached behind her to where a small metal box was sitting on the steps. Inside it was an assortment of things from Dom's shrine: the anchor necklace she'd worn the first day I saw her, the Strokes keychain, the Ramones shirt she hadn't been able to wash. She stood and took my hand and led me back into the pond, her limp barely discernable in the water, where we held hands, our breaths bright white and blooming in the cold, as she released him piece by piece into the depths. The last thing to go was the box itself: DOM GRADE 10 had been scratched into the side. We watched it sink amid a flurry of silver bodies to come to rest on the debris-strewn floor at our feet.

I wondered, as I watched her, if this was what redemption looked like. If this was something like absolution of sin, and now that she'd forgiven herself—if she *had* forgiven herself—if she could move on. But Grace caught me looking at her and said, as though she could read my mind: "Stories with happy endings are just stories that haven't finished yet."

Then she waded through the water and ascended the stairs wearing my jacket and her white dress, the latter of which clung, damp and sheer, to all the curves of her body. She walked out of the train station and up the hill and climbed the hedge and fence barefoot, and when we got to my car, she stripped to her underwear in the street and threw her dress in the gutter.

"I was going to marry him in that," she said flatly, staring at the sopping pile of wet lace. "I'd already said yes." Then, trembling, she got into the car and put on her seat belt and drew her knees to her chest, alive but empty, her hair wreathed in flowers like a walking grave.

We didn't speak on the drive back to her place. I cranked the heat so Grace could warm up, but even though her skin was rashed with goose bumps, she sat perfectly still, a statue of a fallen angel.

All the lights in the house were on when we arrived. Martin and his wife Mary and Grace's mom and two cops were standing on the front lawn. They moved toward the car as I slowed, but Grace shook her head and held up her hand to stop them and they slowed and waited and watched.

Grace turned to me. "I killed their son, and as a reward, they're paying my medical bills and letting me live in their house. That's part of the reason why I can't be with you. I can't . . . spit in their faces like that. I can't watch their son die next to me and then let myself fall in love with someone else a few months later. You understand?" I did understand, sort of, but sort of understanding didn't make it any easier. Would Dom's parents really not want her to move on? Would they really want her to be in so much pain as some sort of sick repayment for what she thought she'd done?

I'd asked her that first night at the abandoned train station what sins she needed absolved, and here was the truth, finally. "You think you deserve to be sad. You think you're working off some kind of cosmic debt by torturing yourself. You think this is your redemption."

"I feel less guilty and less shit about myself when I'm sad than when I'm happy. It's the least I can do for Dom and his parents. Don't you get that? It's the only justice I can offer."

"So you've handed yourself down a prison sentence. For how long? A year? Two years? The rest of your life? How much pain do you have to put yourself through before you've repaid your debt?"

"At least a little bit more."

"Jesus. It wasn't your fault. You didn't kill him. It was an *accident*."

Grace took off her seat belt then and tucked her hair behind her ears and leaned over and kissed me, her almost-bare breasts pressed against my chest. I held her jaw in my hand

and she worked her fingers into my hair, and for a few moments, the world was better, even if it was so fucking broken. But then she pulled away, the way she always did, and looked at me like she was trying to tell me something she couldn't find the words to say.

"Why did you kiss me?" I said to her quietly, because I really, truly didn't understand. "That first night. Why did you kiss me if you knew you'd never be able to let him go?"

"You don't want to know," whispered Grace. "You don't want to know that."

"I do. I have to."

"Because I was drunk and you were there and I missed him." Grace shook her head. "God, how can you still look at me like that after everything I've put you through?" she whispered.

"Because I'm in love with you." There seemed to be no point in hiding it anymore. No shame in saying the words first. It was true. I didn't know the exact point when I'd moved from wanting her to loving her, but I had.

"You don't know what love is, Henry," she said, in the same tone you'd use to tell someone they're an idiot. "You don't even know who I am. You have a teenage crush. That's all."

I didn't say anything. I inhaled deeply and turned my head and stared out the window as Grace gathered her wet shoes and got out of the car wearing nothing but her underwear and my jacket. "Good night," she said, but I only nodded, because I couldn't speak.

Then Martin and Mary and her mom were hugging her and the cops were escorting her inside out of the cold, back into the house where she had to work off her debt to her dead boyfriend's parents, and I was left alone in the dark.

I wondered if she really believed she could make herself and the Sawyers feel better by letting her sorrow infect her, or if she just loved the pain. Loved the grief. I wondered if she let herself feel it in every one of her many billions of atoms because she truly, deeply thought she deserved it.

I messaged my mom to let her know Grace was safe but that I wouldn't be home for a while. Then I drove to the place I'd been avoiding for months now, the place that'd lodged in the back of my mind like a burr but that I hadn't realized I wanted to visit until tonight.

The cemetery wasn't as frightening as I thought it would be. There was no mist, no wolfish howls echoing from the distance, no swooping crows. I walked through the rows of graves quickly at first, jumping at every sound, but eventually I relaxed. I found Dom where I'd seen Grace kneeling a few months earlier. There were still flowers all over his grave, some older, their petals pulled away in the breeze, but fresh ones, too, garlands of them. She'd never stopped coming here. Even when she said she'd try, she never had.

The inscription on his gravestone was simple. The three lines read:

Dominic Henry Sawyer
Aged 17
"If love could have saved you, you would have lived forever."

I traced the letters of his middle name. Henry. We shared so much, Dom and I. A name. A scent. A love. I tried to imagine us as friends, in another life, instead of me being jealous of his bones. But no. Probably not. The love Grace had described was the kind that transcended time and space. In any universe, in any life, it would always be them and I would always be the after. The lesser.

I'd seen a gravestone once where a pair of lovers had been buried in the same plot, fifty-four years apart. For fifty-four years the woman had lived on, alone and heartbroken, waiting for the day she got to join her beloved beneath the dirt.

Would Grace be buried here? In sixty or seventy years, would she come back to this spot and lie with her young, dead boyfriend? Even if she loved again, married, had children, would this be where her body would dissolve back into the universe? Could I handle that? If by some crazy miracle Grace and I did work out, if we went to college together and got married and traveled the world and had kids, would I be able to handle her getting buried with him at the end? How lonely would I be, alone in my grave, the love of my life intertwined with the bones of someone else?

Could I handle being jealous of a dead guy for the rest of my life? And even after my death?

I sat cross-legged on his grave in the dark and picked at the grass, trying to remember—now that I was there—what the hell I'd come to say.

"You absolute dick," I said after a while. It kind of spewed out of me, filled with so much more anger and venom than I expected. "God, she loves you so much, and you went and left her here alone. Do you know how fucking broken she is? I mean, if you're there—if you can hear this—you need to get your ghost ass into gear and go all Patrick Swayze on her right now, because she's hurting like hell and there's nothing . . . there's nothing . . ."

I jammed my eyes closed and took a few deep breaths. It was too cold to cry.

"I can't help her, Dom. I want to help her but I can't because I'm not you. So if you're there—I mean it, for real, I don't care about any ghost code and the natural order of things and all that shit—if you're there, you need to show yourself right now. This is a corporeal realm emergency. Get your cowardly, haunted ass out of that headstone and tell me why the hell you left her."

I waited for over an hour in the dark, until my eyes had adjusted to the deep blackness and my ribs were shivering. Ghost Dom never showed. Zombie Dom never rose from the dead.

"Well, screw you too," I said as I stood up to leave. I walked home in the cold instead of driving, determined to prove to myself—just like Grace was—that feeling pain meant I was somehow, in some way, doing something right.

CHAPTER 25

WHEN I WOKE up in the morning, Grace was the first thing I thought about, this involuntary, gut-wrenching ache that spasmed from my brain into my chest. Grace, and the newspaper, and sucking at English and math because I couldn't make myself care, and how any colleges that might've taken me would see my first semester grades and stamp my application with a big OH HELL NO because I'd screwed everything up, let everything slip so far, and for what? For what?

Mom and Dad, unsurprisingly, chose that Saturday to start doing the concerned-parent routine they hadn't had to do since Sadie left for Yale. They came downstairs not long after sunrise and started lurking around the basement, assessing the damage I'd done to my life. They opened the curtains. Made me get out of bed and out of my pajamas. Put a bowl of cereal in front of me and refused to stop singing "Baby Got Back" until I agreed to eat it, which I did, because *God*.

Under their watchful eyes, I vacuumed the carpets, washed

my clothes, tidied my bookshelves, and transported all my schoolwork upstairs to the kitchen table so they could continue to supervise me while I caught up on the last couple of weeks of Hotchkiss's demonic math problems and the English essay I felt too empty to bullshit my way through. At eleven o'clock, Mom made me go for a jog with her. At lunchtime, Dad made me eat again. Sadie had the day off and came over at around two o'clock, by which point my request for a nap had been granted and I was lying spread-eagle on my bed.

"Hey, Henry, have you seen . . . Are you listening to Taylor Swift?" said Suds from the foot of the stairs.

"Yes, Sadie. This is the second straight hour I've been listening to Taylor Swift. She's the only one who understands me."

"Oh God."

"Who hurt you, Taylor?!" I yelled, gesturing at the ceiling. "How can one person endure so much heartbreak?!"

"Good lord. Scooch. It's time for a chat."

"Suds . . . I really don't want to talk about it. I'm not good at sharing."

"I'm your sister, douche canoe. You don't talk to your friends, you don't talk to your parents. Are you gonna keep all this bottled up inside until it manifests as mental illness?"

"That's pretty much the plan."

"How long have you been lying in that bed for, anyway? You're going to get deep vein thrombosis."

"Leave, Sadie. Leave me to my heartache and my DVT."

Sadie ignored my protests and flopped down on my bed

on top of my rib cage, winding me in the process. Then she poked my cheek over and over again in the same spot, saying, "Speak, speak, speak," until I eventually spoke and said, "Ugh, fine, you wretched woman. It's . . . Grace, and I . . . I don't know what's going on."

"I gathered that from the Taylor Swift marathon." Sadie waited for me to continue. "Care to elaborate?"

"I'm just . . . so confused by it all. And I think I've done some kind of permanent damage to my respiratory system. My chest is tight, like, all the time."

"That's probably the ribs I cracked when I jumped you."

"Is love supposed to feel like this?"

"No, it's not, kid. I don't know about the whole 'love lifts us up where we belong' crap, but it isn't supposed to screw you up either."

"I know. I mean, look at Mom and Dad."

"Mom and Dad are a fairy tale. They don't exist."

"You loved Chris, though."

Sadie took a deep breath. "Yeah. I did. And I mean sometimes I used to wake up in the morning and he'd be lying there with his slack jaw drooling on the pillow and I'd think, *What the hell was I thinking when I procreated with him?* He wasn't perfect. He wasn't even perfect for *me*. It was hard, all the time. But I did love him. And it was worth it. While it lasted."

"So you never thought he was your soul mate?"

"Oh, honey. Are we still believing in soul mates?"

"You *don't* believe in soul mates? How can you look at

Mom and Dad and not believe that two people are made for each other?"

"Jesus, they've really screwed up your perspective on the world, haven't they? They thought being deceptive would protect you, but all it's done is spoon-feed you a fantasy. They're practically cult leaders. They've brainwashed you."

"What do you mean?"

"Henry . . . sweetheart . . ."

"Why are you being such a weirdo?"

"Oh boy." Sadie closed her eyes and bit her bottom lip. "Before you were born, Mom left Dad for, like, three months," she said quickly, her eyes still jammed shut.

I blinked a handful of times. Sadie opened her eyes slowly, one at a time.

"Mom made me promise not to tell you until after you'd graduated college. They wanted you to have a 'stable childhood.' But I can't let you walk around for the next half decade looking for something that doesn't exist. I mean, why do you think I had my twelfth birthday party in a trailer park playground?"

"I never really closely studied the photographs of your twelfth birthday party."

"They've poisoned you with this 'love is patient, love is kind' bullshit since you were a kid. But love is scientific, man. I mean, it's really just a chemical reaction in the brain. Sometimes that reaction lasts a lifetime, repeating itself over and over again. And sometimes it doesn't. Sometimes it goes supernova and then starts to fade. We're all just chemical hearts. Does that make love any less brilliant? I don't think so. That's why I don't get why people always say 'fifty percent of marriages end in divorce' as a justification to not get married. Just because a love ends doesn't mean it wasn't real. Mom and Dad were fighting all the time. I know you've never seen them have so much as a disagreement, but they were really going for each other. Then one night, Mom woke me up and helped me pack a bag and that was it. I didn't get to see my bedroom again until we moved back in three months later."

"Do you know why she left?"

"Because she'd fallen out of love with him. The chemical reaction receded. That's why. That's all. Love is never perfect, Henry."

"Why'd they get back together?"

"Mom found out she was pregnant."

"She came back because of *me*?"

"I don't know. Maybe. Probably. They love each other unconditionally and they're best friends, but they're not *in love* anymore. They haven't been for a long time. So you can't go around thinking that every person you fall for is 'The One.' People don't *have* soul mates. People *make* their soul mates."

"I know that. I *do* know that. It's just . . . I can't imagine ever wanting to put that much effort into another human being again. So much time and energy. So much of myself. How do you start over with someone new?"

"How does a novelist start a new book when the last one is

finished? How does an injured athlete start training again from the beginning?"

"God. Why does anyone do this more than once?"

"Fall in love?"

I nodded.

Sadie chuckled. "Biologically speaking? For the continuation of the human race. Logically speaking? Because the journey is beautiful in the beginning. And no one can see the bend in the train tracks until it's already too late to stop. And when you board the train—"

"Really chugging along with this train metaphor, huh?"

"Shh, it's too late to get off the tracks now. When you board the train, you hope that this will be the one that doesn't crash. Even though it might be, even though it probably *will* be, it's worth getting on anyway, just to find out."

"Why can't I stay at the station?"

"You could. But then you'd never get anywhere."

"Oh wow. That's deep."

"I should have been a philosopher."

"I want her back, Sadie."

"I know you want her back, kid. And I know that people saying things like 'there are plenty more fish in the sea' is only going to make you hurt more. And I could tell you all about the science of what your brain is going through right now. How it's processing a pain as intense as hitting a nerve in your tooth, but it can't find a source for that pain, so you kind of feel it everywhere. I could tell you that when you fall for someone, the bits of your brain that light up are the same as when you're hungry or thirsty. And I could tell you that when the person you love leaves you, you starve for them, you crave them, you have withdrawals from them, like an addict would from a drug. And I know this all sounds very poetic, or exaggerated, or dramatic, but it's not. Heartbreak is a science, like love. So trust me when I say this: you're wounded right now, but you'll heal."

"Damn, Suds. You're bringing out the big guns today."

Sadie tilted her head back and fluttered her eyelids. "You're making me cry, you rascal. Listen to me, spouting all this good advice. Have you ever really been happy with her? Because from the outside, this has looked like a struggle from day one. The dead boyfriend, the disappearing. Is there a full month or week or day that you can look back on where you're like, 'Yep, that's it for me. That's what I want my life to be like. Take me back to those good old days.' Do you have that with her?"

I shut my eyes and thought. I tried to remember a period of more than a few hours that I'd been truly happy with Grace. I remembered anxiety, stress, pain, sadness, the acid from my stomach eating away at my lungs. I remembered loving her, desperately. There was the night we walked home together from the movies, hand in hand, when I'd been sure I was going to marry her. There was the Thanksgiving fair, only the second time I'd seen her wear clothes that didn't belong to Dom. Brief, bright flashes of happiness, no more than lightning strikes in the dark.

I opened my eyes. "Oh, shit," I said quietly.

"That's what I thought."

"I don't know if I can accept that it was all a waste of time, though. That all this pain was for nothing. That what we had was never real."

Sadie flicked my temple. "Aren't you listening, doofus? Love doesn't need to last a lifetime for it to be real. You can't judge the quality of a love by the length of time it lasts. Everything dies, love included. Sometimes it dies with a person, sometimes it dies on its own. The greatest love story ever told doesn't have to be about two people who spent their whole lives together. It might be about a love that lasted two weeks or two months or two years, but burned brighter and hotter and more brilliantly than any other love before or after. Don't mourn a failed love; there's no such thing. All love is equal in the brain."

"Doesn't stop it from hurting."

Sadie smudged a tear from the corner of my eye and ran her fingers through my hair. "I know, kid. Sometimes shit just doesn't work out, you know? Plus, how can she be your soul mate? Didn't you tell me she'd never read Harry Potter? Do you really want to spend the rest of your life with someone like that? I mean, for God's sake, think of your children. What kind of environment would they be growing up in with such a mother?"

I laughed then and Sadie laughed and I closed my eyes and hugged her.

She stayed curled up with me, stroking my hair, the way we'd always done for as long as I could remember.

As I stared at the ceiling with Sadie humming Taylor Swift songs into my skin, I thought of Grace and felt the root canal pain Sadie had talked about ping through my entire body. We had a heavy love, Grace and I, the type of love that would drown you if you waded into it too deep. It was a love that tied little sinkers to your heart one at a time, until the organ was so heavy, it ripped right out of your chest.

"Suds . . . I know it's been a long time since you've been a juvenile delinquent, but do you still remember how to break into the English department at school?"

Sadie grinned her wicked grin. "Old habits die hard."

CHAPTER 26

IT WAS LATE AFTERNOON when I committed breaking and entering for the fifth time in my life. School on the weekend felt like being aboard the *Mary Celeste*—there was the sense that people had been here recently, but that some uncanny tragedy (i.e., exams) had befallen them, driven them away from this place. It was dim and quiet, and even in the parking lot, our footfalls cast up eerie echoes all around us.

"Are you sure this is a good idea?" Lola said as we scaled the outer fence. Ryan was clinging to Sadie's neck like a baby monkey and giggling like this was the best adventure ever. "Nobody's gonna come."

"They'll come," I said. "Somebody will come."

Earlier that week, Heslin had finally been ungrounded for throwing The Party a few months earlier, so naturally a rumor had begun circulating that another party of equal or greater proportions was in store for tonight. Heslin's parents, either idiots or far too trusting of their delinquent son, had gone away and left him in charge of the house. Sure enough, by that very afternoon, there was a Facebook event with some three hundred students attending—excluding me, excluding Lola, excluding Murray. Excluding—surprisingly—Madison Carlson.

We had shit to do.

An hour ago, I'd made a post in Heslin's event. *To all those seeking redemption,* it began, and it ended with a plea to please, for the love of all that was holy, help us save the *Westland Post* from certain destruction. Twenty-five people had liked it so far.

"They'll come," I muttered again as we made our way across the grounds toward Hink's office. They had to.

The locks, it turns out, had been upgraded since Sadie's years as a teenage, prank-pulling delinquent, as had—unbeknownst to us—the video surveillance. So while Sadie knelt at the door trying to pick the lock and Lola and I took turns giving Ryan piggyback rides, none of us spotted the burly security guard jogging toward us.

"Freeze, all of you!" he said.

I caught the momentary flicker in Sadie's eyes as she considered making a run for it but didn't—probably something to do with the fact that her son was still clinging to my back and it'd be less than stellar parenting to abandon him.

So I froze. And Lola froze. And Sadie froze.

It doesn't matter, I thought, over and over again. *It doesn't matter, it doesn't matter, it doesn't matter.* It didn't matter that the newspaper wouldn't go to print, that I'd singlehandedly destroyed a thirty-five-year-old school tradition, that I'd let Hink down at every opportunity. It didn't matter that the three of us would probably be arrested and charged with breaking and entering, that Lola and I wouldn't get into college because of our criminal records, that Sadie would lose her job. It didn't matter—the sun would swallow the Earth and everything we did here didn't matter, shouldn't matter—but it did.

It did.

Grace was wrong, I realized in the half heartbeat of time it took for the wheezy security guard to grab my arm, even though I made no attempt to run. On a grand scale, entropy ruled, but humans were so small that the largest laws of the universe didn't apply to us. They couldn't apply to us. We were too tiny; our lives passed too quickly. None of us would be there for our great cosmic redemption when the sun expanded and ate the Earth and gave all our atoms back to the cosmos. None of us could wait that long.

Regenerative chaos: things fall apart and then come back together and we move on. We had to absolve our own sins. We had to redeem ourselves.

Sadie stood from where she'd been kneeling and turned around and—quite unexpectedly—grinned. "Jim!" she shouted when she saw the guard's face. "No freakin' way! It's Sadie Page, man, remember me?"

"*You,*" said Jim, tightening his pincer grip on my arm. Uh-oh. "They promised me you were gone for good."

"Oh, Jim," said Sadie as she clapped him on the back and pried his fingers from my skin and led him to one of the benches that lined the building. "We've got some catching up to do." And that's how, ten minutes later—after slipping him a fifty-dollar bill and offering to make him coffee in the teachers' lounge if he didn't rat us out—Sadie convinced Jim Jenkins, long-suffering security guard of Westland High, to grant us unlimited access to the English department and, with it, the newspaper office.

Ricky Martin Knupps II was swimming lazily in his bowl as the afternoon sun slanted through the blinds and turned the air into a swirling constellation of gold particles. The room still smelled of her—of us—but the scent had faded over the past week, the evidence of it slowly coming unstuck from the furniture and stacks of white paper and books and computer screens. Soon, it'd be as though we'd never been there at all.

Lola sat at the Mac and got to designing the cover while I sifted through the poorly punctuated articles the juniors had submitted throughout the term, looking for anything that could be salvaged, anything that fit the theme. We worked in silence as we waited.

Fifteen minutes after we broke into the school, the volunteers started to arrive.

If you think the whole grade showed up, then you don't know much about the apathy of teenagers. We can be roused, on occasion, like when a classmate's parent dies or one of us makes it onto *America's Next Top Model*. But failing newspapers don't exactly inspire *Braveheart* levels of loyalty.

Still, seven people showed up in the end, which was seven more than I was expecting (or deserved). All of them prefaced their presence with "I actually can't write, but . . ." To which I explained that I truly, honestly, deeply did not give a shit. I'd already known that Muz and Maddy (as Madison Carlson had instructed me to call her—bizarre) would show, but Suki Perkins-Mugnai, Buck, Chance Osenberg and Billy Costa (of "the Trichomoniasis Trio" fame), and Heslin himself were a bonus. All of them, plus Galaxy and the three other juniors whom I'd sworn to personally murder if they didn't come and help out, made for a motley crew of fourteen.

Fourteen people to do three months of work in two days. How hard could it be?

Sadie helped us lay out an assortment of snacks (the promised payment in the Facebook post) and then Lola and I took our places on the sex couch while everyone sat cross-legged on the office floor, eating Kit Kats and drinking Mountain Dew.

"The theme, as you might've guessed from my Facebook post, is going to be 'redemption,'" I said.

"As in . . . *Shawshank*?" said Suki Perkins-Mugnai.

"That's a shit theme, mate," said Murray. "I still vote for 'species dysmorphia.'"

"Is it really shit, though? Every high schooler wants redemption for something. Suki, I want redemption for that terrible touch football game. La, you should probably want redemption for murdering Ricky Martin Knupps. Chance and Billy, well . . . I mean, you know."

"Um, I thought we agreed to drop the charges to involuntary manslaughter?" Lola said. "As if I don't feel bad enough about it already."

"Look, not everyone can write, but everyone has a story to tell, and everyone wants to be absolved of some sin. I don't care if you write an acrostic poem, or draw a cartoon, or compose a score. Just give me something. Some sort of redemption."

Then I put on my Spotify playlist (no Strokes, no Pixies) and we got to work.

Heslin left around three hours later to supervise (read: get hammered at) his party, but not before writing a soliloquy about how he'd finally redeemed himself in the eyes of his parents for the last party. Suki Perkins-Mugnai left not long after. She wrote two pieces—one, an article about the Gutcrushers, the other a poem about how she hadn't called her granddad before he died because she thought she had more time, so much more time, and he'd used up his last breaths asking for her. Chance Osenberg and Billy Costa didn't want to immortalize the Trichomoniasis Trio in print, but Chance had begged his dad for a new phone right after his parents had gotten a divorce, even though he knew he couldn't afford it, so he wrote a short story about that.

"I was thirteen," said Chance as he emailed it to me. "I was a dick."

Billy wrote about getting so drunk the first time he met his girlfriend's parents that he vomited in their bed. Murray drew a cartoon about dropbears, a thinly veiled metaphor for how much he missed his family in Australia. Madison wrote about losing her puppy when she was a kid, how she still couldn't remember if she'd left the gate unlocked or not. Lola wrote a haiku about "the weenus" in penance for convincing her mother that that's what elbow skin was called, and dedicated a whole double-page spread to the memory of Ricky Martin Knupps, forever swimming in the toxic murder castle in the sky. The juniors wrote about people they'd bullied in middle school, how they felt bad for disappointing their parents, the times they'd made their siblings cry.

Due to the fact that he was largely illiterate, Buck wrote nothing, but he could freehand even better than Lola, so she assigned him to help her with the interior artwork. Until two a.m. he sketched watches and dogs and dead fish and a particularly gruesome anatomical rendering of Billy's left elbow's weenus, before he, too, had to go home.

At three a.m., after two pizza deliveries (courtesy of Sadie) and several trips to the closest 7-Eleven for a grand total of four bottles of Dr Pepper, a carton of Red Bull, seven corn dog rollers, and a backpack full of candy, we finally decided to call it a night.

Murray and Madison Carlson had fallen asleep together on the fake linoleum floor of the hallway. Murray's jacket rolled up under Madison's head, Madison's hand pressed against Murray's chest, very little space between them. An interesting development.

Sadie had crashed on the couch with Ryan swaddled at her chest, the both of them resting slack-jawed as their eyes darted from side to side beneath their thin lids.

"Suds," I whispered as I poked her in the shoulder. "Time to go home."

"I set the home economics kitchen on fire on purpose," said Sadie sleepily as she sat up, Ryan still pressed to her chest, her slender fingers supporting his head. "That's what I'd want redemption for. From my teenage years, anyway."

"Not for all the sex, drugs, and rock 'n' roll?" La said as she stretched on her office chair. She looked how I felt: like 90 percent of my blood had been replaced with high fructose corn syrup, caffeine, and cement dust.

"Oh hell no. I don't want redemption for that. I don't *need* redemption for that. The only thing that ever felt wrong was the fire. I don't think Hotchkiss was ever the same."

"*Mr. Hotchkiss* was your home ec teacher?" I said.

"Yeah. Dude loves baking. Like, does it as an actual hobby. But then one day I made these lemon curd cupcakes—you know the ones, Henry—and he gave me an A for them, but I was in a real 'fuck the patriarchy' mood and was pissed that Family and Consumer Sciences even existed as a subject, it's the twenty-first goddamn century, you know . . . so I kind of . . . set the kitchen on fire." Sadie yawned. "It was the worst thing I did as a teenager. The goddamn worst. I think I saw Hotchkiss's heart break while he tried to fight the flames."

"We have spare pages," Lola said, grabbing a pen and paper and pushing them toward Sadie. "I want to do a spread of handwritten confessions."

Sadie eyed the writing utensils. "What's the statute of limitations for arson?" she said, but she didn't wait for us to Google the answer before she started writing. Ryan woke as she leaned forward.

"Hi, Mama," he said, touching her face.

"Hey, baby," she said as she handed the slip of paper back to Lola. "Ready to blow this Popsicle stand?"

Ryan nodded. While Lola and I turned off the lights, they went and waited hand in hand in the dimly lit hall, the both of them chatting quietly about all the things they were going to do tomorrow. Zoo in the morning. Lunch at the park. A sleepover with Daddy while Mommy went to work.

And I thought, as I watched them, about Grace's accusation the night she'd been drunk at the fair. That I didn't love the real her, just an idea that didn't exist anymore, a shadow of who she really was.

I'd loved the legend of Sadie when I was a kid. I'd loved the folklore that murmured around her like fireflies wherever she went. I still did. But I loved this version—the one that saved people's lives, the one that looked at her tiny son like he was made of bright diamonds, pancakes in bed on Sunday morning, and a thunderstorm after a seven-year drought—even more.

Maybe it was possible to love two different versions of someone at the same time. And maybe, just maybe, some people still wanted redemption for sins they didn't need absolved anymore.

Sunday was grueling. I met Lola outside my house at seven a.m., the streetlights burning brighter than the watercolor sunrise. She pushed a large coffee into my gloved hands and said, "Do not speak to me for two hours," so I didn't.

We met Jim Jenkins outside Hink's office. We sat down. Turned on the computers. Tried not to die. Died a lot. My eyes had apparently lost the ability to produce their own moisture, so I spent the morning alternating between abusing my digestive system with mass amounts of Red Bull and rubbing my eyes red raw.

When La was finally ready for human interaction, the first thing she did was show me the cover: a picture of a girl in black and white, a grayscale universe behind her, an exploding supernova where her head should be. It looked like an old penny dreadful novel. Even with THE WESTLAND REDEMPTION splashed across the image in orange letters, I could still tell that the girl had been traced from Grace, a ghostly imitation of her true form.

"I still had photos left over from the shoot you guys did for me. I can use a different model, find someone on Flickr, if you want."

"It's perfect," I told her. "Print it out, tabloid-sized. Let's stick it up and let everyone see."

So we did. And they did. The juniors arrived at ten a.m., Buck not long after. And then—curiously—two girls who'd been at Heslin's party the night before. He'd told them what we were doing here, encouraged them to drop by. Most of the pages were filled by now, except for Lola's spread of hand-written confessions, which the girls—in their deeply hungover state—thought was a great idea.

They wrote down their sins. They gave them to us. We assured them they would be absolved.

And then another person came. And then another. And then two more. After the eighth person, Lola made a sign that read *Confess your sins for absolution* and stuck it above a drop box in the hall. Murray got wind of the situation and turned up at lunchtime in a priest costume, complete with holy water, and then proceeded to sit by our makeshift confessional, greeting each wayward soul that came our way. We watched our classmates and friends and strangers from other grades come and go throughout the day as news of what we were doing spread on Facebook.

At five p.m. I asked Lola: "How are we doing for pages?"

She said: "We now only have one spare page."

I said: "Shit, what are we going to do with that?"

She rolled her eyes and said: "It's for your redemption, dingbat."

I said: "Oh."

And then I looked up at the supernova girl printed in black and white and thought about how, in retrospect, you can see that something is poison from the beginning. Grace had torn me apart and put me back together so many times that I'd started to believe that was what I wanted. A Kintsukuroi relationship, more beautiful for having been broken. But something can only be shattered so many times before it becomes irreparable, just as a piece of paper can only be folded so many times before it cannot be folded any more.

While I sat there, that root canal pain sparking through my body, phrases like *I wish I'd never met her* and *I wish she'd never kissed me* started to cascade through my thoughts. I might've—had it been a viable option at that moment—gone all *Eternal Sunshine of the Spotless Mind* on her. Bleached her out of my memory. Ripped her from where she'd stitched herself into the lining of my soul.

But I thought, again, of Kintsukuroi. That something must first be shattered for it to be put back together in a way that made it more beautiful than before. I thought of how I liked broken things, things that were blemished or dented or cracked, and why that was probably why I fell for Grace in the first place. She was a broken thing in human form, and now—because of her—I was too.

Grace might always be broken, but I hoped that all my shattered pieces could be glued back together and mended with gold seams. That the tears in my heart would heal into scars that would glisten.

And that's when my phone vibrated in my pocket.

I'm outside Hink's office.

Why?

Lola told me about the theme. I have something I want to put in the newspaper.

"You are a demon," I said to La as I stood, my heart stripped and swollen inside my throat.

To which she replied, "In the sack!"

As I stepped out into the pale-pink-and-lemon-colored nightmare that was the hall, I hoped terrible things for Grace Town in spite of myself. I hoped that she would regret this decision for the rest of her life. That it would pierce her like a hot skewer until the day she died. I imagined her old and thin, her skin draped across her bones like damp paper. I saw her draw her final breath, a look of regret in her eyes for the life she could've had with me, and I felt vindicated.

And in that moment I wanted things for myself that I'd never wanted before. I wanted to be rich. I wanted to be famous. I wanted to marry a supermodel and screw her lingerie-clad body every night. I wanted every achievement of my life to stand in testament as a grand "fuck you" to Grace Town. I wanted to destroy her with my extraordinariness.

But by the time I'd reached the end of the hallway, some of the acid had washed away. *Why is it,* I thought, *that we're so willing to hurt the ones we care about the most?* Two days ago I loved her, and now I wanted to carve away pieces of her soul. Why was that? Because she'd hurt me? Because she didn't love me back?

You can't begrudge people their feelings. Grace had done what was right by her. I couldn't ask for more than that.

She was sitting on the seat where we'd waited the afternoon we'd been called to Hink's office. A beginning and an end, all in one place. "Henrik," she said quietly, motioning to the space next to her, the spot where I'd folded my body awkwardly because of her presence. "I wanted to give you something."

"I can't, Grace. I can't do this anymore."

"I know. I know. Trust me: this is the end."

In a normal conversation, this would be the point that she would've apologized for ripping my heart out of my chest. But Grace was not a normal girl and she didn't understand that the word *sorry* was sometimes enough. Instead, she handed me a small envelope with *For the consideration of the editor* written across the front and said, "You asked me, the day we started at the newspaper, why I'd changed my mind. I never answered you, but I should've, because I already knew."

"Okay."

"Every day since the day he died, all I thought about was him. For the first few weeks after the accident, I expected the grief. I let myself feel every inch of it. I'd lost people I loved before. Almost everyone. I knew how grief worked. The only thing that numbs the pain is time, filling up your head with new memories, driving a wedge between yourself and the tragedy. I waited for things to get easier. I waited for the replays of our happiest days together to stop. I waited for my breath to stop catching in my chest whenever a thunderclap of misery would roll through me.

"But it never got easier. After a while I realized it was because I didn't *want* it to. I carried him with me heavily, and it exhausted me, but I did it because I deserved it. I deserved the weight of him, and the pain, and when his parents' grief was too heavy, I carried some of theirs too.

"And then I met you.

"The first afternoon we talked, I didn't think about him for twenty minutes. I know it doesn't seem like a lot, but it was a record for me, and I felt so light and buoyant afterward. I slept for four hours that night without waking up once. And I knew it was because of you. I don't know how, or why, but when I was with you, you made the grief go away."

"But that still isn't enough."

"Oh, Henry," she said, shuffling closer and taking my cheek in her hand. I closed my eyes at the gentleness of her touch and then her lips were moving against mine, impossibly soft.

"Why do you kiss me like that?" I said when it was over.

"Like what?" she said, pulling back from me slightly.

"Like you're in love with me."

Grace looked from my eyes to my lips and then back again. "It's the only way I know how."

Because Dom had been her first and only everything, before me. When she'd first learned to kiss, it had been with the great love of her life.

And it took until that moment for me to realize, finally, that I was a blip in someone else's love story. That there was a grand love going on here, but it wasn't my own, as I'd hoped; I was a side character in the peripheries, a plot device to keep the main characters apart. That if this were *The Notebook* and Dom were still alive, he would be Allie, Grace would be Noah, and I would be the redheaded chick whose name I can't remember, the one who gets shafted and has to pretend like it's no big deal.

I wasn't just her second choice, which I'd convinced myself I could live with: I was a cameo, a walk-on role, a guest star, and it killed me that it had taken me this long to realize it.

And my first immediate thought, because I'm an idiot, was how much I'd make her work if she decided she wanted me back. That a month from now or a year from now or a decade from now, Grace Town would walk back into my life after paying off her debt to her dead boyfriend, after feeling all the pain his death deserved, and I'd make her chase me the way I'd chased her. She'd come to my house in the middle of a thunderstorm with a boom box held over her head, and I'd finally get to see her sopping wet, drenched in rain, the way

I'd wanted to from the beginning. And she'd fling herself into my arms and, my God, it would be so grand.

But as I watched her watch me, I knew it would never happen. As I looked at her looking into my eyes, I realized how very little I knew about her. All the things I'd been desperate to ask her about, to know about her—her childhood, her mom, her future—I'd never gotten around to asking.

Grace waited for me to speak, but I didn't, because everything there was to say had already been said a hundred times before, and I was tired, so tired, of saying the same things over and over again and them making no difference. So she put her hands on top of her head and exhaled loudly. And then she did something I wasn't expecting. Grace Town smiled. It was a smile that stretched across her whole face, crinkled the corners of her eyes. The sunlight caught her irises and made them almost crystal clear and my heart trembled at how achingly beautiful she was and how much I hated her for not being mine.

"You're an extraordinary collection of atoms, Henry Page," she said, and her smile stretched wider and she laughed that silent laugh that's more of an exhale through the nose than anything else. Then she put her arms down by her side and pursed her lips and nodded once, her smile entirely faded.

And as I watched her stand and leave—again, again, again—I finally understood that I loved a multiverse of Graces.

The flesh-and-blood her, the version of her that still wore

Dom's unwashed clothes and slept in unwashed sheets and ran on her injured leg to make sure it didn't heal too quickly. A tithe of guilt paid in pain. The only justice she could offer him; the only redemption she could offer herself.

The version she'd been, the ethereal creature that now existed only in photographs and half-remembered fantasies.

And the Kintsukuroi dream girl, stitched together with gold seams. The version that was clean and whole and dressed in floral, backlit by the setting sun. The version that hummed the Pixies and the Strokes as we slow danced together under string lights. The one I helped put back together.

A multiverse bound up in the skin of a single girl.

I opened her contribution to the *Post*. It was a piece of paper that'd been torn into little pieces and stuck back together with a patchwork of clear tape on the back. All the little jagged scars that broke up the text had been gone over with gold ink. Pablo Neruda's poem, Kintsukuroi in paper form. Lola must've given it back to Grace, bless her. La. A devil and an angel in one. The title, "I do not love you," had been circled in gold, which I expected to hurt like hell, but it didn't. So I read it again, for the last time.

> *I love you as certain dark things are to be loved,*
> *in secret, between the shadow and the soul.*

I can't lie to you and tell you that standing in front of someone and offering them your soul and having them reject you is not gonna be one of the worst things that ever happens to you. You will wonder for days or weeks or months or years afterward what it is about you that was so wrong or broken or ugly that they couldn't love you the way you loved them. You will look for all the reasons inside yourself that they didn't want you and you will find a million.

Maybe it was the way you looked in the mornings when you first woke up and hadn't showered. Maybe it was the way you were too available, because despite what everyone says, playing hard to get is still attractive.

Some days you will believe that every atom of your being is defective somehow. What you need to remember, as I remembered as I watched Grace Town leave, is that you are extraordinary.

Grace Town was a chemical explosion inside my heart. She was a star that'd gone supernova. For a few fleeting moments there was light and heat and pain, brighter than a galaxy, and in her wake she left nothing but darkness. But the death of stars provides the building blocks of life. We're all made of star stuff. We're all made of Grace Town.

"My redemption," I said to Lola as I slipped her the envelope from Grace.

She opened it. She read it. She grinned.

CHAPTER 27

THE REMAINDER OF the semester went like this: One week later, when I woke up in the morning, Grace Town was not the first thing I thought about when I opened my eyes, but the second. I don't remember what the first thing was exactly, only that she hadn't been it. She didn't split through me like lightning, searing my veins. The infection had begun to clear. The wound was healing.

I knew then that I would survive.

And I did.

If you thought *The Westland Redemption* turned out to be a resounding success, then you haven't been paying attention. The document that went to the printer (two hours early, might I add) was somewhere between *catastrophe* and *disaster* on the Shit-o-Meter. It was the Frankenstein's monster of student publications, which—to be honest—aren't exactly known for their style and clarity in the first place.

It was clearly assembled by a dozen or so people who had

differing ideas of what the end product should look like. Buck's hand-drawn sketches clashed with Lola's sleek design, and I hadn't had enough time to edit all the juniors' copy, so most of their work read like postmodern interpretations of classical grammar at best. But it was big, and it was bold, and its orange, black, and white color scheme was eye-catching, and the drawings were beautiful, and the confessions were funny and stupid and heartbreaking, and Lola had organized it all in such a way that, yes, the more I looked at it, yes, it was actually pretty damn good. Yes, there was real redemption there.

Hink didn't even know we'd made our deadline until I approved the proofs four days later. Once he found out, he proceeded to flip the eff out because we'd violated every rule in the charter. Turns out almost all the sins teenagers want absolved involve sex, drugs, and rock 'n' roll, and Lola and I had to petition the PTA to hold a vote on whether the newspaper could even be released.

The deciding vote ended up coming down to Mr. Hotchkiss. Luckily, a container of lemon curd cupcakes had appeared on his desk two hours before the hearing and put him in an abnormally good mood. He voted in our favor, and kept a framed copy of Sadie's handwritten apology on his desk for the remainder of senior year.

The Westland Redemption was distributed the next day, at which point it proceeded to blow Kyle's legacy out of the water, by which I mean at least 60 percent of the student body picked up a copy. A 15 percent spike in circulation—enough to convince Hink and Valentine that, despite my wantonness, I'd redeemed myself enough to remain in charge of the newspaper for at least one more issue.

When Lola and Georgia broke up without warning or explanation, Murray and I dragged her kicking and screaming through the pain, just as she'd dragged us. We made her sing Christmas carols and drink eggnog. We made her put on a hat and scarf and gloves and drive with us (and Maddy) to the mall to get our picture with Santa. We made her watch *The Nightmare Before Christmas* on Christmas Eve, her small body wedged between ours under the covers of my bed. We made her better. Not quickly. Not by a long shot. But we helped.

After Christmas, my parents announced that they'd decided to take separate vacations. One to Canada, the other to Mexico, but this time there was no unwanted pregnancy at the end to bring them back together. When he returned home, Dad packed his things . . . and moved all the way into his carpentry workshop in the backyard. They still ate breakfast together every morning.

And gradually, as her tithe was paid, the gold seams in Grace Town began to appear. After Christmas break, her limp grew less noticeable, until she stopped walking with her cane altogether. She started driving to school. Sometimes she'd wear a piece of Dom's clothing: a knit cap, a necklace, a jacket. But mostly, she wore her own things. Slowly, as she worked off her imagined debt, she let herself be redeemed. Justice had been served.

We came unstuck from each other's lives. We deleted each other off Facebook and Instagram and Snapchat. We signed custody of Ricky Martin Knupps II over to Ryan, who renamed him "Fish Fish" and loved him more than we ever could. All the ties that had connected us slowly snapped and healed, until we were separate entities once more. Until I remembered her only when an ache of longing throbbed through me: on New Year's Eve when the fireworks went off, when I watched movies by myself in the dark, but mostly when I woke up in the morning and she wasn't there.

And all the while I loved her, just as she loved him.

In secret, between the shadow and the soul.

NOTES

THE VERY CORE of this book was born from the July 11, 2014, Nerve article by Drake Baer called "This Is Your Brain on a Break Up." In particular, the interview with Lucy Brown, a neuroscientist at Yeshiva University, directly inspired Sadie and her career.

Grace's fishpond in the abandoned train station wouldn't exist without the November 30, 2013, *Renegade Travels* article "Exotic Fish Take Over Abandoned Bangkok Mall Basement." The station itself is loosely based on a beautiful, ghostly, disused one in Sydney, which I totally never ever broke into.

"I have loved the stars too fondly to be fearful of the night," which Henry references in Chapter 7, is a quote from "The Old Astronomer" by Sarah Williams.

The comedy sketch starring Ricky Gervais and Liam Neeson mentioned in Chapter 9 is from "Episode One" of BBC Two's *Life's Too Short*.

Henry's PowerPoint is based on several hilarious and persuasive examples from Tumblr ("Why You Should Let Me Touch Your Butt," "Why You Should Let Me Touch Your Boobs," etc.). However, it draws most heavily from one called "Why We Should Do Sex Things," which I first saw on Imgur; I can claim very little of its brilliance. To the anonymous girl who wrote the original: I sincerely hope it got you laid.

The line that Henry's father says about Grace in Chapter 17—"Strangeness is a necessary ingredient in beauty"—is a quote by Charles Baudelaire.

I don't know who originally wrote "Stories with happy endings are just stories that haven't finished yet," but I first heard a version of it in *Mr. & Mrs. Smith*.

"If love could've saved you, you would have lived forever," the inscription on Dom's grave, is, as best I can tell, by no author I can easily identify.

"If you were a carrot, you'd be a good carrot" and "Purple, because aliens don't wear hats" are ripped straight from the glorious cesspit that is the internet, as are, I'm sure, a dozen other offhand pop culture references I've failed to properly attribute here (my references are out of control).

Please don't hold my wantonness against me.

WITH THANKS

TO MY AGENT, Catherine Drayton, for being my first and fiercest ally. If I could list all the synonyms for *grateful* and *fortunate* here, it still wouldn't be enough to accurately convey my thanks.

To the rest of the staff at InkWell Management, particularly Masie Cochran, who read this book first, and William Callahan, for editorial advice that was the very definition of invaluable. Also to the foreign rights squad of Liz Parker, Lyndsey Blessing, and Alexis Hurley, for being so damn good at what you do.

To my editor, Stacey Barney, for, like, *literally everything*. Your insight, your fervor, the depth of your love for Henry and Grace. You make it super hard not to believe in fate and soul mates when my book found its soul mate in you.

Also to Kate Meltzer, for your tireless support, and to the rest of the team at Putnam and Penguin Random House, for welcoming me so enthusiastically to the family.

To Laura Harris from Penguin Australia, for breathing life into Murray and sharing my passion for Taylor Swift.

To Emma Matthewson from Hot Key in the UK—like I said in our emails, ten-year-old me went into cardiac arrest the moment an offer from *you* arrived in my inbox!

To Mary Pender and Kassie Evashevski from UTA, for handling the film rights so brilliantly.

To the readers of my early work who told me I was good when I definitely, categorically wasn't: Cara Faagutu, Renee Martin, Alysha Morgan, Sarah Francis, Kirra Worth, Jacqueline Payne, Danielle Green, and Sally Roebuck. You hardly know how much I needed and appreciated your (terribly misplaced at the time) confidence.

To the whole team at Arc, but especially Lyndal Wilson, for making me a far better writer (and putting up with my frequent shenanigans/disregard for the charter).

To Twitter and Team Maleficent, for being my unwavering cheerleaders: Samantha Shannon, Claire Donnelly, Katherine Webber, Lisa Lueddecke Catterall, and Leiana Leatutufu.

A second shout-out here to the incomparable, indispensible Katie Webber. You lead by example in showing me that the impossible was possible if you only worked hard enough. I am unfailingly proud of you and constantly awed by your dedication to what you do.

To my Cowper Crew, for supporting me through the writing of this book: Baz Compton, Geoff Metzner, but especially Tamsin Peters. Thank you for cups of tea, study corner, chicken soup when I was sick (frequently), and feeding me when I was flat broke (even more frequently). Look how far your little parasite has come!

To my lovely grandmother, Diane Kanowski, who will never read this book because it's far too scandalous, but whom I'm grateful to regardless! Our hundreds of library visits when I was a kid were instrumental in fostering my love of books.

To my parents, Phillip and Sophie Batt, for everything, forever. Putting up with me as a teenager is starting to pay off, right? *Right?* To Mum in particular: there's a line in Pierce Brown's *Morning Star* that says, "Mother is the spine in me. The iron." I think the same of you.

Above all, thank you to my little sisters, Shanaye and Chelsea, for a hundred midnight drives, Skittles and Pepsi Max, songs played on repeat, not telling Mum that one time I quit my job to write, loving my characters more than I do, and generally being outstanding human beings.

You are my favourite people in the world and this book is unequivocally and wholeheartedly for you.

TURN THE PAGE
FOR A SNEAK PEEK AT
KRYSTAL SUTHERLAND'S NEXT BOOK,

House of Hollow

COMING SPRING 2021.

Prologue

I WAS TEN years old the first time I realized I was strange.

Around midnight, a woman dressed in white slipped through my bedroom window and cut off a lock of my hair with sewing scissors. I was awake the whole time, tracking her in the dark, so frozen by fear that I couldn't move, couldn't scream.

I watched as she held the curl of hair to her nose and inhaled deeply. I watched as she put it on her tongue and closed her mouth and savored the taste for a few moments before swallowing. I watched as she bent over me and ran a fingertip along the hook-shaped scar at the base of my throat.

It was only when she opened my door, bound for the bedrooms of my older sisters, with the scissors still held at her side, that I finally screamed.

My mother tackled her in the hall. My sisters helped hold her down. The woman was rough and rabid, thrashing against the three of them with a strength we'd later learn was fueled by amphetamines. She bit my mother. She headbutted my middle sister, Vivi, so hard in the face that her nose was crushed and both of her eye sockets were black for weeks.

It was Grey, my eldest sister, who finally subdued her. When she thought my mother wasn't looking, she bent low over the wild woman's face and pressed her lips against her mouth. It was a soft kiss right out of a fairy tale, made gruesome by the fact that the woman's chin was slick with our mother's blood.

For a moment, the air smelled sweet and wrong, a mixture of honey and something else, something rotten. Grey pulled back and held the woman's head in her hands, and then watched her, intently, waiting. My sister's eyes were so black, they looked like polished river stones. She was fourteen then, and already the most beautiful creature I could imagine. I wanted to peel the skin from her body and wear it draped over mine.

The woman shuddered beneath Grey's touch and then just . . . stopped. By the time the police arrived, the woman's eyes were wide and far away, her limbs so liquid, she could no longer stand and had to be carried out, limp as a drunk, by three officers.

I wonder if Grey already knew then what we were.

• • •

The woman, the police would later tell us, had read about us on the internet and stalked us for several weeks before the break-in.

We were famous for a bizarre thing that had happened to

us three years earlier, when I was only seven, a thing I couldn't remember and never thought about but that apparently intrigued many other people a great deal.

I was keyed into our strangeness after that. I watched for it in the years that followed, saw it bloom around us in unexpected ways. There was the man who tried to pull Vivi into his car when she was fifteen because he thought she was an angel; she broke his jaw and knocked out two of his teeth. There was the teacher, the one Grey hated, who was fired after he pressed her against a wall and kissed her neck in front of her whole class. There was the pretty, popular girl who had bullied me, who stood in front of the entire school at assembly and silently began to shave her own head, tears streaming down her face as her dark locks fell in spools at her feet.

When I found Grey's eyes through the sea of faces that day, she was staring at me. The bullying had been going on for months, but I'd only told my sisters about it the night before. Grey winked at me, then returned to the book she was reading, uninterested in the show. Vivi, always less subtle, had her feet up on the back of the chair in front of her and was grinning from ear to ear, her crooked nose wrinkled in delight.

Dark, dangerous things happened around the Hollow sisters.

We each had black eyes and hair as white as milk. We each had enchanting, four-letter names: Grey, Vivi, Iris. We walked to school together. We ate lunch together. We walked home together. We didn't have friends, because we didn't need them. We moved through the corridors like sharks, the other little fish parting around us, whispering behind our backs.

Everyone knew who we were. Everyone had heard our story. Everyone had their own theory about what had happened to us. My sisters used this to their advantage. They were very good at cultivating their own mystery like gardeners, coaxing the heady intrigue that ripened around them into the shape of their choosing. I simply followed in their wake, quiet and studious, always embarrassed by the attention. Strangeness only begat strangeness, and it felt dangerous to tempt fate, to invite in the darkness that seemed already naturally drawn to us.

It didn't occur to me that my sisters would leave school long before I did, until it actually happened. School hadn't suited either of them. Grey was blisteringly smart but never found anything in the curriculum particularly to her liking. If a class called for her to read and analyze *Jane Eyre*, she might instead decide Dante's *Inferno* was more interesting and write her essay on that. If an art class called for her to sketch a realistic self-portrait, she might instead draw a sunken-eyed monster with blood on its hands. Some teachers loved this; most did not, and before she dropped out, Grey only ever managed mediocre grades. If this bothered her, she never showed it, drifting through classes with the sureness of a girl who'd been told her future by a clairvoyant and had liked what she'd heard.

Vivi preferred to cut school as frequently as possible, which relieved the administration, since she was a handful when she did show up. She back-talked teachers, cut slashes in her uniforms to make them more punk, spray-painted graffiti in the bathrooms, and refused to remove her many piercings. The few assignments she handed in during her last year all scored easy As—there just weren't enough of them to keep her enrolled. Which suited Vivi just fine. Every rock star needed an origin story, and getting kicked out of your £30,000 per year high school was as good a place to start as any.

They were both like that even then, both already in possession of an alchemical self-confidence that belonged to much older humans. They didn't care what other people thought of them. They didn't care what other people thought was cool (which, of course, made them *unbearably* cool).

They left school—and home—within weeks of each other. Grey was seventeen, Vivi was fifteen. They set off into the world, both bound for the glamorous, exotic futures they'd always known they were destined for. Which is how I found myself alone, the only Hollow left, still struggling to thrive in the long shadows they left behind. The quiet, bright one who loved science and geography and had a natural flair for mathematics. The one who wanted desperately, above all else, to be unremarkable.

Slowly, month by month, year by year, the strangeness that swelled around my sisters began to recede, and for a good long while, my life was what I'd craved ever since I'd seen Grey sedate an intruder with a simple kiss: normal.

It was, of course, not to last.

Chapter 1

MY BREATH SNAGGED when I saw my sister's face staring up at me from the floor.

Grey's fine, hook-shaped scar was still the first thing you noticed about her, followed by how achingly beautiful she was. The *Vogue* magazine—her third US cover in as many years—must have arrived in the mail and landed faceup on the hall rug, smack bang, which is where I found it in the silver ghostlight of the morning. The words *The Secret Keeper* hovered in mossy green text beneath her. Her body was angled toward the photographer, her lips parted in a sigh, her black eyes staring at the camera. A pair of antlers emerged from her white hair as though they were her own.

For a short, witching moment, I'd thought she was actually there, in the flesh. The infamous Grey Hollow.

In the four years since she'd left home, my eldest sister had grown into a gossamer slip of a woman with hair like spun sugar and a face out of Greek mythology. Even in still pictures there was something vaporous and hyaline about her, like she might ascend into the ether at any moment. It was perhaps why journalists were forever describing her as *ethereal*, though I'd always thought of Grey as more earthy. No articles ever mentioned that she felt most at home in the woods, or how good she was at making things grow. Plants loved her. The wisteria outside her childhood bedroom had often snaked in through the open window and coiled around her fingers in the night.

I picked up the magazine and flicked to the cover story.

Grey Hollow wears her secrets like silk.

When I meet her in the lobby of The Lanesborough (Hollow never allows journalists near her apartment, nor, it's rumored, does she host parties or entertain guests), she's dressed in one of her hallmark enigmatic creations. Think heavy embroidery, hundreds of beads, thread spun from actual gold, and tulle so light it drifts like smoke. Hollow's couture has been described as a fairy tale meeting a nightmare inside a fever dream. Gowns drip with leaves and decaying petals, her catwalk models wear antlers scavenged from deer carcasses and the pelts of skinned mice, and she insists on wood-smoking her fabric before it's cut so her fashion shows smell like forest fires.

Hollow's creations are beautiful and decadent and strange, but it's the clandestine nature of her pieces that has made them so famous so quickly. There are secret messages hand-stitched into the lining of each of her gowns—but that's not all. Celebrities have reported finding scraps of rolled-up paper sewn into the boning of their bodices, or shards of engraved animal bone affixed alongside precious gems, or riddles painstakingly painted in invisible ink, or minuscule vials of perfume that crack like glow sticks, releasing Hollow's heady eponymous scent. The imagery that features in her embroidery is alien, sometimes disturbingly so. Think gene-spliced flowers and skeletal Minotaurs, their faces stripped of flesh.

Much like their creator, each piece is a puzzle box, begging to be solved.

I stopped reading there, because I knew what the rest of the article would say. I knew it would talk about the thing that happened to us as children, the thing none of us could remember. I knew it would talk about my father, the way he'd died.

I touched my fingertips to the scar at my throat. The same half-moon scar I shared with Grey, with Vivi. The scar none of us could remember getting.

I took the magazine up to my bedroom and slipped it under my pillow so my mother wouldn't find it, wouldn't burn it in the kitchen sink like the last one. Before I left, I opened my Find Friends app and checked that it was turned on and transmitting my location. It was a requirement of my daily morning runs that my mother could track my little orange avatar as it bobbed around Hampstead Heath. Actually, it was a requirement if I wanted to leave the house *at all* that my mother could track my little orange avatar as it bobbed around . . . wherever. Cate's own avatar still hovered south, at the Royal Free Hospital, her nursing shift in the emergency room dragging—as per usual—into overtime.

Leaving now, I messaged her.

Okay, I will watch you, she pinged back immediately. Message me when you're home safe.

I set off into the predawn winter cold. We lived in a tall, pointed house, covered in rough white stucco and wrapped with leadlight windows that reminded me of dragonfly wings. Remnants of night still clung to the eaves and collected in pools beneath the tree in our front yard. It was not the kind of place a single mother on a nurse's salary could usually afford, but it had once belonged to my mother's parents, who both died in a car accident when she was pregnant with Grey. They'd bought it at the start of their marriage, during World War II, when property prices in London had crashed because of the Blitz. They were just teenagers then, barely older than I was now. The house had been grand once, though it was sagged and sunken now, and smelled of rising damp and the past.

In my favorite old photograph of the place, taken in the kitchen sometime in the sixties, the room was fat with lazy sunlight, the kind that lingers for hours in the summer months, sticking to the tops of trees in golden halos. My grandmother was squinting at the camera, a kaleidoscope of glittering green cast across her skin from a stained glass window that had since been broken. My grandfather stood with his arm around her, a cigar in his mouth, his pants belted high and a pair of Coke-bottle glasses on his nose. The air looked warm and smoky, and my grandparents were both smiling. They were cool, relaxed. If you didn't know their story, you might think they were happy.

From the four pregnancies she'd carried to term, my grandmother had given birth to only one living child, quite late in her life: my mother, Cate. The rooms of this house that had been earmarked for children had been left empty, and my grandparents had not lived long enough to see any of their grandchildren born. There are things in every family that are not talked about. Stories you know without really knowing how you know them, tales of terrible things that cast long shadows over generations. Adelaide Fairlight's three stillborn babies was one of those stories.

Another was the thing that had happened to us when I was seven.

Vivi called before I'd even reached the end of the street. I took the call on my AirPods, knowing without looking at my screen that it was her.

"Hey," I said. "You're up early. It can't even be lunchtime in Budapest."

"Ha ha." Vivi's voice sounded muffled, distracted. "What are you doing?"

"I'm out for a run. You know, the thing I do every morning." I turned left and ran along the footpath, past empty sports fields and the carcasses of trees that stood tall and stripped in the cold. It was a gray morning, the sun yawning sluggishly into the sky behind a pall of clouds. The cold needled my exposed skin, drawing tears from my eyes and making my ears ache with each heartbeat.

"Ew," Vivi said. I heard an airline announcement in the background. "Why would you do that to yourself?"

"It's the latest rage for cardiovascular health. Are you at an airport?"

"I'm flying in for a gig tonight, remember? I just landed in London."

"No, I do not remember. Because you definitely didn't tell me."

"I'm *sure* I told you."

"That would be a negative."

"Anyway, I'm here, and Grey's flying in from Paris for some photo shoot today, and we're all hanging out in Camden before the gig. I'll pick you up when I get out of this godawful airport."

"Vivi, it's a school day."

"You're still at that soul-destroying institution? Wait, hang on, I'm going through immigration."

My usual path took me through the green fields of Golders Hill Park, the grass sprinkled with a confetti bomb of yellow daffodils and white-and-purple crocuses. It had been a mild winter and spring was breaking already, rolling across the city in mid-February.

Minutes dragged by. I heard more airline announcements

in the background as I ran along the western border of Hampstead Heath, then into the park, past the blanched milk-stone of Kenwood House. I headed deeper into the twisting wildwood warrens of the heath, so tight and green and old in places, it was hard to believe you were still in London. I gravitated to the untamed parts, where the trails were muddy and thick fairy-tale trees grew over them in archways. The leaves would soon begin to return, but this morning I moved beneath a thicket of stark branches, my path bordered on both sides by a carpet of fallen detritus. The air here smelled sodden, bloated with damp. The mud was thin from recent rain and flicked up the back of my calves as I pushed on. The sun was rising now, but the early-morning light was suffused with a drop of ink. It made the shadows deep, hungry-looking.

My sister's garbled voice on the phone: "You still there?"

"Yes," I replied. "Much to my chagrin. Your phone manners are appalling."

"As I was saying, school is thoroughly boring and I'm very exciting. I demand you cut class and hang out with me."

"I can't just—"

"Don't make me go to the administration and tell them you need the day off for an STD test or something."

"You wouldn't—"

"Okay, good chat, see you soon!"

"Vivi—"

The line went quiet at the same time a pigeon shot out

of the undergrowth and into my face. I yelped and fell backward into the muck, my hands instinctively coming up to protect my head even though the bird had already fluttered away. And then—a small movement on the path far ahead. There was a figure, obscured by trees and overgrown grass. A tall man, pale and shirtless despite the cold, far enough away that I couldn't tell if he was even looking in my direction.

From this distance, in the gunmetal light, it appeared as though he was wearing a bull skull over his face as a mask. There were horns protruding from his head and the bleached bones of his face were stripped of flesh. I thought of my sister on the cover of *Vogue*, of the antlers her models wore on the catwalk, of the beasts she embroidered on her silk gowns.

I took a few deep breaths and lingered where I sat in the mud, unsure if the man had seen me or not, but he didn't move. A breeze cooled my forehead, carrying with it the smell of woodsmoke and the wild wet stench of something feral.

I knew that smell, even if I couldn't remember what it meant.

I scrambled to my feet and ran hard in the direction I'd come from, my blood hot and quick, my feet slipping, visions of a monster snagging my ponytail playing on repeat in my head. I kept checking behind me until I passed Kenwood House and stumbled out onto the road, but no one followed.

The world outside the green bubble of Hampstead Heath was busy, normal. London was waking up. When I finally caught my breath, my fear was replaced by embarrassment that a wet brown stain had spread over the back of my leggings. I stayed alert while I ran home, the way women do, one AirPod out, a sharp slice of adrenaline carving up the line of my spine. A passing cabdriver laughed at me, and a man out for his first cigarette of the day told me I was beautiful, told me to smile.

Both left a prickle of fright and anger in my gut, but I kept running, and they faded back into the white noise of the city.

That's the way it was with Vivi and Grey. All it took was one phone call from them for the strangeness to start seeping in again.

At the end of my street, I messaged my middle sister:

DO NOT come to my school.

Chapter 2

AT HOME, I found my mother's red Mini Cooper in the driveway and the front door ajar. It keened open and closed on its hinges, breathing with the wind. Wet footprints tracked inside. Our ancient demon of a cat, Sasha, was sitting on the doormat, licking her paw. The cat was older than me, and so threadbare and crooked she was beginning to look like a bad taxidermy job. She hissed when I picked her up—Sasha had never liked me or Vivi or Grey, and she made her feelings known with her claws—but she was too decrepit these days to put up much of a fight.

Something was off. The cat hadn't been allowed outside for probably ten years.

"Cate?" I called quietly as I pushed the door open and stepped inside. I couldn't remember when or why we'd stopped calling our mother *Mum*, but Cate preferred it this way, and it had stuck.

There was no answer. I put Sasha down and scuffed off my muddy shoes. Soft voices echoed down the stairs from the floor above, snippets of an odd conversation.

"That's the best you can do?" my mother asked. "You can't even tell me where they went? How it happened? If they were buried or burned or—"

A tinny speakerphone voice responded: a man with an American accent. "Listen, lady, you don't need a PI, you need a psychiatric intervention."

I followed the voices, my footfalls quiet. Cate was pacing by her bed, still in her emergency room scrubs, the top drawer of her nightstand open. The room was dark, lit only by a dim honey lamp. Night shift at the hospital called for her room to have blackout curtains, so the space always had a slightly sour smell to it from the constant lack of sunlight. In one hand, Cate held her phone. In the other, a photograph of herself with a man and three children. This happened every year around the anniversary: My mother hired a PI to try and solve the mystery the police were no closer to unraveling. Inevitably, the PI always failed.

"So that's it, then?" Cate asked.

"Jesus, why don't you ask your *daughters*," the man on the phone answered. "If anyone knows, it's them."

"Fuck you," she said sharply. My mother rarely swore. The wrongness of it sent a prickle into my fingertips.

Cate hung up. A glottal sound escaped her throat. It was not the kind of noise you'd make in the presence of others. I was immediately embarrassed to have stumbled on something so private. I went to turn away, but the floorboards creaked like old bones beneath my weight.

"Iris?" Cate said, startled. There was a prick of something odd in her expression when she looked up at me—anger? fear?—but it was quickly replaced with concern when she spotted my muddy leggings. "What happened? Are you hurt?"

"Oh. No. I was mauled by a rabid pigeon."

My mother let out a breath. "And you were so scared that you shat your pants?"

I threw her a *very funny* pout. Cate laughed and perched on the edge of her bed and beckoned me with both hands. I went and sat cross-legged on the floor in front of her so she could fix my long blond hair into two braids, as she had done most mornings since I was little.

"Everything okay?" I asked as she ran her fingers through my hair. I caught the prickly chemical scent of hospital soap, overlaid with sweat and bad breath and other telltale hints of a fifteen-hour shift in the emergency room. Some people thought of their mothers when they smelled the perfume she wore when they were children, but for me, my mother would always be this: the cornstarch powder of latex gloves, the coppery tang of other people's blood. "You left the front door open."

"No, I didn't. Did I? It was a long shift. I spent a long time with a guy who was convinced his family was controlling him with anal probes."

"Does that count as a medical emergency?"

"I think I'd want some pretty rapid intervention if that was happening to me."

"Fair point." I sucked my bottom lip and exhaled through my nose. It was better to ask now, in person, than over text later. "Is it okay if I come home a little later tonight? Vivi's in town for a gig and Grey is flying in from Paris. I want to spend time with them."

My mother said nothing, but her fingers slipped in my hair and tugged hard enough to make me gasp. She didn't apologize.

"They're my sisters," I said quietly. Sometimes, asking to see them—but especially asking to see Grey—felt like asking for permission to take up shooting heroin as an extracurricular activity. "They aren't going to let anything bad happen to me."

Cate gave a short, complicated laugh and started braiding again.

The picture she'd been looking at was facedown on the blanket, like she hoped I wouldn't notice it. I turned it over and studied it. It was of my mother and my father, Gabe, and the three of us girls when we were younger. Vivi wore a green tweed duffle coat. Grey was dressed in a Bordeaux faux-fur jacket. I was in a little red tartan coat with gold buttons. Around each of our necks hung matching gold heart pendants with our names pressed into the metal: IRIS, VIVI, GREY. Christmas presents from the grandparents we had been in Scotland to visit when the photo was taken.

The police had never found these items of clothing or jewelry, despite extensive searches for them.

"It's from that day," I said. I hadn't seen any photographs from that day before. I hadn't even known there were any. "We all look so different."

"You can . . ." Cate's voice split, fell back down her throat. She let out a thin breath. "You can go to Vivi's gig."

"Thank you, thank you!"

"But I want you home before midnight."

"Deal."

"I should make us something to eat before you go to school. And you should definitely have a shower." She finished my braids and kissed me on the crown of my head before she left.

When she was gone, I looked at the photograph again, at her face, at my father's face, only a handful of hours before the worst thing that would ever happen to them happened. It had carved something out of my mother, shaved the apples from her cheeks and left her thinner and grayer than before: For much of my life, she had been a watercolor of a woman, sapped of vibrancy.

It had carved even more out of Gabe.

Yet it was the three of us girls who'd changed the most. I hardly recognized the dark-haired, blue-eyed children who stared back at me.

I've been told we were more secretive after it happened. That we didn't speak to anyone but each other for months.

That we refused to sleep in separate rooms, or even separate beds. Sometimes, in the middle of the night, our parents would wake to check on us and find us huddled together in our pajamas, our heads pressed together like witches bent over a cauldron, whispering.

Our eyes turned black. Our hair turned white. Our skin began to smell like milk and the earth after rain. We were always hungry, but never seemed to gain weight. We ate and ate and ate. We even chewed in our sleep, grinding down our baby teeth and sometimes biting our tongues and cheeks so we woke with bloodstained lips.

Doctors diagnosed us with everything from PTSD to ADHD. We collected an alphabet of acronyms, but no treatment or therapy ever seemed to be able to reset us to how we'd been before it happened. We weren't sick, it was finally decided: We were just strange.

People always found it hard to believe now, that Grey and Vivi and I had come from our parents. Our father had brown hair and light eyes. Our mother was short, round-faced, dark-haired. Somehow, combined, they'd produced . . . us. We were each five eleven, a full ten inches taller than our tiny mother. We were each inconveniently beautiful, with high cheekbones and eyes like does. People told us as children, told our parents how exquisite we were. The way they said it, it sounded like a warning—which, I supposed, it was.

We all knew the impact of our beauty and we all dealt with it in different ways.

Grey knew her power and brandished it forcefully, in a way I had seen few girls do. In a way I was afraid to mirror myself, because I had witnessed the repercussions of being beautiful, of being pretty, of being cute, of being sexy, and of that attracting the wrong kind of attention, not only from boys and men but other girls, other women. Grey was an enchantress who looked like sex and smelled like a field of wildflowers, the human embodiment of late-summer evenings in the South of France. She accentuated her natural beauty wherever possible. She wore high heels and delicate lace bras and soft smoky eye makeup. She always knew just the right amount of skin to show to achieve that cool-sexy look.

More than anything else, this is how I knew my eldest sister was different from me: She walked home alone at night, always beautiful, sometimes drunk, frequently in short skirts or low-cut tops. She walked through dark parks and down empty streets and along graffiti-smeared canals where itinerants clustered to drink and take drugs and sleep in piles. She did this without fear. She went to the places and wore the things that—if anything happened to her—would later prompt people to say she was asking for it.

She moved through the world like no other woman I knew.

"What you don't understand," she said to me once when I told her how dangerous it was, "is that *I* am the thing in the dark."

Vivi was the opposite: She tried to banish her beauty. She shaved her head, pierced her skin, inked the words FUCK OFF!

across her lissome fingers, a spell to try and ward off unwanted desire from unwanted men. Even with these enchantments, even with a zigzag nose and a sharp tongue and unshaved body hair and the dark grooves beneath her eyes carved out by drink and drugs and sleepless nights, she was achingly beautiful, and ached after accordingly. She collected each wolf whistle, each smacked butt cheek, each groped breast, kept them all beneath her skin, where they boiled in a cauldron of rage that she let out onstage on the strings of her bass guitar.

I fell somewhere between my sisters. I didn't actively try to wield or waste my beauty. I kept my hair washed and wore no scent but deodorant. I smelled clean but not heady, not sweet, not tempting. I wore loose-fitting clothing and no makeup. I didn't take up the hem of my uniform. I didn't walk alone at night.

I went to put the photograph back in Cate's open drawer. A manila folder, distended with paper, sat beneath her socks and underwear. I pulled it out, flicked it open. It was filled with photocopies of police files, their edges curled with age. I saw my name, my sisters' names, caught snippets of our story as I riffled through, unable to look away.

The children claim to have no memory of where they have been or what happened to them.

Officer Mackenzie and Officer Mason refuse to be in the same room as the children, citing shared nightmares after taking their statements.

The flowers found in the children's hair are unidentifiable hybrids—possible pyrophytes.

The cadaver dogs continue to react to the children even days after their return.

Gabe Hollow insists that all three children's teeth have changed: that baby teeth have grown back in places where they were already lost.

My stomach pressed against my throat. I snapped the folder shut and tried to shove it back into the drawer, but it snagged on the wood and split open, heaving paper onto the floor. I knelt and gathered the sheets back into a pile with shaking hands, trying not to look at its contents. Pictures, witness statements, pieces of evidence. My mouth was dry. The paper felt corrupted and wrong in my fingers. I wanted to burn it, the way you'd burn a blighted crop so the rot couldn't spread.

And there, at the top of the stack of documents, I found a photograph of Grey at eleven years old, two white flowers—real, living flowers—growing out of the paper as if they were bursting from her eyes.

Chapter 3

I WAS HUNGRY when I arrived at school, even after Cate had cooked me breakfast. Even now, years after whatever trauma had first sparked my unusual appetite, I was *still* always hungry. Just last week, I'd gotten home ravenous and laid waste to the kitchen. The fridge and pantry had been stocked with food after Cate's fortnightly grocery shopping: two loaves of fresh sourdough bread, a tub of marinated olives, two dozen eggs, four cans of chickpeas, a bag of carrots, chips and salsa, four avocadoes . . . The list goes on. Enough food for two people for two weeks. I ate it all, every bite. I ate and ate and ate. I ate until my mouth bled and my jaw ached from chewing. Even when all the new groceries were devoured, I downed an old can of beans, a box of stale cereal with a liter of milk, and a tin of shortbread.

Afterward, my hunger finally sated, I stood in front of my bedroom mirror and turned this way and that, wondering where the hell the food went. I was still skinny, not so much as a bump.

At school, I felt high-strung and jumpy. When a car door slammed in the drop-off line, I smacked my hand to my chest so hard, the skin was still stinging. I straightened my uniform tie and tried to center my thoughts. My fingers felt grimy and smelled of something putrid, even though I'd washed them three times at home. The smell came from the flowers on the photo. I'd plucked one from my sister's eye before I left. It was an odd bloom, with waxy petals and roots that threaded into the paper like stitches. I'd recognized it. It was the same flower Grey had turned into a pattern and embroidered on many of her designs.

I'd held it close to my nose and inhaled, expecting a sweet scent like gardenia, but the stench of raw meat and garbage had made me dry heave. I'd left the files and fetid bloom in my mother's drawer and slammed her bedroom door shut behind me.

I breathed a little easier at school, felt like I was coming back to myself—or at least to the carefully curated version of myself I was at Highgate Wood School for Girls. My backpack, groaning at the seams with books on Python and A-level study guides, cut hot tracks into my shoulders. The rules and structure here made sense. The weirdness that lurked in old, empty houses and the wildwood thickets of ancient heaths found it hard to permeate the monotony of uniforms and fluorescent lighting. It had become my sanctuary away from the baseline strangeness of my life, even if I didn't belong here with the children of some of London's richest families.

I hurried through the busy corridors, bound for the library.

"You're five minutes *late*," said Paisley, one of the dozen students I tutored before and after school. Paisley was a pint-sized twelve-year-old who somehow managed to make the school uniform look boho chic. Her parents had been paying me decent money for weeks to try and teach her basic coding. The annoying thing was, Paisley was a natural. When she paid attention, she picked up Python with an easy elegance that reminded me of Grey.

"Oh, I'm deeply sorry, Paisley. I'll give you a free extra hour after school to make up for it." She glared at me. "That's what I thought. Where's your laptop?"

"I heard you're a witch," she said as she returned to tapping away at her phone, curls of mousy hair falling out of her bun and into her eyes. "I heard your sisters were expelled for sacrificing a teacher to the devil in the auditorium." Wow. The rumors had gotten out of control in the last four years, but honestly, I was more surprised that it had taken this long for one to reach her.

"I'm not a witch. I'm a mermaid," I said as I set up my laptop and opened the textbook to where we left off. "Now show me the homework I set for you last week."

"Why is your hair white if you're not a witch?"

"I bleach it that way," I lied. In fact, the week after Grey and Vivi left, I'd tried to dye it darker. I'd bought three boxes of black dye and spent a rainy summer evening drinking apple cider while I painted my hair. I'd waited the forty-five minutes the instructions recommended, then a little longer just to be sure, before rinsing it out. I was excited to see the new me. It felt like the transformative scene in a spy movie when the protagonist is on the run, forced to change their appearance in a service station bathroom after they go rogue.

When I wiped away the fog of condensation on the mirror, I shrieked. My hair was its usual milky blond, entirely untouched by the dye.

"*Homework*," I ordered again.

Paisley rolled her little eyes and dug her laptop out of her Fjällräven bag. "There." She turned her screen toward me. "Well?" she demanded as I scrolled through her code.

"It's good. Despite your best efforts, you're picking this up."

"What a terrible shame this will be our last session."

God, what kind of twelve-year-old talked like that?

I tsked her. "Not so fast. Unfortunately for both of us, your parents have paid through the rest of the term."

"That was until they found out who your sisters are." Paisley handed me an envelope. My name was written on the front in her mother's loopy handwriting. "They're super into Jesus. They won't even let me read Harry Potter. Suddenly they don't seem to think you're such a good influence on me." She packed her things, stood to leave. "Bye, Sabrina," she called sweetly on her way out.

"Wow," came a disembodied voice. "Some people are *so rude.*"

"Oh," I said as a small bottle-blond figure made her way out of the stacks and pulled up the chair across from me. "Hello, Jennifer."

In the months after Grey and Vivi had left school, when the loneliness of being without them sank so deeply into my body that every heartbeat ached, I'd desperately wanted to make friends with some of my peers. I'd never needed friends before, but without my sisters, I had no one to eat with at lunchtime and no one but my mother to spend time with on the weekends.

When Jennifer Weir had invited me to her sleepover birthday party (reluctantly, I suspected—our mothers worked together at the Royal Free), I'd cautiously accepted. It was an appropriately posh affair: Each girl had her own mini tipi set up in the Weirs' vast living room, each frosted with fairy lights and set among a floating sea of blush and gold balloons. We watched three of the *Conjuring* movies into the early hours of the morning and ate so much birthday cake and so many delicate baked goods that I thought someone might vomit. We talked about the boys who attended nearby schools and how cute they were. We snuck into Jennifer's parents' liquor cabinet and did two shots of tequila each. Even Justine Khan, the girl who'd bullied me and subsequently shaved her head in front of the school, seemed not to mind my presence. For a handful of pink, sugary, alcohol-softened hours, I dared to allow myself to imagine a future that looked like this—and it might have been possible, if not for the now infamous game of spin the bottle that had landed both Justine and me in the emergency room.

Jennifer Weir hadn't spoken to me since that night, when I left her house with blood dripping from my lips.

"Did you want something?" I asked her.

"Well, *actually*," Jennifer said with a smile, "I bought tickets to the gig at Camden Jazz Café tonight. I heard your sister was going to be there."

"Of course she's going to be there," I said, confused. "She's in the band."

"Oh no, silly, I meant your other sister. *Grey*. I was wondering . . . I mean, I would totally *love* to meet her. Maybe you could introduce me?"

I stared at her for a long time. Jennifer Weir and Justine Khan (together, they called themselves JJ) had been making my life a living hell for the better part of four years. Where Jennifer outright ignored me, Justine made up the difference: *witch* scrawled across my locker in blood, dead birds slipped into my backpack, and—one time—broken glass sprinkled over my lunch.

"Anyway," Jennifer continued, her saccharine smile beginning to go sour, "think about it. It wouldn't be the worst thing that could happen to you, you know—being my friend. I'll see you tonight."

When she was gone, I read Paisley's note, in which her parents explained they'd heard some "concerning accusations" and asked for their advance back. I tore it up and dumped it in the bin, then checked the countdown timer on my phone to see how many days were left until graduation: hundreds. Forever. The school had a long memory when it came to the Hollow sisters, and it had been my burden to bear since the month both of my sisters had skipped town.

My first class of the day was English. I took my usual seat at the front of the classroom, by the window, my annotated copy of *Frankenstein* open on my desk, its pages frilled with a rainbow of multicolored sticky notes. I'd read it twice in preparation for this class, carefully underlining passages and making notes, trying to find the pattern, the key. My English teacher, Mrs. Thistle, was deeply conflicted by this behavior: On the one hand, a student who did the assigned readings—*all* of them, always, frequently more than once—was something of a phenomenon. On the other hand, a student who wanted the *right answer* for a work of literature sent her half-mad.

It was drizzling outside. A flicker of strange movement caught my eye as I set up my things, and I looked through the glass over the wet gulch of grass between buildings.

There, in the distance, was a man in a bull's skull, watching me.

**TURN THE PAGE
TO READ AN EXCERPT FROM
KRYSTAL SUTHERLAND'S**

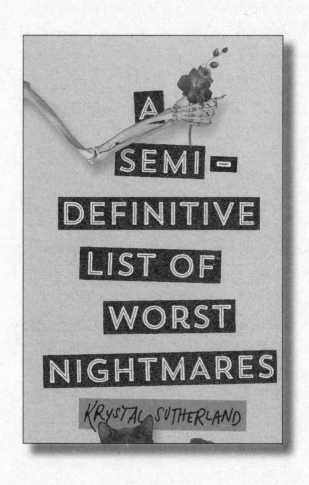

1

THE BOY
AT THE BUS STOP

ESTHER SOLAR had been waiting outside Lilac Hill Nursing and Rehabilitation Center for half an hour when she received word that the curse had struck again.

Rosemary Solar, her mother, explained over the phone that she would no longer, under any circumstances, be able to pick her daughter up. A cat black as night with demon-yellow slits for eyes had been found sitting atop the hood of the family car—an omen dark enough to prevent her from driving.

Esther was unfazed. The spontaneous development of phobias was not a new phenomenon in the Solar family, and so she made her way to the bus stop four blocks from Lilac Hill, her red cape billowing in the evening breeze and drawing a few stares from strangers along the way.

On the walk, she thought about who normal people would call in a situation such as this. Her father was still interred in the basement he'd confined himself to six years ago, Eugene was AWOL (Esther suspected he'd slipped through another gap in reality—it happened to Eugene from time to time), and her grand-father no longer possessed the fine motor skills required to oper-ate a vehicle (not to mention that he couldn't remember that she was his granddaughter).

Basically, Esther had very few people who could bail her out of a crisis.

The bus stop was empty for a Friday night. Only one other person sat there, a tall black guy dressed like a character from a Wes Anderson movie, complete with lime-green corduroy pants, a suede jacket, and a beret pulled down over his hair. The boy was sobbing quietly, so Esther did what you're supposed to do when a complete stranger is showing too much emotion in your presence—she ignored him completely. She sat next to him and took out her tattered copy of *The Godfather* and tried very hard to concentrate on reading it.

The lights above them hummed like a wasp's nest, flicker-ing on and off. If Esther had kept her eyes down, the next year of her life would've turned out quite differently, but she was a Solar, and Solars had a bad habit of sticking their noses where they didn't belong.

The boy sobbed dramatically. Esther looked up. A bruise was blooming across his cheekbone, plum-dark in the fluorescent light, and blood trickled from a split at his eyebrow. His patterned button up—clearly donated to a thrift store sometime in the mid-1970s—was torn at the collar.

The boy sobbed again, then peeked sideways at her.

Esther generally avoided talking to people if it wasn't

completely necessary; she sometimes avoided people even when it *was* completely necessary.

"Hey," she said finally. "You okay?"

"Think I got mugged," he said.

"You *think*?"

"Can't remember." He pointed to the wound at his forehead. "Took my phone and wallet though, so think I got mugged."

And that's when she recognized him. "Jonah? Jonah Smallwood?"

The years had changed him, but he still had the same wide eyes, the same strong jaw, the same intense stare he had even when he was a kid. He had more hair now: a shadow of stubble and a full head of thick black hair that sat up in a kind of pompadour style. Esther thought he resembled Finn from *The Force Awakens*, which was, as far as she was concerned, a very good way to look. He glanced at her, at the Jackson Pollock painting of dark freckles smattered across her face and chest and arms, at the mane of peach red hair that fell past her hips. Trying to place her. "How do you know my name?"

"You don't remember me?"

They'd only been friends for a year, and they'd only been eight at the time, but still. Esther felt a twinge of sadness that he'd apparently forgotten about her—she had certainly not forgotten about him.

"We went to elementary school together," Esther explained. "I was in Mrs. Price's class with you. You asked me to be your valentine."

Jonah had bought her a bag of Sweethearts and crafted a handmade card, on which was a drawing of two fruits and a line that read: *We make the perfect pear.* Inside, he had asked her to meet him at recess.

Esther had waited. Jonah hadn't showed. In fact, she'd never seen him again.

Until now.

"Oh yeah," Jonah said slowly, recognition finally dawning on his face. "I liked you because you protested Dumbledore's death outside the bookstore like a week after the movie came out."

How Esther remembered it: little Esther, seven years old with a bright red bowl cut, picketing the local bookstore with a sign that read, SAVE THE WIZARDS. And then a snippet from the six o'clock news, a reporter kneeling next to her, asking her the question: "You do realize the book was published years ago and the ending can't be changed?" and her blinking dumbly into the camera.

Back to reality: "I hate that there's video evidence of that."

Jonah nodded at her outfit, at the bloodred cape held at her throat by a ribbon and the wicker basket resting at her feet. "Looks like you're still strange. Why are you dressed like Red Riding Hood?"

Esther hadn't had to answer questions about her predisposition for costumes for several years. Strangers on the street always assumed she was on her way to or from a costume party. Her teachers—much to their vexation—could find no fault with her outfits as far as the school's dress code was concerned, and her classmates were used to her coming in dressed as Alice in Wonderland or Bellatrix Lestrange or whatever, and didn't really care what she wore so long as she kept smuggling them cake. (More on this in a moment.)

"I was visiting a grandparent. It seemed appropriate," she said in reply, which appeared to satisfy Jonah, because he nodded like he understood.

"Look, you got any cash on you?"

Esther did have cash on her, in her Little Red Riding Hood picnic basket. She had $55, all of it earmarked for her Get the Hell Out of This Podunk Town fund, which now stood at $2,235 in total.

Back to the previously mentioned cake. You see, in Esther's junior year, East River High had instituted sweeping changes in the cafeteria until only healthy food was available. Gone were the pizzas and chicken nuggets and tots and fries and sloppy joes and nachos that made high school semibearable. The words "Michelle Obama" were now muttered in exasperation every time a new item was added to the menu, like leek and cauliflower soup or steamed broccoli pie. Esther had seen a budding business opportunity and made a box mix of double chocolate fudge brownies. She brought them into school the next day, where she sold each one for five dollars and made a cool profit of fifty bucks. Since then, she'd become the Walter White of junk food; such was the extent of her empire that her customers at school had dubbed her "Cakenberg."

She'd recently expanded her territory to Lilac Hill Nursing and Rehabilitation Center, where the most exciting things on the menu were overcooked hot dog and bland mashed potato. Business was booming.

"*Why?*" she said slowly.

"I need money for a bus fare. You give me cash, and I can use your phone to transfer funds from my bank account directly into yours."

It sounded slippery as all hell, but Jonah was bruised and bleeding and crying, and she still halfway saw him as the sweet young boy who'd once liked her enough to draw her a picture of two pears.

So Esther said: "How much do you need?"

"How much you got? I'll take it all and transfer you that."

"I have fifty-five dollars."

"I'll take fifty-five dollars."

Jonah stood up and came to sit next to her. He was much taller than she thought, and thinner too, like a stalk of corn. She watched as he opened the banking app on her phone, logged in, filled in her account details as she gave them to him, and authorized the transfer.

Funds transfer successful, the app read.

So she leaned down and opened her basket and gave him the fifty-five dollars she'd made at Lilac Hill today.

"Thank you," Jonah said as he shook her hand. "You're all right, Esther." Then he stood, and winked, and was gone. Again.

And that's how, on a warm, damp evening at the end of summer, Jonah Smallwood swindled her out of fifty-five dollars and pickpocketed, in the space of approximately four minutes:

- her grandmother's bracelet, right off her wrist
- her iPhone
- a Fruit Roll-Up from her basket that she'd been saving for the ride home
- her library card (which he later used to rack up $19.99 in replacement fees for defacing a copy of *Romeo and Juliet* with lobster graffiti)
- her copy of *The Godfather*
- her semi-definitive list of worst nightmares
- and her dignity

Esther kept replaying the cringeworthy memory of her Dumbledore protest in her head, and didn't realize she'd been robbed until her bus arrived six minutes and nineteen seconds later, at which point she exclaimed to the driver, "I've been robbed!" To which the driver said, "No riffraff!" and closed the doors in her face.

(Perhaps Jonah didn't steal all of her dignity—the bus driver took what shreds he hadn't managed to scrape away from her bones.)

So you see, the story of how Esther Solar was robbed by Jonah Smallwood is quite straightforward. The story of how she came to love Jonah Smallwood is a little bit more complicated.

2

THE HOUSE OF LIGHT AND GHOSTS

IT TOOK Esther a total of three hours, thirteen minutes, and thirty-seven seconds to walk to her house, which was on the outskirts of the outskirts of town. The town had expanded in the opposite direction than the developers expected, thus stranding the neighborhood in the middle of nowhere.

On the long walk there, the sky cracked open and heaved water, so that by the time Esther got to her front steps, she was sopping, muddy, and shivering.

The Solar house was glowing, as always, a fluorescent jewel in an otherwise darkened street. A soft breeze licked through the trees that had taken root in the front yard, a forest in the middle of suburbia. Some neighbors had complained about the constant lights a few years back. Rosemary Solar had responded by planting eight oak trees in the lawn, which had grown from saplings to giants that enshrouded the property in the space of about six months. As they grew, she hung their branches with nazars, hundreds of them, the blue, black, and white glass tinkling an eerie song whenever the wind moved. The nazars were to ward off evil, Rosemary said. So far, the only people they had managed to scare away were Girl Scouts, Jehovah's Witnesses, and trick-or-treaters.

Eugene was sitting on the front steps that lead up to the brightly lit porch, looking like he'd time travelled from a Beatles concert, complete with Ringo's haircut and John's fashion sense.

Esther and Eugene were the twins who no one could ever believe were twins. Where his hair was dark, hers was light. Where he was tall, she was short. Where he was lithe, she was buxom. Where her skin was pocked with freckles, his was clear.

"Hey," Esther said.

Eugene looked up. "I *told* Mom you were still alive, but she's already looking up caskets online. Your funeral color scheme is going to be pink and silver, or so I'm told."

"Ugh. I have specifically requested a tasteful black and ivory funeral, like, *a hundred* times."

"She's been watching the emergency death slideshow she made last year, adding new pictures. It still finishes with 'Time of Your Life.'"

"God, so basic. I can't decide what would be more tragic—dying at seventeen, or having the most cliché funeral ever."

"Come on. A pink and silver funeral isn't cliché, just tacky as hell." Eugene had genuine worry in his eyes. "You okay?"

Esther wrung out her long hair; it grew red as blood when wet. "Yeah. I got mugged. Well, not really mugged exactly. Conned. By Jonah Smallwood. Remember the kid who left me hanging on Valentine's Day in elementary school?"

"The one you were desperately in love with?"

"The very same. Turns out he's a rather talented pickpocket. He just stole fifty-five dollars *and* my Fruit Roll-Up."

"Twice scorned. I hope you're planning vengeance."

"Naturally, brother."

Eugene stood and swung his arm over her shoulder and they walked inside together, under the horseshoe nailed above the lintel, the sprigs of dried pennyroyal dangling from the doorframe and the remains of the previous night's salt lines.

The Solar home was a cavernous old Victorian, the kind where even the light had a hazy, faded quality. It was all dark wood paneling and red Persian carpets and walls the distinct pale green color of rot. It was the kind of house where ghosts moved in the walls and neighbors believed the inhabitants might be cursed; for the Solars, both were true.

These are the things people would notice, if strangers were ever allowed inside:

- All of the light switches were kept in the *on* position
  with electrical tape. The Solars loved light, but
  Eugene loved it most of all. For his benefit, the halls
  were decked in string lights, and lamps and candles
  covered every spare surface of furniture and, quite
  often, much of the floor.
- Scorch marks from the Great Panic Fire of 2013
  when the power went out and Eugene bolted
  out of his bedroom into the hall, knocking over

approximately two dozen of the aforementioned candles in the process and setting the drywall alight.

- The steps to the second floor were sealed off by a jumble of discarded furniture, mostly because Peter Solar had been midway through completing upstairs renovations when he had his first stroke and all work had quickly stopped, but partly because Rosemary believed the second floor was genuinely haunted. (Like a ghost was only going to haunt half a house and politely let the residents chill downstairs without any *Paranormal Activity* action. C'mon.)
- There was nothing on the walls, apart from the taped-up light switches and blinds to cover the windows at night. No pictures. No posters. Definitely, definitely no mirrors. *Ever.*
- The rabbits in the kitchen.
- The evil rooster named Fred that followed Rosemary Solar everywhere and was, according to Rosemary anyway, a goblin straight out of Lithuanian folklore.

Lisa Fahey

krystal sutherland grew up in Australia, directly across the road from the local public library, where she spent almost every day after school having adventures between the pages of books. Now her own novels for young adults have been published in over twenty countries. She served as an executive producer on *Chemical Hearts*, the Amazon Studios film adaptation of her first book, which stars Lili Reinhart and Austin Abrams. The TV rights to her second novel, *A Semi-Definitive List of Worst Nightmares*, were optioned by Yellow Bird US. Her third book, *House of Hollow*, is set for publication in spring 2021. She has lived in Sydney, San Francisco, Amsterdam, and Hong Kong, but she currently calls London home.

You can find her on Instagram at @km_sutherland or online at krystalsutherland.com